In the Shadows

BY THE SAME AUTHOR

The Actor

In the Shadows

CHRIS MACDONALD

MICHAEL JOSEPH

PENGUIN MICHAEL JOSEPH

UK | USA | Canada | Ireland | Australia
India | New Zealand | South Africa

Penguin Michael Joseph is part of the Penguin Random House group of companies whose addresses can be found at global.penguinrandomhouse.com

Penguin Random House UK,
One Embassy Gardens, 8 Viaduct Gardens, London SW11 7BW

penguin.co.uk

First published 2026
001

Copyright © Chris MacDonald, 2026

The moral right of the author has been asserted

Penguin Random House values and supports copyright. Copyright fuels creativity, encourages diverse voices, promotes freedom of expression and supports a vibrant culture. Thank you for purchasing an authorized edition of this book and for respecting intellectual property laws by not reproducing, scanning or distributing any part of it by any means without permission. You are supporting authors and enabling Penguin Random House to continue to publish books for everyone. No part of this book may be used or reproduced in any manner for the purpose of training artificial intelligence technologies or systems. In accordance with Article 4(3) of the DSM Directive 2019/790, Penguin Random House expressly reserves this work from the text and data mining exception

Set in 13.4/16pt Garamond MT
Typeset by Falcon Oast Graphic Art Ltd
Printed and bound in Great Britain by Clays Ltd, Elcograf S.p.A.

The authorized representative in the EEA is Penguin Random House Ireland, Morrison Chambers, 32 Nassau Street, Dublin D02 YH68

A CIP catalogue record for this book is available from the British Library

ISBN: 978–0–241–70832–3

Penguin Random House is committed to a sustainable future for our business, our readers and our planet. This book is made from Forest Stewardship Council® certified paper

For O, S and J.
Shine on you crazy diamonds

In the Shadows

The quest to solve rock's greatest mystery

By Winter Blakely-Harris

Prologue

Just before midnight on 28 October 1977 police burst through the locked door of a top-floor bedroom at 1 Cheyne Walk, a Georgian townhouse overlooking Chelsea Bridge. Inside they found the dead body of a twenty-five-year-old man curled on its side on the fox-fur coverlet of a Queen Anne four-poster bed. A blanket made with the fur of a fox. Not for the last time in this book, you will have to accept these were very different times. The young man was in a bad way, legs, arms, torso pockmarked with sores and deep bruises the colour of thunder. Without the make-up, the costumes or the stick-on fake gills, the police didn't recognise him. It wasn't until twenty-one-year-old Sergeant Bryn Halleran arrived soon after, giving an involuntary cry of shock on seeing the dead man, that first responders realised they were looking at the corpse of Nereus Forbes.

They wouldn't have failed to recognise him today. Half a century after his death, Nereus Forbes has become one of the most iconic figures of the twentieth century. Known by every age group, in every social strata as a singer, songwriter, fashion icon, pansexual trailblazer and all-round universe-conquering rock god. His album *The Apotheosis of Poseidon* has been ranked in the top ten of the greatest albums of all time by no fewer than forty-six publications. The song 'Lady Theia' tops innumerable greatest-song-of-the-twentieth-century lists. By the latter half of the 1970s, Nereus Forbes was arguably the most famous man in the world. The true circumstances of his supposedly accidental death remain rock's greatest mystery.

And for the last two years I've become obsessed with solving it. I've ignored my job, alienated my husband and attracted the attention of the wrong people, putting both myself and my children in harm's way, all in the name of uncovering the truth. The irony being, I've spent most of my life trying to avoid the figure of Nereus Forbes. Although I was just five when he died, Nereus always represented everything I wanted to be but wasn't. He knew he was extraordinary and made his extravagant dreams happen, whereas I spent my youth listless, unsure of what I wanted, trying and failing in many careers before settling as an academic and classicist. Now in my fifties, I spend my days combing through works by thousand-year-old poets, trying to make sense of the world. At half my age, Nereus Forbes had already conquered it.

It takes hubris to think you can find answers to a mystery which has taken on near-mythic status in the history of popular culture but when I started down this path, I didn't feel like I had a choice. Two weeks after my fiftieth birthday, my older daughter Sara had something put through the letterbox of her student house in Brighton. It was an early picture of Nereus in what would become his trademark Bronze Stingray cloak from a concert in Ghent. Scrawled across the image in what she first thought was blood but turned out to be crimson nail polish, was the word 'God-killer'.

My daughter did not kill Nereus Forbes. But there's a subset of his ever-growing fanbase who are convinced his death wasn't an accident as was reported, and that he was in fact murdered. Every murder needs a prime suspect and theirs is Nereus's former guitarist, closest musical collaborator and best friend, Graham Harris – who also happens to be my father.

To understand Nereus's death I have to take you back to the beginning, to the making of an icon, his subsequent destruction and my parents' role in both. This is a tragedy of greed, ownership, music and love. A story which came to take over my entire life. A mystery I came to believe I would never find the definitive answer to. Until I did.

I present it to you as I unravelled it from a wealth of investigation I undertook alongside a WhatsApp group full of subredditors, online sleuths and Nereus fanatics; from tapes my father Graham Harris recorded as a young man for a purported memoir; from extensive research of contemporary sources and various interviews I conducted, chief amongst them with my mother, Sadie Blakely. I have reimagined certain exchanges for narrative purposes which I hope you'll excuse. Nereus died nearly fifty years ago and, although I may seem like a minor character, this is in fact my story.

Neil Forbes and The Marshalls EP

'Drying of the Light', the fourth song on *Neil Forbes and The Marshalls* is the highlight of an underwhelming debut and can be viewed as a divining stick towards the dizzy heights of artistry Nereus would reach. Despite the disconnect with Graham Harris's stomping guitar-lick, Nereus's ethereal voice soars perilously close to the sun. The somewhat saturnine lyrics contain the first example of his use of archetype, in this case the abandoned archer Philoctetes from Homer's *Iliad*. His protagonist seems to take pleasure in his isolation while still yearning to be rescued by his former brothers in arms. It's a dichotomy Nereus would come back to. Man as alone, contented as outlier while simultaneously desperate to connect with a humanity just out of reach.

From *Sounds and Sweet Airs* by DeVaughn Reeve

I.

On the afternoon of 31 October 1977, a dozen journalists in crumpled suits jostled under too-few black umbrellas to avoid a pelting rain-shower no one on their papers had forecast. They'd been scrambled to 61 Regent Street at the last minute and, as they observed their steamed-up watches ticking past two o'clock and were further soaked by a Routemaster bus, were all considering whether they'd be able to sneak off to the nearest dry pub and finesse the story on the fly. But 61 Regent Street was the office of Pacifica Holdings, the company operating the affairs of Nereus Forbes – despite the lukewarm reception to his most recent album, Nereus always provided good copy. The rock star had just returned to Britain following a disastrous concert on Kekova Island near Turkey and the talk was that his manager, Thomas Tee, had gathered them to make a public statement about what had gone down.

Fifteen minutes later, the glossy ochre door opened and Thomas Tee walked out holding a silver umbrella, obscured by the rain. It was only when he stopped in front of the assembled journalists and lifted his umbrella that they realised Tee had tears in his eyes. The pack scrambled for their notebooks. The rain vanished.

'My client and friend,' Thomas began, 'died three days ago. From a respiratory issue.' His thousand-cigarette voice cracked with emotion as he continued his statement asking the world to play Nereus's music, to celebrate him and continue his legacy. He closed with a bastardisation of a line from Plautus.

'Those who the gods love die young,' he said, before snapping his umbrella shut and returning through the yellow door into his offices.

When the story hit the evening editions that afternoon, the reaction was seismic. Thousands gathered at Nereus's childhood homes in Shepherd's Bush and Belgravia. There were forty-eight-hour singing vigils in Battersea Park, on the opposite side of the river from where he died on Cheyne Walk. A driftwood effigy was made by Italian fans and launched into the sea from his birthplace in the Peloponnese – a now-annual event that's become a folk festival in its own right.

But the shock, reverence and grief were soon replaced with speculation. Why had it taken three days to reveal Nereus's death? What sort of respiratory problem had killed him? Why had the police been involved? Not wanting the rumours to spiral, the Metropolitan Police released the official cause of death as 'asphyxiation due to aspiration of vomit'. Investigators explained there had been a homecoming party at the house the night before Nereus's death, hinting at heavy drinking. But the police's attempts to control the story were upended when someone at the coroner's office leaked the toxicology results showing Nereus had three-and-a-half times the lethal dose of a new strain of heroin in his system. Though the cause of death would have been the same, it seemed narcotics rather than alcohol were to blame.

We know about rock stars' excessive drug use now but Britain was still a deeply conservative and largely Christian country then. Drug users were demonised as dissolute junkies, explaining why Nereus's team would have wanted to keep the circumstances vague to protect his legacy. Likewise, with the police and government struggling with a growing influx of heroin trafficked from Pakistan, they wouldn't have wanted further lurid drug stories in the press. But anyone who cared about Nereus, his friends, collaborators and most of all his fans, knew the singer was a long-term heroin user. A connoisseur almost, the kind of addict who could never have made such a significant mistake as an accidental overdose.

Suicide was suggested in some quarters but police had already reported the scene looked haphazard, casual. There was no note, no instructions, no affairs left in order. To officials, it simply didn't look like Nereus had taken his own life. In addition, everyone who saw him that day said he was more lucid than he'd been in months, fired up by some plan for a new creative direction. And even if all that had been a front, Nereus must have known an overdose was a risky, painful and unreliable way to go. Which left those fans still bereft and traumatised by his death only one explanation as to how such a practised drug-user could have died from an overdose – someone else gave him the fatally potent hit of heroin meaning Nereus Forbes was murdered.

The theory was never given credence in the mainstream media, but in the first twenty-four hours, before the results of the autopsy had come back, police investigated Nereus's death suspecting possible foul play. With the input of neighbours, chief amongst them Caroline French, a retired public-school headmistress, they built a timeline of the comings and goings to Nereus's house that night.

On the 27th, the day before his death, Nereus and his entourage returned from the Turkish island of Kekova. His girlfriend, the German model, singer, medium and seventies sex-pot Greta Handverk, hosted a homecoming party at 1 Cheyne Walk. Around twenty people attended. All but Greta had left by seven o'clock in the morning on the 28th.

Nereus then had five subsequent visitors. At ten, his manager Thomas Tee arrived. It's unclear when Thomas left. At midday, Nereus's pianist Matthew Salvini then arrived with Hungarian aristocrat and drug dealer to the stars, Dominik Szlonik. They stayed for twenty minutes, raised voices were heard. At a little after one, Greta Handverk left but was then seen re-entering the building sometime around half past three. No one saw her leave again, but she was seen by multiple witnesses at the Colony Room in Soho at four thirty, so can't have left Cheyne Walk later than quarter past four.

Between four and four thirty a teenage neighbour, Abby Grade, saw an unidentified red-haired woman banging on the door of Nereus's house, looking through ground-floor windows, loitering around the wall of his garden, trying to see a way around to get to the back of the house. Alerted by the commotion, Caroline French went to see what the loiterer was doing but by the time she got outside, the red-headed woman had disappeared. Caroline went for a walk to a local café. When she returned to Cheyne Walk around six o'clock, she saw a green Jaguar parked on the street outside number 1.

The car remained there until she checked the road before retiring to bed at nine thirty. When police arrived just before midnight, following an anonymous tip-off, the Jaguar had gone. No other cars arrived. No other visitors were witnessed in the interim. Meaning whoever was in the car was the last person to see Nereus before police found him dead and the person most likely to have given the anonymous tip-off. With time of death estimated somewhere between three and six in the afternoon, it's unclear whether Nereus would have been alive or dead when the car arrived.

Despite not having the car's registration, it didn't take long for detectives to discover that the only person Nereus knew who owned a green Jaguar XJ8, the model Caroline described, was Neil's former guitarist Graham Harris. But when they got to Methuselah, Graham's country pile near Horsham in West Sussex, he wasn't there. Nor was the Jaguar.

His not being at home rang alarm bells so they began a search for Graham which ended swiftly when, after calling round the airlines, they discovered his name on a manifest for a flight to Nice the day before. Further investigation revealed his ticket had been bought on his behalf by the Jordanian royal family. He was due at their Monaco residence to teach his long-term pupil Princess Bismah. The flight left Heathrow at six o'clock in the evening, hours before police would discover Nereus dead.

Although there were tentative efforts to contact the Jordanian royal family to check whether their guitar teacher had in fact been on the flight to Nice, as soon as Nereus's toxicology results arrived indicating an overdose, and only an elderly neighbour's report of an unknown car indicating Graham had any involvement, the police saw no reason to continue looking for him. But Graham then didn't return to Britain. He would never return. At the point I started looking into the case nearly fifty years later, no one knew where Graham was, or if he was even still alive.

Although the police and those closest to Nereus were happy to declare his death a tragic accident, Graham's disappearance, alongside the sighting of what seemed to be his car, remains hugely suspicious. The two former collaborators had almost nothing to do with each by the time of Nereus's death. Yet that same weekend Graham made the decision to leave the country, never to return. Leaving his life behind, his five-year-old daughter, me, who he must have known would have been irrevocably damaged by never having a father. Graham had to have done something, something terrible perhaps, to force him to leave me behind for good.

But why would Graham kill Nereus?

Straight after my own daughter rang and showed me the poster she'd received, desperate to conceal how shaken she was by it, I sat at my laptop and stormed onto the internet forums, trying to track down the person who'd sent it to her. I was astonished at what I found there. It was an entire world. A community of fans, trolls, obsessives on subreddits, music rag comments sections, and self-published books. A labyrinth of wild theories, well-researched hypotheses and flat-out guesses put forward as empirical fact, all dedicated to one thing – finding Nereus's killer.

I shouldn't have engaged with them but reading how certain they were that Graham killed Nereus, I felt compelled to call them out. I hadn't seen my father since I was five, he'd only ever existed for me as an absence, but I still didn't want him to be a murderer. So I asked them why. I got a litany of answers but at the heart of all of them was something very simple. Nereus was a genius. Graham wasn't. And he couldn't handle it.

When I went back and asked if they thought he really could have killed his best friend because he was jealous of his talent, asperryman3, the user I suspected had posted the threatening picture to my daughter in the first place, wrote – 'you'd be amazed what people can do out of jealousy.'

2.

It wasn't enough for me. It couldn't be. The man had left me. I had to work out why he might have killed Nereus, or if he didn't, what else could have happened to force him into exile. I set about looking for my father. Something I hadn't done before, for reasons I'll come to in due course. But I had no reliable leads, no wherewithal to find someone who'd been missing for so long and, in truth, no idea if he was even still alive.

So I took the less emotionally fraught path and began looking into what led to Nereus's death. And after six weeks of research, I got my first significant break from an elderly Swede called Kim Jakobson. I was put on to Kim, a collector of Nereus memorabilia, by the Victoria and Albert Museum who housed the Nereus archive following their blockbuster 'Pacifica' exhibition.

I emailed Kim and was astonished when he replied informing me he still had in his possession a box of nine reel-to-reel tapes Graham Harris had recorded for a book of his life. Kim had never listened to them as he had no device which would play them and said he'd send them over. I transferred Kim ninety pounds to expedite delivery, and the next morning I was staring through bubble wrap at a row of rusted metal boxes containing my father's voice, his story. I hoped, the truth.

I had ordered a reel-to-reel tape player, set it up in the summerhouse in my garden and was alone the first time I heard my father's voice since I was five years old. I hadn't remembered it, not really, but I knew it. I knew it did something to me, moved molecules and chemicals within me. I didn't cry but as I blinked myself back into a rational enough space to really listen, to begin to make notes, to analyse what he was saying, it took a long while for a feeling of profound hollowness to leave me. Throughout the recordings, journalist Lincoln Trevick asks Graham several times what his ambitions were. Graham dismisses it, not having grown up with grand plans. But there's a moment he admits that from a young age he always wanted to make music which would last. 'Something which, after you hear it, lives in the heart. Forever.'

3.

There's a fragment of a Super 8 recording of Graham Harris playing with his teenage band The Marshalls in a Scarborough bandstand in 1966. A sixteen-year-old Graham's playing guitar and singing with Danny Greig on drums and Harry 'Fraz' Fraser on bass guitar. There's no sound but Graham's fingers on the fretboard of his guitar move at such an extraordinary speed, I had to check there wasn't something wrong with the tape the first time I watched it. He seems lost in the music when he plays, head down, eyes closed, but when it comes time for him to face his audience, open his eyes and sing, his body stiffens. It could be self-consciousness or it could be explained by what happens next.

A wide-set man in his fifties marches onto the stage, berating the band, seemingly about their hair, no more than a grown-out short back and sides by our standards, before going for their amplifiers to stop the gig. But Graham gets in his way. They square up before the man shoves his guitar-neck and all hell breaks loose. Graham pushes the man in the chest as Danny leaps over his drums to join the fight. A rabble storms the stage, before the film ends abruptly. It's interesting to note it's the man roughhousing Graham's guitar which sparks the melée. But guitars cost a lot in the sixties and Graham didn't come from money.

Born in 1949 in the picturesque fishing town of Whitby, the only child of fisherman Paul and Sunday School teacher

Barbara, Graham's life was defined by his talent from before he could remember. He stunned his mother's church fundraising committee by climbing onto the piano in St Saviour's Church Hall and playing an almost perfect rendition of 'The Lord is my Shepherd' when he was just four years old. From that moment, his mother Barbara made it emphatically clear that Graham's innate ability had nothing to do with him but was a gift from God.

'The Lord put you on His great green earth for one reason,' Graham recounts his mother saying to him on the recordings for his memoir. 'To spread His glory.' Within a few weeks Barbara had the St Saviour's organist teaching Graham and after six months he was performing in church meetings, the Rotary Club and Women's Institute before expanding to venues throughout the rest of East Yorkshire. A review in the *Scarborough Recorder* describes 'a jumpy-looking child playing the pianoforte as if heaven itself had possessed him'. Photos I found showed a stocky kid in a too-small suit and bow tie, sitting stiffly at the keyboard with hunted eyes.

'Nerves were so bad I was sick in the toilets every time before playing,' Graham remembers. 'My mother had a bag of Granny Smiths for the smell.'

Graham couldn't understand how his piano playing could bring a room full of adults to tears, always thinking he must have done something wrong, or why blue-rinse ladies and bewhiskered men cooed over him for hours after each show. 'They grabbed my cheeks, examined my fingers. Had the stink of the freak show.' He was always desperate to go home after playing, but the adulation over tea and crustless sandwiches was the only thing Graham remembered making his mother happy so he never asked.

'I was a kid. It's what I did each day. Why would I question it?'

With school, working with his father on the boats and travelling throughout the North to perform, Graham didn't have time to question anything. But that would change one night in November 1961 when he woke up and saw what looked like flames flickering through the slats of the garden shed at the end of their garden. Knowing he'd be blamed if there was a fire, he crept downstairs to see. As soon as he got outside, he heard music coming from the tiny outbuilding. Though he knew how angry his mother would be risking a cold with a concert the following day, Graham couldn't help following this sound.

It wasn't the Bach and Haydn he played, nor even the Chopin or Liszt his teacher let him play for fun. He got closer and heard raps of snare-drums, stabs of horns, a twanging melody with the soul of a human voice. He got to the shed, put his eye to a gap in the wooden boards and saw an almost unbelievable sight. His father in candlelight, sat on the floor listening to a record on a phonograph Graham didn't know they owned, nodding his head along to a song. A pop song. Sung by women. 'Please Mr. Postman' by The Marvelettes.

Graham was so shocked he fell forward into the shed, before turning and running back up to his room. He hid under his blanket but his father never came in to chastise him for snooping, nor acknowledged it the next day. But seeing his father like that, a ghost of a man from his time fighting in France in the Second World War, shifted something in Graham. He became obsessed with what he heard that night and a few days later, skipped school when he knew his mother and father wouldn't be home, went down to the shed and began listening to his father's secret stash of records.

Although Elvis and the Everlys were all over the airwaves at the time, Barbara didn't allow a wireless in the house so Graham had barely heard rock and roll. His father had an aficionado's collection, exported to him by an American soldier he'd fought with, Graham later surmised. When the young boy listened to the songs it felt like his whole biology was at war with itself. Sister Rosetta Tharp, then Howling Wolf, Chuck Berry; their unrestrained screaming energy bursting through the speaker rattled him like his bones were ice in a cocktail shaker.

'Like being slapped awake,' he said. 'Feelings, new sensations, trembling in me. I'd find my cheeks wet, crying, when the records ended.'

The true Road to Damascus moment was a year later in 1962 at a Little Richard gig in Newcastle he snuck up to with Danny Greig and Harry Fraser, the school friends he'd go on to start his first band, The Marshalls, with.

Danny and Fraz were born on the same street within a day of each other, their mothers sharing the same taxi to the maternity ward. Despite Fraz stretching to six foot at twelve while Danny was the shortest person in their year, the two boys always seemed to come as a pair. Being in and out of school with his concert tours, Graham hadn't made many friends but when he overheard Danny and Fraz talking about rock and roll, still niche at the time in Yorkshire, he saw his chance.

'Heard Ray Charles?' he said. Danny and Fraz narrowed their eyes. 'I'll play it to you.'

'We thought he meant a record,' Danny Greig, who died in 1997, writes in his memoir *Kicked and Snared*. 'But he drags us into the school hall, starts bashing out "Hit the Road Jack" on the upright in the corner. We were going to scarper, thought we'd get the cane, but then he started singing and we just couldn't leave, it was that good. Radio Luxembourg didn't play much black music, and this Ray Charles cat was wild. Graham kept on playing, teachers came to listen, bit of a crowd gathered. After that, we were just mates with Graham. He was something else.'

The trip to Newcastle to see Little Richard was Graham's idea. Planned like a bank heist, the three of them snuck out under cover of darkness and were driven up by Fraz's older sister, bursting into the concert venue moments before the flamboyant showman took to the stage. It was like nothing they had ever seen.

'The band are there, handsome guys in suits blasting saxophones, whipping the crowd into a frenzy. Then he's there, Little Richard, shock of black hair, pencil moustache, and starts hammering the piano like he's trying to break it. Then he's singing, screaming more like, staring at us with his wild eyes.' After the first few songs, Richard jumped up on top of the piano to sing 'Tutti Frutti', kicking his legs, thrusting his crotch at the audience. 'We were thirteen, it was grotesque to us. That sexuality.'

'We didn't know he was gay,' Danny writes. 'Wasn't something we knew about. But we could feel it was dangerous. We resisted for a while, but the energy was so infectious.'

'Crowd were near speaking in tongues, eyes rolling back in their heads,' Graham recalls. 'Ten years going to church and I'd never felt anything like it. We got swallowed into the crowd and before we know it our arms were round each other, hugging. Hugging each other. Thirteen-year-old lads in Yorkshire in the fifties. We did not hug.'

The boys emerged blinking into the night two hours later entirely changed. The world had been grey and now all seemed technicolour. And Graham had a purpose.

'I wanted it,' he remembers. 'More than anything in my life I wanted to surround myself with that music, be in it, fill every pore, every brain cell. I wanted to be on stage playing to people who were searching for something new, write songs which could change them as fundamentally as that night changed me.' But for the shining light of his mother's whole church community, this newly awakened desire was an existential disaster.

'Mother called rock the devil's music. It felt like I'd been tempted like Jesus in the wilderness. How much I wanted to give in to it totally wrecked my head.' He didn't sleep for weeks. Took to his knees four or five times a night to pray to God to rid him of these sinful ambitions.

But he couldn't resist. Six weeks after the gig, ragged by long nights of broken sleep, Graham found himself pulled into Woolworths where he asked the assistant to take down a plastic-stringed guitar for him to try. The piano would always be rigid lines to him, precision. It represented doing things right.

'Soon as I held the guitar into my body, I could feel that wasn't who I was.' Graham Harris taught himself to play in snatched trials at Woolworths until he saved enough to buy it. The devil had won. He was lost for good.

4.

By the time he met Neil Forbes eight years later in February 1970 at the Pine and Whistle in Archway, London, Graham had been plying his trade as guitarist and lead singer of The Marshalls for five years.

A few months after the Little Richard gig, Graham stole a set of drums from the store cupboard of St Saviour's, set it up in Fraz's granny's garage which looked out onto the sea on the road to Middlesbrough and the band was born. Graham whipped the boys into shape and after a few months they were doing Bill Haley covers on the promenade and within a couple of years playing gigs at tourist spots along the East Yorkshire coast.

Despite an elaborate network of cover stories, word eventually got back to Barbara. Fifteen-year-old Graham arrived home one evening in June, to find his house, normally rabid with his mother's church friends, silent. His mother sat at the kitchen table, the moon coming through the back door of their worker's cottage. Eyes blazing, she pulled a suitcase from under the table and held it out to him.

'Jill Allis saw you playing with those delinquents,' she said. 'In public.'

'We were playing a few songs,' he said. 'Getting paid for it.'

'Ladies of the night get paid for it.'

'It's music,' Graham said, shaking his head.

'That filth is not music.'

'People like us.'

'They like watching children singing about showing your baby a good time?'

'If you'd just listen –' She grabbed Graham by the shoulders of his shirt.

'You think I don't know how long you've been doing this? I prayed it would go away but no. You've debased this house, failed our Lord, humiliated me.' She held the suitcase out. Graham looked at his mother's rictus grin, the deep lines of constant judgement etched around her mouth. Her road to heaven had left her miserable and trapped. The crowds who buzzed off their music were making their own heaven on earth.

Graham took the suitcase and moved into Fraz's uncle's house where he had to give up all his earnings for the privilege of sleeping on a damp sofa in his back room. 'As living situations went, it couldn't have been much worse. But I didn't have to sneak around anymore. Started writing songs. I was free.'

The other Marshalls left school with Graham soon after he was kicked out to gig full time, the trio making a name for themselves in former bingo halls with cigarette-butt carpets, thrilling tramp-drunk crowds in their Sunday best. Every night it was like they were playing a zombie wedding. They adored it.

One night in early 1969, Hull-based promoter Jack Donald, who'd begun booking The Marshalls, took Graham aside, suggesting he move up to London.

'Since Jimmy Page and Zeppelin, everyone's on the lookout for real talent,' he said. 'Streets be paved with diamonds for someone like you.'

Although it was a tough sell at first to the others – 'London might as well have been Timbuktu to us,' Danny Greig wrote – Graham painted a picture of money, girls and broader horizons. He didn't dare to dream of fame. It was decided the lads would move down in February of 1969. Graham didn't tell his mother, though he ran into his father the day before they left – he said nothing but wedged two pound notes in his son's top pocket.

They travelled down on the train and moved into a two-room flat above a fish and chip shop in Bermondsey. They began their big city adventure green-eyed and full of excitement, joining foreigners and Irish in lines for casual labourers, calling numbers from pinboards in Denmark Street music shops for gigs, leaving demos on desks at recording studios in the West End. But within a few months, it seemed that if there were diamonds in the streets for people like Graham, it wasn't the ones The Marshalls were walking.

Promoter Jack Donald hadn't reckoned on all the other kids, well-heeled Home Counties chaps who'd found a Gibson Les Paul in their stocking and had the same idea. Compared to them, The Marshalls must have seemed like the Norse hordes. Graham's work on the fishing boats had given him the sort of broad shoulders and barrel chest you'd only ever get from a childhood of manual labour. Though his strawberry-blond hair grew out in thick waves, with beard and a chunky moustache to match, you can see in every photograph that beneath the foliage, and this was always galling to me because I didn't inherit it, Graham was properly gorgeous. He had a jawline that had the girls at Atlantic and Universal refer to him as Desperate Dan and eyes the colour of a Pacific Island sea, sparkling with an unplaceable depth. The other boys weren't as good-looking, Danny short and stocky while Fraz still beanpole thin, but they were equally hairy. So the three, with their Yorkshire accents and thrift-shop suits, a year or two behind the now more slouchy than swinging London, stood out amongst their peers, and not in a good way.

After a year in London, forced to play gigs in Streatham,

Bromley, Kingston, to bored audiences for no money, Danny and Fraz started pushing to move back home. Graham was about to give in when he got a call from Otis de Kock saying he was coming to see them at the Pine and Whistle. Otis was young for a record company exec but had a reputation for brilliant taste and an eagle ear for what the public wanted to listen to. In his late thirties, half-South African, half-Lebanese, he wore open kaftans with lots of chest-hair and was known to many as 'Telly' after the actor Telly Savalas, largely due to his glistening baldness.

'He always seemed more like a pal who'd sidled in to see what all the music hoo-ha was about than a company man,' Nereus said of Otis in a 1971 CBS interview.

'Didn't interfere,' Graham said of Otis. 'Could always tell whether he liked it from those caterpillar eyebrows. Had a life of their own.' Graham had met Otis in the control room at a session a few months after he'd arrived in London and he'd booked him as a guitarist three or four times after. On the phone Otis told Graham he was coming to see them as he was on the lookout for a band to support Paul Denly. Denly was a bubble-gum Beatles knock-off, not Graham's scene, but he sold out venues.

'The gig was a last-chance saloon,' Graham says on the tapes.

Standing at an existential crossroads, The Marshalls took to the small stage at the far end of the North London pub and were greeted by thirty or forty punters who barely looked up from their pints of mild when they clanged into the first chords of 'How Blue Ya Are', a Muddy Waters-inspired song they started every set with. After another original and a couple of covers – 'We'd do anything ten years old as long as the Stones hadn't' – a few of the audience had turned to listen, and buoyed by Otis's arrival at the bar, his bald pate picked out in the lights like a halo, Graham tried to find his inner showman and attacked their set with a bravado his bandmates didn't often see.

'I was in my head in the early days,' Graham recalls. 'Ashamed to be up there, doubting why people would want to watch me. But if that night hadn't worked out, we could have been back North in a week.'

As their time on stage was coming to an end, Graham spotted Otis surveying the flat crowd, and with nothing to lose he kicked into an unashamedly indulgent guitar solo which he sang along to – a doubling inspired by jazz pioneers like T-Bone Walker. Graham closed his eyes, fingers stopping, releasing, flesh against string against wood as he howled jazz-scat gibberish.

'The air seemed to suck out of the room,' Danny remembers. 'We'd not heard him do it. Audience were into it, hanging on every phrase. Could hear a pin drop. But after a minute or so we noticed something happening.'

The band saw the crowd parting, shuffling, grins spreading amongst them. Graham paused, letting a note ring out, and stared down to see a tall figure in the middle of them, head thrown back, singing along in a high, piercing voice.

An annoyed Graham blinked away the distraction, went back into his solo, but the singer in the crowd didn't stop. And as soon as he left a space, his tune came back to him, embellished and turned around. The audience were jostling over each other to hear whoever this interloper was. Graham stopped, teeth gritted as he saw Otis peering into the melée. He looked at the singer.

'With that long dark hair, dead-pale skin, lips like an allergic reaction,' he recalls, 'I didn't know what it was I was looking at.'

Graham played again, sang, as fast as his fingers could go but although he couldn't hear it from where he was, the interloper seemed to be keeping up. Not to be beaten, Graham locked eyes with the person who'd crowbarred themselves into his big chance, played an almost impossibly complex riff and left a pause. The kid sang it back, note perfect.

'We started sparring, call and response, like Plant and Page started doing with Zeppelin. I wanted to crush the kid but he kept coming back.'

The two began harmonising, overlaying notes.

'They knew exactly where the other was going,' Danny wrote. It grew to be a magical moment. A fan who'd been there that night said they got goosebumps so severe they worried they were having a stroke. The two built towards a finish, Graham moving down towards the stage, kneeling, as they challenged each other higher and higher. The moment crescendoed, both of them getting wilder, more elaborate.

'I was raging at first but couldn't help enjoying it by the end.'

'Graham was about to run out of frets, so me and Fraz came back in.'

The Marshalls and their heckler finished the set with a chaotic cacophony before ending in silence. The crowd exploded, hands above heads clapping, whistles, whoops for a band they'd never heard of. The lads joined Graham at the front of the stage, hands above their heads, soaking it all up.

'I had the shakes,' Graham recalls. 'Ever since seeing Little Richard we'd been trying to get that feeling. I looked into the crowd for whoever it was, still didn't know if it was a boy or a girl, couldn't tell from the voice.' But Graham couldn't find the interloper. He ducked under the blinding lights to find them in the audience, but by the time he spotted the singer, Neil Forbes, the boy who would one day be Nereus, was walking out the front of the venue, deep in conversation with Otis de Kock.

5.

'Nereus knew what he was doing,' pop culture professor and Nereus expert Dr Hailee Yamine said when I asked why he was at the Pine and Whistle that night.

'But why there, listening to a band no one had ever heard of?'

'He'd got a tip-off that a red-hot music exec was going to be at a backwater venue and precisely because no one had heard of The Marshalls, knew he'd be able to put himself in the shop window.' Though I knew she was right, I didn't like Dr Hailee's answer. When I'd been thinking about Graham and Neil's first meeting, I'd harboured a theory, a romantic hope he'd somehow heard The Marshalls music, had gone as a fan and felt impelled by some connection with Graham to join in.

'He was seventeen,' I protested. 'Could he really be so calculating?'

'Nereus grew up hearing Greek myths like bedtime stories,' Dr Hailee continued. Neil Forbes was brought up by his mother, celebrity classicist Penelope Kanelides. Born Nearchos in Patras in southern Greece, she changed his first name on moving to the UK then kept her short-lived husband Alasdair Forbes' surname to further assimilate into British life. 'She'd put him in front of movies while she was working at University College London. A young kid watching David Lean, *20,000 Leagues Under the Sea*, *King Solomon's Mines*, Nereus had a sense of the epic, of theatricality baked into his bones from the cradle. He knew how vital it was to make an unforgettable first impression.' Although I didn't want it to be true, a look into where Nereus was in his life at the time seemed to bear out Dr Hailee's theory.

Neil had left Christopher Wren Technical High School the year before the gig at the Pine and Whistle. Although he had loved the curriculum which allowed him to focus on art, technical drawing and the sort of practical skills his private primary school had tried to steer him away from, he'd made the decision to pursue music. 'He was always happiest drawing,' school friend Fred Gaunt wrote in a 1986 *Telegraph* interview. 'But he said Jagger was the closest thing we had to Achilles so he didn't have much choice.' It surprised me when I read this. Not just the unashamed ambition, but also how he saw music as a means to some other end. Almost the polar opposite of Graham who saw it as a higher calling in itself.

Regardless of Neil's motivations, he chased his dreams in his own inimitable way. Although he'd been known throughout Mayfair and St James' through his mother, in the year before Neil met Graham, he stepped out on his own, going to a different gig every night at the Marquee Club, Bag o' Nails and Les Cousins, staying out afterwards crafting a precocious persona which enamoured him to the great and the good of seedy Soho.

'Neil was relentless when he wanted something,' my mother Sadie Blakely had told me, although she was yet to meet him at that point.

'Didn't Graham know?' I asked when we talked about the night he interrupted their gig. 'If Neil was just there for Otis, wasn't Graham angry?'

'He never looked at the world like that,' she said. 'Wanted to see good in people.'

'Did he never trace it back though?' I said. 'After. Knowing he'd been used like that, from the start?'

'The impression Neil made dazzled,' she said. 'Graham could never see past it.'

Sadie's view is borne out by the tapes. Even much later, Graham never seems to question why Neil was there stealing their thunder.

'Not sure the industry knew what we were,' he says at one point, explaining their early struggles – seeming to blame himself. But I wondered, after years working together, such incidents accumulating, what Graham might have done if he had managed to see Neil's real intentions? What a proud man might do if he realised he'd spent the best years of his life as nothing more than another means to an end. But if that were to be the case, after five years of not having seen each other by 1977, what was it that helped Graham see the light?

6.

Although the tour Otis dangled in front of The Marshalls didn't materialise, the triumphant end to the gig in Archway galvanised the Whitby boys.

'That feeling when we had the audience, being at one with them. I'd never felt anything like that sort of connection,' Graham recalls. He spent the last of their money on rehearsal space for the band, trying to work up some of his original tracks while they'd spend their evenings turning up at venues with their gear, offering to play ten-minute sets for free, to try to recapture a fraction of what they'd felt that night.

Their renewed efforts seemed to pay off, because five weeks later, they received a call from Otis offering them two weeks of sessions, their first as a full band, at a rehearsal space in Bethnal Green. The band cramped onto the Underground with their gear and bounced up to East London, excited to see who they'd be working with, having heard rumours Otis de Kock had been courting Rod Stewart to move to his new Apollo Records label. When they arrived at the address they'd been given and found a somewhat decrepit former church, they tempered their expectations.

'Work's work,' Graham told the grumbling Marshalls.

Otis wore a Cheshire Cat grin as he emerged from the vestry and took them inside to a set of double doors opening into the nave. Through the glass The Marshalls saw a woman in a purple fur coat sitting at an upright piano, a halo of cigarette smoke circling above her. Danny, the most girl-mad of the three, barged through, eager to get first dibs on the girl they were there to accompany.

'But when she turned round,' Danny writes. 'We realised "she" wasn't a she.' Graham couldn't believe what he was seeing. It was the singer from the crowd at the Pine and Whistle, he knew it from the bee-stung lips. Although Danny and Fraz didn't recognise Neil Forbes, they too were shocked at the sight of this boy with long black hair in a woman's coat and, most shockingly, wearing make-up. The Marshalls had encountered transvestites in Old Compton Street, knew Jagger wore eyeliner on stage, but seeing a boy in blusher, kohl, mascara in the cold light of day, without an iota of shame, was a lot to take in.

'This is Neil Forbes,' Otis said, making the introductions. 'He has some songs for an EP we're doing which need a little fleshing out.' The Marshalls said nothing. Not only was Graham surprised to see their interloper, but he was so befuddled by his appearance he could barely look at him.

'Hope you boys will be gentle with me,' Neil said, in a ham-fisted attempt to break the ice. 'It's my first time.' The ice remained unbroken. Neil was frightfully well spoken, leaning on his consonants with a sibilant S. When I listened to early interviews, the one that's often memed where he questions why port and owls are the only thing we describe as 'tawny', his voice seems put on, like a bad impression of the camp entertainers of the day, Kenneth Williams, Larry Grayson, entirely different from how he spoke later in the press.

'You can't imagine how shocking it all would have been,' Sadie told me. 'Graham grew up being told sex before marriage would condemn you to the pits of hell. A boy in make-up dropping smutty innuendos might as well have been the devil himself.' On top of which, once Graham had overcome his shock at Neil's appearance, he realised how angry he was.

'We'd spent a year grafting,' he recalls. 'I'd have given a limb to record an EP. Yet the best we could get is holding the hand of this posh kid in his mum's coat.'

Sensing the antipathy, Otis clapped his hands and asked Neil to play them something. Neil threw off his coat, strode into the middle of the studio and hovered his hand in the air above an oversized guitar. The Marshalls knew it was five times the price of their instruments. He carried himself like a seasoned rock god. If he hadn't been so blindsided by his appearance, Graham might have even been impressed. Neil attacked the strings, swished his hips, an impish grin into the middle distance like he was playing to tens of thousands.

It was atrocious. Shockingly so. He couldn't play the guitar at all. It was too much for Graham to take. He stormed through the double doors, into a small kitchenette opposite the nave where Otis found him.

'Is this a stitch-up?' he said, flicking the hot tea-urn.

'Just come back in and –'

'Is that what people want? Strutting around like –' He looked through the door to see a shell-shocked Danny and Fraz sat at their instruments as Neil clutched the microphone, gyrating against it like they were lovers. 'That circus freak?'

Otis smoothed his eyebrows with his thumbs, not used to being talked to so directly.

'He asked for you,' Otis said.

'What?'

'He asked for you. Requested it. Has decided to dedicate the majority of his rather paltry advance to paying you.'

'Why?'

Otis shrugged. 'I explained we could get people in to record parts. Much cheaper than employing a whole band, but Neil insisted.' Graham couldn't make sense of it. Why was this strange boy he'd never met before giving up so much to work with them?

He moved closer to the door, looked at Neil still sashaying as he sang and, with the fog of injustice cleared, listened to his song. His voice was high, sweet, ephemeral and feminine. Graham found himself clenching his jaw at the sound, trying to imagine playing with him. Neil spotted him, held his gaze, singing to him almost. Graham noticed Neil's make-up as if for the first time and cast his eyes to the floor.

I wonder if Neil saw Graham's discomfort, disgust even, because something seemed to burst in him and he really sang.

'Let me drown again in your oasis,' the celebrated refrain from 'Stranded Heart'.

'I could sing,' Graham says on the tapes. 'But this was like nothing I'd ever heard. Vibrated differently. And the words. I always found lyrics torture. It didn't make sense to me that a teenager could make a simple phrase mean nothing and everything at once.' Neil finished on a high, ethereal note before the whole church, it seemed, a site of so many of Graham's childhood musical experiences, rested into silence.

Neil put clasped hands to his mouth like he'd done something naughty. A bewildered-looking Danny and Fraz looked at Graham outside, pleading with him to come back in and make sense of the man, if he was a man, in front of them.

Otis, at Graham's side, gave him a sideways look.

'I can find you all something else,' he said. 'If you don't think you'll gel.'

Graham studied Neil, trying to imagine if he could really spend weeks at close quarters with someone like him. But he could still feel the energy of his voice in the building, still had that refrain in his head, remembered how it felt being on stage singing with him in Archway, the electricity bursting around them.

He put his hand on the door, caught sight of Neil's purple nail polish, took a deep breath, and walked through.

7.

When I heard the description of their first proper meeting on the tapes, I couldn't understand how Graham got over the insult of being passed over for the cross-dressing oddball that stole their thunder during their big audition. Who couldn't even play guitar.

'Graham was a proper musician,' my husband Bobby said. 'You can hear it on the tapes. If you hear a voice like Nereus's, something new, you just want to get cooking with it. You're not thinking about who did what first, credit or hierarchy.' Bobby is two years younger than me. He has a shock of silver hair he's had since before we married in our late twenties, having been bright blond beforehand. He trained as a tonmeister, literally a sound master, and has gone on to specialise in recording and mixing live music events all over Europe. He works with bands every day so understands them in a way I never could. And yes, I am aware of the irony of trying to avoid being Graham Harris's daughter for my whole life and marrying someone obsessed with music to an almost granular level. I had thought Graham being forced to give up leading his band to work for Neil might have sown the bitter seeds which would bloom into murderousness years later, so I found my husband's artistic idealism frustrating. And, I would soon discover, misplaced.

The keyboard warriors I'd started to engage with enjoyed spinning new theories far more than solving existing ones, so one night I challenged the *nereusforever* subreddit to give me some evidence of the jealousy they were certain drove Graham to murder. A few days later Lennox Dixon, an attorney from Wisconsin I'd already recognised as one of the saner posters, sent me a screenshot of the cover page of a set of legal documents sent by Clyne, Willis and Knight in November 1974 to Nereus's company, Pacifica Holdings. I didn't know what I was looking at until I cross-referenced the name of the law firm with my notes and found Graham had instructed them in a house purchase. It seemed that in 1974, Graham Harris's lawyers had taken steps towards some legal action against Nereus.

Not finding any details about it in the public domain or at the National Archive at Kew, I contacted the Royal Courts Records Office but found nothing about any case between the two men. I reached out to top intellectual property lawyer Helen Grady, a friend of a colleague in my department, who told me almost all cases between musicians who'd worked together related to disputes over royalties. However 'proper' a musician Graham Harris might have been, in the space of four years, with Nereus having become wealthy beyond all of their imaginings, it seemed Graham had begun to care rather a lot about credit.

Investigators look to 'The Four Ls' when deciphering motive in a murder. Lust, love, loathing or loot. This legal dispute, probably over royalties or credit for the music, could be tied to either of the last two. Graham may have wanted the share of money he thought he was owed, or simply been driven to murderous fury that he hadn't got the recognition he deserved. Either way, the document presented the first concrete evidence of professional enmity between the two men.

Asperryman3 and various others who seemed adamant Graham did it, jumped on Lennox Dixon's letter as proof but my husband didn't buy it.

'Graham had been round the block. He would have known you can't get songwriting royalties for instrumental parts, however much he was doing.'

'Credit within creative work is incredibly unfair,' Helen Grady told me. 'In something collaborative like music, no one person is truly the sole author. There are so many elements which go into any work of art. Not just who else is in the room with the creator that day but everything that's gone before. Their education, family background, conversations they've had, what's happening in the news, the weather, in their bedroom the night before. But the line has to be drawn somewhere. Disputes usually come about from that side of things not being done assiduously enough.'

There's no record of the contract Graham signed for the Neil Forbes EP, no evidence as to whether Neil had joined The Marshalls or whether Graham, Danny and Fraz were employed as day-players. But, whether by accident or design on Nereus's part, something I've rarely been able to ascertain when it comes to his actions, the line of authorship in the band's early days hadn't been drawn at all.

8.

During the newly thrown-together band's first days in the Bethnal Green church, credit wouldn't have been at the front of their minds. They had two weeks to learn Neil's songs and The Marshalls quickly realised he didn't have many. At least none he was willing to share.

'He'd start things,' Danny Greig writes. 'Fragments. Then stop, walk around shaking his head, smoking about a hundred ciggies.'

'He had this notebook,' Graham says. 'Smythson, gold lettering on the front. He'd break off mid-song to write in it. One morning I grabbed it off him. Try to force him to work on something until it was done.' But inside, Graham couldn't find any songs to work on. There were no words, no musical notation, chord progressions, only sketches.

'How are we meant to play this?' he said, finally snapping. He stormed out for some fresh air, where he looked through Neil's pictures. Pencil-drawn seascapes, rows of cypress trees, wooded glens, waterfalls. Combinations of these scenes from nature with drawings of human bodies, making centaur-like beings, but instead of a horse's body it'd be rocky outcrops, glaciers.

I found the notebook in the Nereus archive at the V&A. The pictures in it are strange, sensuous, incredibly affecting. There's one of a craggy cliff-face above the sea, scarred rock which became part of a human back with sculpted shoulders that tapered down to lower-back muscles like a fillet of beef.

I wanted to bite it. There's a very overt sense of the artist trying to make something both new and old. I tried to imagine buttoned-up Graham looking at the sensual pictures, many of which focus on the intricacies of the male form. Perhaps he was disturbed by the workings of his collaborator's mind. Or disarmed by them, moved even. Because when Neil joined him outside, saying his mother wanted to meet him and asking him to dinner, Graham found himself saying yes.

'The mythical man!' Penny Forbes announced as she opened the door, wrapping Graham's enormous frame in a hug so loving, it almost felt like assault. Penny came from Pilos, a small town on an almost circular bay at the southern tip of the Peloponnese in Greece and exuded such Mediterranean warmth she could have been picked out of central casting. She thrust a giant balloon of brandy into Graham's hand and led him to the living room of her Belgravia garden-flat, where half a dozen extraordinarily dressed people of various ages knelt round a low table, covered in ornate Middle-Eastern carvings.

'I felt like I'd walked into a different dimension,' Graham says, remembering his first encounter with Penny's admirers. And in many ways he had, as it was only then that he realised how celebrated Neil's mother was. On arriving in England, Penelope Kanelides' lectures on Greece and the ancient world soon became famous amongst artists and literati who began attending in their droves. In a time when novelists and academics regularly appeared on prime-time television, her short book on the duplicity and agency of Helen of Troy made Penny a minor celebrity. As with any female success of the time, she became conflated with her work and was pursued by a coterie of intellectual alpha-types. When Neil was nine she married bad-boy sculptor Alasdair Forbes, who brought her into an exclusive clique which intersected art and the aristocracy. They divorced after four hellish years down to Alasdair's alcoholism and philandering misogyny and Penny had been happily single for the better part of a decade when Graham met her.

As the mezze was brought out, which Graham didn't touch because he couldn't make head nor tail of so many plates of sauce, he noticed how Neil's mother dominated like a blazing fire. She caught Graham's eye at points, gave him smiles which felt halfway between concerned matriarch and brazen flirtation. Everyone there was in love with her and the other men, a ceramicist, a Swiss conductor and an architect, took umbrage at how much attention she was giving Graham, talking across him, giggling in his direction. Meanwhile, Julie Stark, the bottle-blonde model and It girl two away from him, quite overtly rolled her eyes anytime he spoke. Feeling out of his depth, Graham resigned himself to keep quiet until he could make his excuses, but a thin man in his seventies wearing a purple scarf, an art collector called Anton Nantua-Jones, wouldn't let him.

'What's our Northern friend's view on Bacon?' Anton said, inviting Graham to join in the conversation he'd long lost the threads of.

'Bacon?' Graham said. 'I like it.'

'It?'

'With eggs and that.' The room held its breath for a moment, eyes wide with cruel delight before erupting into laughter.

'I'm sure Francis would be delighted,' Anton said, barely able to get the words out, 'to hear how well he goes "with eggs and that".' They had been talking about Francis Bacon's recently announced Paris exhibition moments before. Humiliated, unable to even look at Penny, Graham got up to leave but Neil pushed him back down.

'This is the most talented man I've ever met,' Neil shouted, silencing the diners instantly. 'I'd rather hear his thoughts on cured meats than whatever shite you parasites have cribbed from *The Times*.' Graham tugged Neil's sleeve, desperate for him to sit down so the episode would end. But instead, Neil stormed out of the room and returned with a guitar which he thrust into Graham's chest.

'What you doing?' Graham murmured, face flushing. Neil looked in his eyes and began to sing, putting words to a melody he'd been humming in glimpses for the previous few days. Graham looked round the table, who didn't seem to find the impromptu performance unusual, and somehow began playing a song he'd barely heard. Neil stepped onto the table, wilfully knocking glasses and plates into the guests' laps as he walked towards his mother. He knelt in front of her, sang the rest of it directly to her.

The room broke into raucous applause when they finished, Anton holding his hands up to Graham in a mimed apology. Penny grabbed her son's head and whispered something, tears in her eyes.

Later, Graham was in the hall taking in the grandeur of Neil's beautiful home. The walls were decorated with textured wallpaper depicting Amazonian scenes. He could hear space-age jazz on a turntable, the smell of patchouli from spirit burners in corner nooks. This was Neil's life, his childhood. Exotic, cultured, an open world of experience. From the hallway he heard a melody coming from a room further down the corridor. He followed the sound and peeked around the door jamb to see Penny and Neil lying together on a chaise-longue.

'She was singing to Neil, in Greek, two of them lounging there like there was no one else in the world.' Graham thought of his own upbringing. The two-up-two-down terraced worker's cottage, magnolia walls, crosses and statuettes of Christ the closest thing they had to decor. His father, who was at

Dunkirk and D-Day, struck near-silent by the trauma of what he'd seen there. And a mother who reacted to the loneliness of a shell-shocked husband by throwing herself into St Saviour's Church with its oppressive conservatism.

'My childhood was soundtracked by the church cohort in our kitchen outdoing each other for how scandalised they were by the morals of the youth like they'd never been young themselves.' From the little Graham talks about Barbara, their relationship seemed akin to a boss and her employee, defined by hierarchy and fear. She wanted her son to fear her, fear God, driven entirely by her own fears of how he reflected on her. She repressed him, stifled him, even physically, stuffing him into starched suits and putting his brilliance on display like an exhibit. There was no love. What happens to that overwhelming need for care and affection a child has when it's met by a brick wall? The hurt goes inside, the pain brews into resentment, anger, murderous rage perhaps.

And how must it have felt seeing Penny and Neil together in that intimate moment, warmth, love, respect passing between them like electricity round a circuit, when not only had Graham not had it in his own life, but growing up in a straight-laced working-class town in the shadows of two world wars, he'd possibly never even seen it.

I imagined Graham staring at the cracks in the ceiling of his chip-oil stinking Bermondsey flat after he'd returned from Penny's bohemian bazaar feeling those same sharp stabs of jealousy. The subredditors thought Graham might have been driven to murder because he felt inferior in terms of talent, but maybe he was driven by something deeper. Graham could work on his talent, play until his fingers calloused to stone, study the masters, write ten thousand songs. But the thing he could never have had is Neil's life.

9.

Graham's tapes gave me a picture of the man but when it came to why he left Britain, and Nereus's actual death, it was all conjecture. Everything I knew about what might have happened that night was from the notoriously unreliable people on the internet and various Nereus biographies which offered nothing more than creative re-renderings of the story put out into the public domain at the time. I needed someone who was there so I reached out to former Detective Inspector Bryn Halleran.

Bryn was one of only two policemen still alive who worked on the case, and the only one who would speak to me. He'd commented on a couple of threads on the *nereusforever* subreddit, usually pouring cold water on preposterous theories with actual facts, so I decided to reach out. Seventy-two when we first met, with close-cropped grey hair and a square nose like a bullseye in the middle of his face; despite fashionable thick-framed glasses I could tell Bryn had been a policeman from a thousand yards. He had told me on the phone he'd continued investigating Nereus's death for a few months after the police's official verdict of 'death by misadventure'.

'There were a couple of things I couldn't square,' he said when I asked why he couldn't let the case go. 'But mainly, it was because no one on the force apart from me seemed to care that Nereus had died at all.' Bryn was a fan, a big one. 'Saw him in Brixton,' he told me. 'Earl's Court, up to

Cambridge even. Loved everything about him. But to most I worked with, Nereus was just the pervert from the papers.' I asked how it felt finding Neil's body that night. 'Like finding a family member,' Bryn said. 'Sounds stupid, but that's how much it hurt.'

One of the main things Bryn couldn't square about Nereus's death related to the time of death.

'Forensics were rudimentary back then,' he told me. 'Time of death was done by body temperature, stage of rigor mortis. Not fail-safe at all. But the time they gave always seemed tight.'

'In what way?'

'Someone with a high tolerance like Nereus wouldn't have died from an overdose instantly. For him to be dead at six, which is the latest time they gave, he's having the hit at least half an hour before but probably more like one or two hours.'

I did the maths. His girlfriend Greta Handverk was believed to have been there between three thirty and four fifteen latest. If Graham was there, the earliest would have been between around five and six, when the green Jaguar was first sighted. The red-headed woman came by between four and four thirty and is thought to have left, though we can't be certain she didn't gain access to the house in some way. If Greta was involved in his death, maybe the two of them taking heroin together, she would have to have left immediately afterwards to have been seen by multiple people in Soho at four thirty. If we think Graham's responsible, he has to have done the deed the minute he walked through the door.

'What does that tell us?' I asked Bryn.

'That if Graham was involved, he went there that night in order to do it.' I blinked. This went against everything I had thought. Neil and Graham's relationship had long broken down by then; from what I knew they hadn't seen each other for at least three years. If Graham did something to him, I had assumed he was provoked into a crime of passion. Going there with the express intention of calculated murder didn't make sense.

'But why?' I asked. 'Why would he go there to kill him after so many years?'

'That never bothered me.'

'How could it not?' Bryn took a deep breath, sucked his teeth.

'I saw men come back and murder their wives after ten years, nothing to provoke them,' he said. 'Men of my generation, there was no therapy, no mental health awareness. Only thing you could do is brood. You do it long enough, who knows what it drives you to do. But, as my superiors said back then, we had a drug addict who died of an overdose on the wrong side of a locked door. However much I felt like there was more to it, the most obvious answer is usually the right one.'

10.

After the impromptu performance at Penny's soirée of what would become 'Abigail's Way', the songs began to flow, though Danny and Fraz were still unconvinced by Neil's strange behaviour.

'He'd look right at us and apply lipstick,' Danny writes, 'like we were a mirror, or pick up bits of my kit as props in some ballet he was making up.' This came to a head when Neil stopped them mid-song one afternoon and told them they were playing 'slugs and snails' where he needed 'a centipede stepping along the spine of a leaf', leading the proud Northerners to storm out.

'They're not your butlers,' Graham told Neil after his school friends had left. 'Make an effort, pretend if you have to.' Graham placated the lads back to work but his words had clearly touched Neil because a black Bentley was waiting outside for them at the end of the day to whisk them to the most exclusive private member's club in London – Annabelle's.

Known as a regular hang-out of Frank Sinatra, John Wayne, European royalty and the cogs of international power, the boys from Whitby couldn't believe it when the doorman embraced Neil and waved them past the queue inside. They watched in amazement as he worked velvet banquettes of middle-aged men in Saville Row suits, kissing their wives or mistresses on the lips, twirling an ancient-looking heiress on the starlit dance floor. Though Graham felt stiff amidst the loucheness of these power-players, uncomfortable with Neil touching the glitterati with the intimacy of a decades-old lover, Danny and Fraz couldn't get enough of this glamorous new world. Especially when they arrived at 'their' table to find a bevy of models. 'We'd never seen girls like it,' Danny writes in his memoir. 'Like goddesses dropped to earth.'

'If Neil wanted to get the chaps onside,' Graham recalls on the tapes, 'he couldn't have planned it better.'

As the drinks flowed, the girls seemed to get over their doubts about the boys' accents and passé suits, and paired off with them. Leaving Graham with Julie Stark, the It girl he'd met at Penny's soirée.

'How is it he knows everyone?' Graham asked as they watched Neil bouncing from table to table like a delighted cricket.

'We grew up in places like this,' she said, barely interested.

'As kids?'

'Our mothers and fathers didn't build their lives in Mayfair to be at home eating soup of an evening listening to the wireless,' Julie said.

'But this is no place for a child,' he said. Julie looked at him with an incredulous smirk.

'What a funny chap you are,' she said, not remotely amused, before taking the ice bucket off to be replenished. Graham continued to watch Neil, imagining him as a boy in such nightclubs trying to appear at home. Since meeting Penny's coterie and seeing mother with son, Graham had been so envious of their life, but for the first time he realised he and Neil had both been forced to live in an adult's world too soon.

Later Neil saw Graham at a booth alone while Danny and Fraz were ensconced with their girls, Julie nowhere in sight, and suggested they go on somewhere. 'Just the two of us.'

Fifteen minutes later, their cab pulled up at a black door

in Soho where they were greeted by a lady in her seventies dressed head to toe in Chanel who Neil introduced as Tabby.

'I thought she was an elderly relative,' Graham recalls. 'Only when two women in silk gowns got up from a game of chess and ran over, I realised he'd brought me to a brothel.' An out-of-the-frying-pan-into-the-volcano situation for Graham.

The taller of the two took Neil off through one of six burgundy doors while the other took Graham's hand and led him to the bedroom opposite. The girl was petite with freckles and curly dark hair and introduced herself as Harriet. She got Graham a drink, put on a record. Little Richard. One of his slower ones.

'From up North?' she said. Graham nodded, standing awkwardly by the door still.

'I'm from Somerset, Taunton.' Which explained her lilting accent.

'What, um, brought you up here?'

'Bright lights, make my fortune, same as you.'

'And is this –' Graham knew he shouldn't ask about her profession, but it was anathema to him that someone who seemed so sweet could choose to have sex with people for money.

'This is what I do,' she said, sliding off her bolero jacket to reveal a red lace brassiere. 'I'm very skilled and you're very good-looking. Want to come over?' Graham approached the bed, a hulk of a man frightened like a child. He doesn't say much about what happened next in the tapes, but it didn't seem to go as you might expect.

'She was easy to talk to,' he says. 'I liked her. The whole thing didn't seem right though. Little Richard playing felt like I was at home again. Had my mother in my head.' Although I had no way of knowing, I thought there was a good chance

Graham was a virgin at that point and can't imagine the crushing shame he must have felt to be put in a situation like that.

Neil came in some time later and found Graham sitting on the edge of the bed, fully clothed while he was in his girl's silk robe, hair mussed, reeking of abandon. 'I'm sorry,' Graham said, expecting Neil to be disappointed, annoyed at wasting his money.

'Harriet told me she had a wonderful time,' he said. Graham looked at him and felt such gratitude at the easy absolution. 'We won't tell the boys about what a lovely night we've had though. They'd be so jealous. Now, I've got a key to the old church hall. Shall we go make some music?'

They fleshed out two more songs that night and were still playing together when Danny and Fraz arrived dishevelled but delighted the next morning. After three rounds of toast and many more cups of tea Neil may have laced with brandy, the four played the new music together and it was good. The room shone from glowing smiles through the hangovers and sleeplessness. They were becoming a band.

'He'd chosen to take me into his secret world and looked after me. He was everything I'd been brought up to detest, but I couldn't help it. It made me feel special.'

11.

Roughly six months into what Bobby had begun to refer to as my 'inquisition', my phone started glitching. Green lines of light would appear and then stop. It would turn off for no reason, vibrate without there being a notification. I put it down to it being an iPhone 5. My tech-obsessed nineteen-year-old daughter Delphi, who still lived with us when she wasn't at her girlfriend's, was always begging me to get a new one but I'd grown attached to it, blanketed in dust as it was in its silver-mosaic case. But by that point the conspiracists' mindset had infected me by osmosis and I plugged the phone's symptoms into my forums.

'They're tracking you,' the user who called himself asperryman3 replied on Reddit within seconds. In no time, he'd posted dozens of links to articles about malware, Government surveillance, and somewhat surprisingly, a *New York Times* article about the Harvey Weinstein case. I didn't read them, dismissing asperryman3 as I'd learnt to early on in proceedings. But a few nights later, as I made my way to the Underground after one of the first times I'd met some of my new online people in real life at a pub in Clerkenwell, I felt sure I was being followed.

A man wearing one of those flat caps Jason Statham favours, a scarf pulled up to his face, was walking on the opposite side of the street and I felt sure he was staring at me. I caught him looking at one point and he quickly marched down a side street out of view. At least that's what it seemed like. He could have thought I was giving him the eye and wanted to make his feelings crystal clear. But it unsettled me and, with the glitching phone, when I got home that night, I started to look into a theory I'd always thought to be outlandish.

Nereus was twenty-five when he died but he's often conflated with the famous '27 Club' of musicians who died at the beginning of the seventies. And like them, there are many out there who believe the CIA were involved with his death. Or MI5, or the police, or the British Government, or Spectre – essentially any shadowy agency people have seen in films.

Candi Garner, who posts as candishack, a trans woman, card-carrying anarchist and proud LGBTQ+ advocate, is a firm proponent of the theory the British Government wanted Nereus dead.

'He made being different, androgynous, trans look way better than the cis Victorian bullshit they were pushing back then,' Candi told me. 'He created a mania at his concerts, like a prophet. Gave people licence to be who they wanted to be. What's more dangerous for a government trying to control its people than that?' Rock stars had long been accused of corrupting the youth but there was no doubt Nereus's genderfluidity presented British society with something they saw as darker and more troubling than long hair and leather jackets. The decriminalisation of homosexuality in 1967 had created a full-on culture war around the sex lives of Britain's youth and with his outlandish outfits and stage persona, Nereus swiftly became the symbol of the country's slide into iniquity. Which is why, Candi is certain, he became a target.

Although I've never bought into governments putting contracts out on musicians, there is one significant detail from the case which could be seen to support the theory. In the days after his death was announced, police put huge emphasis on how he choked on his vomit, that the room was littered with spirit bottles, several glasses, that his clothes were stained with whisky and even that his hair smelled strongly of liquor.

In the autopsy, however, the coroner reports that though there was a reasonable amount of alcohol in his body, there was more whisky found in Nereus's lungs than in his stomach. How did the alcohol get on his clothes, his hair and most significantly in his lungs, if he didn't seem to drink much? Candi and many others think the only explanation for it is that someone tried to force the alcohol down his throat, causing him to choke on it and get it all over him, in an attempt to disguise the true cause of death. Despite this, I still found it impossible to accept they'd go to all that trouble, or take such a sizeable risk, just because Nereus was felt to be 'corrupting the nation's youth'.

But when I looked into Tabby Jocasta's brothel, where we know Neil was a regular, another theory occurred to me. In the 1980s, Tabitha Drake, Ms Jocasta's real name, appears several times in papers relating to the Hawthorn Inquiry – an investigation into government ministers' and international diplomats' involvement with prostitutes. I couldn't quite believe they'd kill Nereus for some ephemeral sense he might 'send the country to the dogs', but if he knew something someone in the corridors of power needed to remain secret, is it too much of a stretch to imagine they might want that problem to go away?

I didn't want it to be true. I couldn't see where Graham's disappearance would fit into that story. And, more pertinently, I didn't want someone to be following me.

12.

Two weeks after the night at Annabelle's, the band was at Bricktop Studios recording the Neil Forbes and The Marshalls EP. Graham was in heaven. Clive Dors, the engineer of the sessions who continued to work with Nereus throughout his short career, wrote that Graham was a 'natural in the studio', arranging songs and playing virtually all the additional instrumental lines. Short of the lyrics and top-line melodies, it seemed like he did almost everything.

With the six songs they'd worked on still mostly unfinished, Neil and Graham grew close, spending almost every minute outside the sessions working together in the parlour at Penny's house. She taught Graham mah-jong while Neil slept off his hangovers and would bring museum books filled with pictures of articles of antiquity if they seemed stuck which, despite Graham's initial doubt, always seemed to unlock something. The two men would kick through leaves walking into the sessions together, talking incessantly.

'Neil wanted to know about my dad and the war. Loved anything about the church, the gospel, catechisms. Obsessed with Lot's wife turning into a pillar of salt.' At weekends, Graham would sneak out of their Bermondsey flat while Danny and Fraz slept to join Neil at the Tate, talks at the ICA, even an art-house cinema to watch Tom Courtney in an adaptation of *One Day in the Life of Ivan Denisovich*.

'I was hungry for it because I didn't finish school,' Graham recalls. 'Being with Neil was like university.' Graham's world was expanding and in the studio everything was sounding wonderful. By the end of their three weeks at Bricktop, he was convinced they had made something truly special. But as the band listened to the final mix, while Danny, Fraz, Clive and Otis's assistant Lisa were popping Asti Spumante, Neil stood up and left without a word. Concerned, Graham forsook the celebrations and took a bus to his house.

'You must go talk to him, darling,' Penny said as she wrapped him in one of her hugs at the front door. 'He's fallen into one of his funks.'

Graham found Neil slumped on a pile of velvet cushions in his bedroom, two bottles of red wine down. His room was vastly different from the rest of the house. Walls covered with charcoal sketches, posters ripped from travel magazines: the Acropolis, Mayan temples, but also homewear and fashion, Eames chairs, William Morris wallpaper. Graham felt like he was looking at Neil's mind.

'What do you want from music?' Neil asked.

'What do you mean?'

'Your aim. What is it you're aiming to do when you pick up a guitar, write a song?'

'I don't know.' Graham leant on the doorframe. 'Make something which might stay with the people who hear it. Change them. Make their life a little better.'

'I want to change the world.' Neil jumped up from where he was and put a large, dishevelled folder in Graham's hands. 'Never shown anyone this.' He went to the other side of the room and stared out the window at a sycamore in the garden fighting with the wind. Graham opened the folder and found the pages of a home-made book. We might have called it a graphic novel, though that wasn't a known term back then, so to Graham it was a comic called *The Fall of Pacifica*.

That original first edition Graham read took pride of place at the Nereus exhibition. I had to wear white cotton gloves to handle it, while Yin Li, the senior curator, watched me like I was a teenage shoplifter. The illustrations are incredible, drawing stylistically on influences ranging from nineteenth-century Japanese Shunga erotic art to the original runs of Marvel's Fantastic Four.

The story is about Poiseidon, a dissolute prince of an advanced underwater civilisation, a utopia based on Plato's myth of Atlantis. When the sea level rises, it brings Pacifica into contact with the people of Earth, the Terranians. Pacifica wages war on the inferior Terranians but amongst the bloodshed, Poiseidon realises the only way to save both civilisations from environmental disaster is in becoming a messianic figure who sacrifices himself to find a mineral which provides eternal energy. It ties Jules Verne up with the beginnings of climate science, the global fear of nuclear annihilation with messianic religious dogma, undeniably brilliant for an eighteen-year-old.

What's more typical of a teenage boy is the second half, however, where it seems Poiseidon's sacrifice involves his engaging the Terranians in a seemingly endless orgy to find the chosen person with whom he can somehow conceive and birth whatever the magical mineral is. It's filthy. I was shocked and I wasn't brought up by the ultra-conservative Barbara in 1950s Yorkshire. As Graham skipped towards the end, at once scandalised and fascinated by the caverns of Neil's mind, Neil sat at an electric piano and began singing a song about Poiseidon half-drowning in the air.

'Is that this?' Graham held up the folder at the end of the song, trying to make sense of Neil's sullen drunkenness and the bizarre book.

'Back in Greece,' Neil said. 'I somewhat drowned. Three years old.' Neil swung his head round to face Graham. 'I heard a voice in the water,' he continued. 'Like windchimes deep inside my head. Gentle hands pushed me up to the surface, lifted me right up, out of the surf. I've no doubt I would have died.'

'What was it?' Graham asked. Neil turned to him, blinked.

'An angel, I suppose.' Graham smiled, about to ask what he really thought it was before realising Neil was being sincere.

'That's what I want to do,' he said, indicating the folder in Graham's hand. 'I see *The Fall of Pacifica* as an album, a show, an opera for the people, a huge spectacular at the scale of gladiatorial bouts at the Coliseum.' Graham looked at the pages of lurid illustrations in his hands, wondering if Neil might not be completely mad.

'Coming to the end of something like today –' Graham said, not sure how to be tactful about the idea of putting his mermaid fantasia to music. 'It's normal to feel put out. But songs we've done, about girls, getting your heart broken, love, that's what people want to listen to. Trust me.'

Graham was wrong. It would be generous to call the 'Neil Forbes and The Marshalls' EP a flop, because when it came out on 19 May 1970, barely anyone noticed. The few critics who did couldn't square Neil's ghostly, theatrical voice with The Marshalls' prosaic rock sound while the songs were found to be, in the words of a critic in the *Daily Mirror*, 'somehow both formulaic and naïve'. It hit Graham hard.

'I thought it would launch things,' he said. 'Thought things might start coming easier.' On top of which, the lack of response to the EP meant no summer tour to promote it which felt to Graham not just the end of the line for the project but also for his relationship with Neil.

'With nothing else to work on, I couldn't justify going over to Penny's. And I didn't hear from Neil at all.' Graham would lie awake at night staring at mould blooming in the corner of his bedroom, wondering whether the friendship with Neil he'd begun to find so nourishing might have been purely transactional. The partnership hadn't borne fruit and Neil seemed to have forgotten him.

But three weeks later, as the boys were eating dinner after an afternoon in the pub, a car horn blasted repeatedly outside their window. They looked out to see Penny's Bentley, Neil leaning over the driver, pounding on the horn. The Marshalls came out onto the street, pulling their coats on, Fraz still holding his half-eaten pie. 'Get in, get in,' Neil said. 'Chop, chop.'

'What's going on?' Graham said.

'What's going on?' he said, wildly gesticulating them into the car. 'What's going on is we're going to be on television gentlemen, is what's going on.'

13.

There have been whole books written about the performance of 'Platinum Scales' on *Top of the Pops* that night. For Graham the experience was disorienting the moment Neil picked them up.

They arrived late, The Marshalls still tipsy from their afternoon at the pub, while Neil was so manic they could barely keep him inside the car.

'Mother heard two bands had dropped out with Hong Kong flu and pitched us for the spot,' Neil said as they were rushed through a labyrinth of corridors by a furious assistant. He had been evasive on the journey, giving Graham the feeling there might be more to this miraculous opportunity.

His anxiety increased when he saw a schedule on the wall saying they were there to play 'Platinum Scales' – a song he'd never heard of. He raced ahead to ask Neil about it, but by the time he caught up, he'd disappeared inside a dressing room. When Graham followed him in, he found himself face-to-face with a rail of aquamarine jumpsuits with silver fish-scale detailing along the arms and legs. His stomach sank as he realised what was happening.

'The song you played me in your bedroom?' he said. 'From your book? The mermaid song?' Neil shrugged, a coy smile. Otis de Kock stood smoking a thin cigar next to Penny, both clearly in on the ambush. From out of nowhere a young woman with freckles and a coffee-coloured Mary Quant bob appeared in front of Graham. She held out one of the shimmering blue bodysuits, the most outlandish piece of clothing Graham had ever seen let alone been expected to wear. He turned round and walked out, not intending to stop until he'd got back to Bermondsey.

'Can I help you get into that?' The girl with the bob said from just outside the dressing room, stopping Graham halfway down the corridor.

'She had a big grin on her face,' he said. 'All dimples, batting her eyelashes. Reminded me of a very pretty Jersey cow.' It was odd for me to hear Graham say this on the tapes, because the young design student of Penny's who had helped to sew together the original Poiseidon costumes was my mother, Sadie Blakely.

'It wasn't love at first sight,' she told me. 'But, this big man all puffed up like that. He was sweet.' She walked over, held the outfit up against him.

'You don't like it?' she said, mock innocence.

'Not my style.' Graham struggled with letting his hair grow long, and insisted The Marshalls played in button-down shirts all the way until they were in London. One night Fraz wore a scarf to a gig in Croydon and Danny had to stop Graham yanking it off him. With his mother's voice always there at the back of his head, putting on a spangly jumpsuit would have been a horror he wouldn't have even comprehended.

'Your style got you on TV recently?' Sadie said.

'If wearing that is what it takes, I'll pass.'

'I made "that",' she said, shoving it into his chest. 'Don't be offensive, we've only just met.' He spotted Penny in the door frame giving him the most withering of looks. Graham took the hanger and stormed back into the dressing room.

'I'm not sure he was ever really going to leave,' Sadie said. 'Though Neil can't have been certain, because he sent his mother and me.'

Once in their outfits, immensely tight and sparkly but not as bad as they'd looked on the rail, they had one rehearsal under the lights where Graham, possibly to overcome how emasculated he felt, took control.

'Graham always seemed at home in those environments,' Sadie said. 'Could ignore everyone else's stress, the pressure. Getting up on stage had been his whole life.' Back in the dressing room Neil stood at the mirror as they waited to go on, applying too much theatrical greasepaint, his usual devil-may-care sparkle dulled to rust. Graham was almost pleased to see a chink of vulnerability beneath the bravura – Neil was scared.

'Think of it like just you and me up there,' Graham said, taking the make-up stick out of his hand. Neil grabbed his wrist.

'You, me and the future history of the world,' he said. Graham smiled, grabbed at Danny and Fraz and the four men walked down the corridor to the sound stage, hugging each other like brothers in arms. As they took their places on stage, they wouldn't have heard the presenter introducing them to the audience not as The Marshalls, nor even Neil Forbes and The Marshalls but as just Nereus Forbes.

I've watched the performance dozens of times. The costumes look twee, like something from *Dr Who*. Elvis had been doing rhinestone jumpsuits for years, TV comedians like Tommy Cooper had cross-dressed, wearing far more outlandish costumes. No, the power of those three minutes of television all comes from Neil. How unashamedly strange he is, looking into the camera, going from smiling to sultry come-to-bed eyes as he sings.

'No one was behaving like that on national television,' cultural professor Dr Hailee told me. 'The fearlessness, the total lack of apology.' It's electrifying to watch even decades later.

The performance was better than Graham expected. The audience seemed drawn to the oddness of their outfits. Wearing a rock-star pout throughout, Graham seems unaware of Neil's canoodling with the camera. About halfway through he even starts enjoying himself, eyes closed as he sings his harmonies. But then Neil's at his microphone, looking straight into his eyes as he sings. Graham tries to hold Neil's look, but you can sense he's somewhere else. With Barbara, her church, every fisherman in Whitby, every promoter, venue owner in the North. His father. Imagining them watching him being mooned over by a merman in drag make-up. Neil stares down the barrel of the camera and puts his arm round Graham's shoulder, pulls him closer as they sing into one mic. Graham smiles through clear discomfort. Then Neil sneaks his hand over, dips it onto Graham's bare chest and plants a kiss on his cheek, just missing the side of his mouth. It's not a peck you'd give your grandmother. It's lips pressed firmly into Graham's beard like a possessive lover. Graham freezes, rictus grin, doesn't move away until they finish the song. Neil might as well have stuck his tongue down his throat. Sadie remembers the audience gasping, almost as one. It was shocking, transgressive, yet very sexy. It would change everything.

14.

There have been multiple sightings of Graham Harris over the years. Greece, Thailand, Montana, even Medellín and the Colombian jungle. But Graham wasn't Elvis or Amelia Earhart. If it had been Nereus who disappeared, there'd be a ten-thousand-strong army searching for him, but none of the people I met in the months after I began looking into the story had any real sense of where he might be, nor seemed much to care.

I asked Bryn to check Graham's name and social security number on various police portals and public sector databases but nothing came up, meaning he'd either changed his name or, more likely, hadn't been back to the UK since he left. I reached out to the office of the Jordanian royal family but no one would speak to me about whether he arrived with them, or where he might have gone if he had. I had a map on the wall of the summerhouse which I'd turned into my centre of operations, on which I tracked with push-pins where he might have logically gone on from Monaco. I checked the sightings of him against well-known backpacking routes of the period, and ease of travel with the Iron Curtain still firmly down. But it yielded nothing.

My daughter Delphi, who I would often find amongst my research in my garden-bunker, was convinced he'd be in North Africa on the hippy trail.

'It's the only place a seventies rock star would go to hide,' she said. But Graham wasn't a typical rock star. London felt exotic to him, I couldn't see him making a life for himself in Marrakesh. I met with several private investigators who specialise in tracking down people gone missing abroad. Most of them wouldn't take my money as I had no leads, no sense of where he might be and, crucially, he disappeared so long ago. The only person who even entertained looking for Graham suggested it would end up costing me tens of thousands of pounds.

When I asked my mother if she had any sense of his whereabouts, she was characteristically blunt on the matter.

'He'll be dead,' she said. She pointed out that Graham would be seventy-five, he smoked, drank, didn't know how to cook, or look after himself, and that she couldn't imagine him doing aqua aerobics. Although the tapes and various accounts of Graham didn't paint a heavy drinker, I had to concede a man of his generation holed up alone for years without any support was unlikely to have kept in great shape. I didn't want it to be true, but Graham having died was a possibility. In a world with the internet, social media and obsessive online fandoms, I had to accept it might be the most likely explanation for why no one knew where he was.

The one thing I did feel sure about, though, was that my father had loved me. I don't remember details from before I was five, but I know what parental ambivalence looks like; when my girls were young I'm sure I was guilty of it from time to time. I never felt that from Graham, he always seemed thrilled when he was with me. His love for me, unequivocal. Even if Graham had nothing to do with Nereus's death, he left my life forever that day. Which, I've come to realise, meant Graham Harris made a choice. And I wasn't what he chose. Which is why, as I began to meet with my motley crew of internet folk in the Crown Tavern in Farringdon, Central

London – insurance investigator Stan Derbyshire, Candi the activist, former Detective Bryn, with Lennox the lawyer from Wisconsin dialling in on Zoom, later joined by Dr Hailee – I found it hard to accept jealousy or gripes over money or credit as motive enough to commit murder. Humiliation, however, making a Christian-raised Yorkshireman from fishing stock look gay in front of the entire nation, I found harder to dismiss.

Particularly after what I discovered from Nereus's former neighbour Abby Grade. She was fourteen when Nereus died, sixty-one when we met. She had crab-apple cheekbones and flowing grey hair which reminded me of a druidic village elder. I tracked her down to her home town of West Wittering in West Sussex hoping she might shed some light on the mysterious red-headed visitor she told the police she'd seen outside 1 Cheyne Walk the day Nereus died.

'The woman was around a lot,' Abby told me. 'With Nereus, but with all of them. The bands.'

'A groupie?'

'She was in her thirties. Their tastes skewed younger.' Abby's voice had a louche irony, the sound of an eyeroll. 'Fans were always knocking on his door, but she seemed desperate to get in the house, agitated. Only reason I mentioned it.' Abby had no idea who she was but told me about Chelsea in those days, the bands, movie stars, models and aristocrats sat outside the pubs amongst window-boxes of dazzling flowers, drinking and the rest until they couldn't anymore. The red-headed woman was often there, but so were many, many others.

'Did you ever see her with Graham Harris?' I asked on a whim, expecting nothing as he hadn't been amongst Neil's milieu for several years by that point. 'No, but I did see him visiting Cheyne Walk,' she said.

'You did?'

'A month or so before Nereus passed.'

'Are you sure it was then?'

'We went to Cornwall until the end of August every year but I hadn't gone back to school. So it must have been the first week of September.'

I was shocked. The received wisdom was that Graham and Neil hadn't seen each other since 1972. The legal document we found hints at some involvement between them later, but I hadn't found any suggestion they were in contact so close to his death.

I retreated to my summerhouse when I got home that afternoon to listen to the last of Graham's tapes again, which finished a week and a half before the murder, but found no hint he'd seen Neil a couple of weeks before. I flicked through my notes for anything I'd missed which might indicate why he'd been there but again drew a blank.

In the first week of September, Nereus would have been back from his US tour for around ten days. The Concert at the Sunken City was announced mid-September. I asked myself why Graham might conceal the visit from his biographer. Surely, if his and Neil's story was coming to its close, them seeing each other after so long could be a good ending, the perfect button. In the tapes Graham comes across as open, honest, disarmingly so at times. The omission felt significant.

Abby told me Graham's Jaguar was still there at midnight the night she saw him a month before Nereus's death. Graham had stayed at Neil's house into the night. I leant back in my mildewed office chair and gazed up at the maps, newspaper articles and photos I'd pinned to the walls and connected with fishing wire like I'd seen on police programmes. I hadn't done it right. It looked like the work of a half-cut spider. Delphi referred to my mind map at dinner one night as 'the most rudimentary mid-life crisis I've ever seen'.

I stood up and unpinned the picture of the two men from that *Top of the Pops* performance, just before the kiss. Neil's hand on Graham's chest. Graham's jaw clenched, eyes seeming somewhere else entirely. I tried to decipher what was going through his head. Discovering he'd been to see Neil in secret in September 1977, perhaps staying the night, I began to wonder whether it might not have been public humiliation which made him so angry that night at the TV studio but that Neil had awoken something in him. Love, lust, loathing, loot. He got together with Sadie, they had me, but that doesn't preclude the idea he could have had feelings for Neil. That he was, perhaps, in love with him.

Within a few weeks of first having this thought, after I'd talked to my mother and had memories of my childhood stirred up in me like burnt scraps at the bottom of a pan, I began realising I might have wanted Graham to have killed Nereus. That perhaps that was the reason I'd become so fixated on finding out what really happened. But only if Graham had done it for love. Out of a deep, tragic love. Because if Graham hadn't killed Neil, if he wasn't fleeing an irredeemable act he'd been driven to by a love that dare not speak its name, why else would he have chosen to abandon me?

Dance of the Satyrs

Although it didn't deliver the grand-standing originality of *Apotheosis, Dance of the Satyrs*, the first album as Nereus Forbes, was a hard-hitting triumph of art-rock brilliance. While 'Platinum Scales' grabbed the attention for its sense of world-building, the stand-out track is 'Found Them There'. A classic top-line melody of sickly sweetness commands Nereus's paean to polyamory, giving profundity to lyrics which in other hands might have seemed lascivious. Its raunchy guitar riff is only just brought back by the school-hall sound of Blakely's piano part. A song greater than the sum of its parts, it has a depth which haunts the listener and begs to be played again and again.

From *The Star of the Sea* by Tony Nagdadis.

15.

From the moment Graham left the country, my mother and I became a two-person coven. We moved to Kent, outside Tunbridge Wells. She got a job as a seamstress at a haberdashery. I spent my afternoons after school running my hands along reels of silk and velvet, using off-cuts to make sculptures which would attract families of moths into the wardrobe in my bedroom where I stored them. I would press pincushions into my palm because I liked the way it felt. Things were fluid. There were no bedtimes, no rules of what I should wear, whom I should choose to hang out with. That's not to say my mother wasn't fiercely protective.

When I was thirteen, Sadie got wind that a boy had been rude to me, making inappropriate comments about my newly developed body. She hung him up on a school fencepost by his blazer like she was Henry VIII putting his head on a spike. She could be strict with me too but only ever if I was lying or being secretive. Honesty was the only thing she ever demanded of me. Which was why I didn't question when she said she had no idea where my father was when I asked as a child. And why my finding something she'd hidden in the attic when I was twenty-three created such a fracture between us.

I lived at home at the time, commuting to London where I was studying film. We had been given a project to make a collage piece about childhood and one afternoon when my mother was at work, I climbed into the attic hoping to find some images or artifacts to base my film around. After blowing years of cobwebs away from packing boxes and screaming after uncovering a colony of woodlice under a stack of records, I began leafing through old photos. I found one of myself as a baby in Sadie's arms in front of a fully blossoming tree, but that aside, there was very little from before I was about six, none of me with Graham.

Having taken a few pictures from their sleeves in the musty albums and an old pocket watch I thought might be my grandfather's, and sneezing repeatedly from the dust, I began climbing back into the light, when I spied a polka-dot box shoved roughly into the eaves at the far end of the room. Having never seen it before, I crouched down and yanked it from under some decrepit Easter decorations. Sitting on the floor, I took off the lid, more mould than cardboard, and saw a faded image of a teddy bear holding a bunch of balloons. It was a birthday card. I opened it and a folded fifty-pound note fell out. I can't remember if it was current or had been discontinued. I read the message.

'Dear Winnie, Happy Birthday Sweetheart, I love you.' There were a dozen more cards in the box, more even. I opened them to find the same bank note in each. And the exact same message. I knew straight away they were from Graham.

I confronted my mother with the cards the minute she came home.

'They're from years ago,' she said.

'The last one's from two years ago. I counted.' They stopped at twenty-one. Sadie cleared her throat, no remorse at being caught out in the lie.

'Why?' I asked. 'Why would you keep them from me?' Sadie pursed her lips, eyes darting to see if I was holding anything else. She was looking for the envelopes, the postmarks. 'You thought I'd try to find him? You hid the cards my dad sent me every year because you thought I'd try to find him.'

'Wouldn't you?' I was speechless. I never asked my mother about Graham because I understood the sacrifices she'd made, giving up her glamorous London life to raise me as a single mother. She had encouraged me not to think of him, to create an identity distinct from being a girl without a father and I'd gone along with it obediently, even when I was desperate to know more about him. The cards felt like a betrayal I'd never even considered before. I demanded she tell me where he was but she wouldn't.

'No good can come of it,' she said. 'Decisions are made and we move on.' I left home and moved into Bobby's flat in Kingston the next day.

My mother and I spent a little over a year not speaking until I realised how self-defeating it was severing ties with my only remaining parent. She was unapologetic, which didn't surprise me, and the matter became one of those hearty bones of contention which can linger in families for decades. Never talked about but never forgotten. As the years passed, we continued being involved in each other's lives. She was a hands-on grandmother when called into action, Sara and Delphi both adored her. But our relationship never returned to how it was before I found the cards.

So it was daunting meeting her for lunch one day and telling her about the threatening poster, Graham's tapes, the people on the internet convinced Nereus was murdered. And I was right to be daunted because her assessment, given between bites of home-made flatbreads and tzatziki, was withering.

'You're wasting your time,' she said, flicking the bob she'd kept her whole life, now laced with silver. 'Only nutters think it wasn't an accident.' Undeterred, I told her I had questions about that time I felt she owed me answers to.

'Is it not a little late to try to find yourself?' she said with the sort of lacerating insight only a mother can have. I bowed my head, trying not to let her rile me.

'I have never told your granddaughters about the birthday cards,' I said as calmly as I could. 'I've never told them you blocked any chance I had to have a relationship with my father, who clearly wanted one. I've never told them about the space it left in my life, the space I filled with booze, men I didn't like, two university degrees and about five different careers.' Sadie walked towards the patio door. I couldn't see her face, but I could tell I was making an impact. 'Young girls don't like other women being controlled, having their agency, their choices taken away. I don't think they would forgive you. Delphs might, but Sara . . .' My eldest, who wanted to be a human rights lawyer, was my mother's favourite.

'It won't fix anything,' Sadie said in a thin voice, staring out into my garden. I wondered whether she meant me or our relationship. I wasn't sure I cared. She sighed, put a hand on the glass, condensation clouding around her fingers. 'Fine.'

16.

Sadie was nineteen the night Neil put his hand inside Graham's shirt in front of the nation. She was studying textile design and fine art at the school that would later become the world-renowned Central Saint Martin's. Penny, a visiting lecturer, took an instant liking to her when she interrupted a talk she was giving on Plato's *Symposium*.

'Don't we have enough men telling us the meaning of life, without trawling back through the archives?' she said. Penny invited her to one of her soirées that night, where she first met Neil.

'Mama said your designs are magnificent,' he said. 'Very Bauhaus.' She didn't know what to make of Neil with his long hair, eyeliner and full lips. She'd watched him being flirtatious, overly tactile with other girls at the party, but he couldn't make eye contact with her, more prey than predator.

'He saw me as Penny's protégée,' she told me. 'He'd never do anything to upset his mother.'

'What did you think of him?' I asked.

'Apart from the fancy dress, he seemed like every other entitled mummy's boy I'd met.'

A few weeks later, just after the release of the EP, Neil invited Sadie to Quaglino's where he showed her his graphic novel and asked her to make the costumes from it. Sadie wasn't sure she wanted to involve herself with this strange boy and his Jaques Cousteau erotic fiction.

'But he was a good salesman,' she said. 'Talked about kids needing something new, hoped they could build a better world. It was the Cold War after all. He was frightfully sincere. And he was paying.' Sadie didn't have the luxury of turning Neil down, her father had cut her off the year before.

Sadie's father Benjamin Blakely had been a successful businessman before becoming a Conservative MP in 1959. Her mother Adeline grew up in colonial Zimbabwe, daughter of a mine manager and his wife, returning to England in 1948 on a scholarship at the London School of Economics. But after meeting and marrying Benjamin, ten years her senior, he demanded she give up her studies to have Sadie, then three years later, her brother, Cameron.

It was not a happy marriage. Adeline hated being a politician's wife and would tell her daughter stories of men's weakness and fragility like ancient fables. Benjamin duly enforced everything she'd said in 1965 when he was exposed as having extramarital affairs with not one, but two of the young women who worked for him at the Houses of Parliament. In the wake of the Profumo Affair a few years before, the press jumped on more vinegary Tory sleaze like seagulls on a toddler's chips. More than the affair, it was the public humiliation which damaged Sadie the most. Her mother had no means of her own, was forced to stand by and excuse a cheating husband she despised for the sake of keeping a roof over her children's heads. Sadie was determined not to fall into the same trap.

Having drawn obsessively since she could hold a pencil and dressed her little brother up in costumes far beyond the age she should have, she left school at seventeen and moved to London to study design. And like the stand-up guy he was, Benjamin Blakely cut her off permanently – his design having been to marry her off to one of his influential and much older friends.

Knowing Sadie's upbringing, I'm often surprised she had me. I asked her about it one afternoon after I'd finished my first year at film school.

'We got pregnant,' she told me. 'Graham and I were in love then. It seemed the most natural thing in the world.'

This came back to me when I heard Graham talking about the aftermath of the *Top of the Pops* performance on the recording. It's what brought me to reach out to Sadie, knowing I wouldn't be able to tell the story of what happened between Neil and Graham, understand our part in it, without her perspective. Although things had turned sour between them by the time of Neil's death, Graham and Sadie had been in love. She had lost him too when he left. And I wondered whether she'd fallen for him then and there, because she went to him once the cameras had swung away after their performance.

He had ducked under Neil's arm and stormed backstage where Sadie found him in the dressing room trying to tear off his spandex costume.

'Let me, you'll rip it,' she said. He stopped, jumpsuit round his waist.

'You saw it, what he did?' he asked as she reached him, standing by the mirror.

'Come on,' she said, sitting him down and pulling the jumpsuit off him.

'How could he make me look like that?' Graham asked as she wiped sweat-drenched make-up from around his eyes. 'The whole world watching?' Sadie looked at him in the mirror, took in his bearishness for the first time. She smiled.

'It's mostly down to the incredible outfits of course,' she said. 'But the only thing you "looked" up there, was kind of incredible.'

17.

Though Sadie may have thought the show a triumph, for every person who loved the performance on *Top of the Pops*, there were many more appalled by it. The BBC had two hundred and ninety complaints. Mary Whitehouse, the campaigner for standards in British life, briefly made it one of her bêtes noires. Neil's hand drifting into Graham's shirt, the kiss on his cheek, made the inside pages of four different tabloids. An article in the *Mail* makes particularly grim reading, talking about how such public shows of homosexuality were the inevitable consequence of having decriminalised same-sex relations in 1967, imploring 'good Christians' to make a stand.

For Otis de Kock and Apollo Records, the furore was a boon. They could have paid all London's new-fangled PR companies and not got half the publicity. With the outfits, make-up and the way he interacted with the camera, Neil smashed every convention of how a singer should perform. Whether people loved it or hated it, the world wanted to know more about Nereus Forbes.

Otis called a meeting the day after the show and The Marshalls walked in to find Neil drinking champagne with the Apollo Records impresario, wearing a kimono over his fish-scale jumpsuit, hair still in the Viking braids Sadie had plaited for their TV appearance.

'The under-the-sea thing was there to stay,' Danny Greig writes.

'They're giving us an album,' Neil blurted, arms wide in celebration almost as soon as they walked through the door. Graham looked around at assistants primping towers of cakes and sandwiches, dumbfounded.

'I'd gone in for peace talks after what Neil'd done,' Graham said. 'But it was party time.' Once the drinks were poured, Otis went through plans for the album, including his intention to release in time for Christmas.

'How can we write a whole album in a couple of months?' Graham said, almost choking on a scone.

'Neil has seven songs already,' Otis said. 'Including "Platinum Scales".' Graham looked at the singer, incredulous.

'They all came out in a flurry after the EP,' he said. Graham sank back into his seat and Otis brought in a colleague to discuss the marketing plan; the first point of discussion was the band's name.

'A producer grabbed me to check the spelling for the autocue,' Neil said, addressing the band like he was performing Shakespeare. 'I had an epiphany there would never be a rock star called Neil. I told the chap Nereus. I honestly, hand on heart, expected them to call us Nereus and The Marshalls.'

'You just came up with it?' Graham said.

'Must have been mother in my head.' In Greek mythology, Nereus is the Titan who had dominion over the seas. Graham wasn't sure how true this was, but having looked through the archives and all the biographies, it's the only origin for the name I've been able to find. But Sadie didn't buy the story for a second.

'Everything he did was premeditated.' Regardless of how it came about, it was the name the country was now talking about so wasn't up for debate.

Doesn't fit with The Marshalls though,' Otis chimed in.

'Bit 1950s. The Mermen?' Graham looked at Danny and Fraz, gripping the underside of his chair.

'No, it has to be masculine,' Neil said, a half smile at Graham. 'Earthy. Let me be the fruit in the salad.'

They settled on The Satyrs – Greek woodland deities, famous for sexually assaulting mortals and nymphs alike. Though those in the room would have phrased it as being raunchy, manly types. When Neil suddenly jumped up on the table a little later, declaring the album should be called *Dance of the Satyrs,* seemingly making the band's new name central, everything seemed settled.

Danny and Fraz were over the moon, drinking top-shelf booze with pretty young secretaries in the office of a music exec – they finally had a record deal. Graham, however, couldn't enjoy it as much.

'Things had moved so slowly for us since we'd come to London,' Graham says on the tapes. 'So to get everything so quick. And how it had come, the outfits, the song. It was nothing like I'd imagined.'

'He didn't like looking gay on national TV,' Sadie said. 'But it was really that Graham had begun to trust Neil before that. Open himself up to him. Was a big deal for him. After the kiss, perhaps he thought he was wrong to.'

Otis produced a contract and a Mont Blanc pen which Danny leant forward to take, but Graham stopped him.

'We'll take a few days,' he said, surprising everyone in the room.

'Of course,' Neil said, a slight tension behind his eyes. 'You must.'

But in the intervening days, Neil barely left Graham's side, playing him the songs and asking for his input, trying to make it clear that despite his having written the songs, he still wanted Graham to be creatively central to the album.

There were together in Penny's parlour one morning when her housekeeper came in to tell Graham he had a phone call. Danny from the telephone box outside their flat.

'It's your mother,' Danny said. 'You've got to go home.'

'What? Why?'

'All she said was that you need to see what you've done.'

Graham ended the call, confused, apologising to Neil that he had to go home straight away.

'Something's happened,' he said.

'I want to come,' Neil said. It was just dawning on Graham that his worst nightmare had come true – that Barbara had seen him, had seen the kiss. Taking Neil home would be like pouring petrol on a fire. 'Mothers adore me.'

'You've never met one like mine.'

'Nor she anyone like me.' Neil swished his kimono. Though he'd barely spoken to her since moving out, Graham had heard his mother had become more hardline in her views about his life choices. There was something about Neil's shamelessness, his ebullience, that made Graham want him there if he had to face whatever she was calling him back for.

'Can't go worse I suppose,' he said. Neil clapped his hands, did a little jig and Graham realised it might go a lot worse.

They jumped on a train and travelled up North together and got off at Whitby, Neil imagining himself in Bram Stoker's *Dracula* as they walked the streets from the station to the terrace of workers' cottages where Graham had grown up. As soon as they got halfway up the street, Graham saw why he'd been summoned.

The word 'Pervert' had been daubed across the front of his childhood home in ten-foot letters with red paint.

They stood outside the house, staring up at the word. Neil put a hand on Graham's shoulder which he shrugged off. Net curtains twitched in nearby houses.

'You should go,' Graham said, unable to tear his eyes from the graffiti. He was about to tell Neil about a pub a few streets away when his mother emerged from the front door. Barbara's eyes widened at Neil in his get-up next to her son, a well of rage behind the rictus grin she wore knowing the street would be watching.

'Mrs Harris,' Neil said, dancing over and extending his hand. Graham batted it down, walked past, trying to block his mother's view of Neil.

'Mother, I'm –'

'Can't be undone,' Barbara said, moving aside and indicating a ladder she'd brought into the hall. Graham shuffled past her to grab it.

'He sees you,' she said through clenched teeth. 'This is his judgement.'

'I'm sorry,' he murmured on his way back outside.

'Never in my worst nightmares,' she mumbled to herself, 'did I think my own blood could become –' She swallowed the thought, retching almost.

'No,' he said. 'No, it – it was a joke.'

'A joke? We were in our beds when they did this,' she said, nodding up to the vandalised house. 'We could have been murdered.'

'Steady on, Barbara,' Neil said, lighting a cigarette. Barbara's eyes raged with fury before she collected herself, put a bucket and brush outside and closed the door gently. 'Thought her lot were all about forgiveness.'

Graham shook his head, ignoring Neil, before setting the ladder up against the house, climbing up and beginning to clean off the letters.

With bucket in one hand, brush in the other, he worked ferociously, brick dust mixing with paint specks, gumming up the brush, pouring rust-red over his fingers, his shirt. From his vantage-point he could make out fishing boats by the quay where he used to work, the bandstand where The Marshalls first performed. He glanced down at Neil lounging against the houses in his ridiculous clothes, bored and idle, and wondered how he'd travelled so far from who he really was. He looked at his work, the word faint but still clear enough to read.

'And I realised, properly, that it was me it was talking about. In the eyes of whoever wrote it, *I* was the pervert. Because of what Neil did, people in my home town thought me such a deviant they took it on themselves to defile my house, scare my parents. Who knows what the rest of the world was saying.'

With the skin on his hands raw from the stiff brush, Graham accepted that he'd lost his way. He resolved to tell Neil he wasn't going to sign the contract, he wasn't going to make the album, that it was over between them, but by the time he got down the ladder Neil wasn't there. He looked up and down the street, worried the same people who'd vandalised the house might have jumped his friend, but then he saw his mother's front door ajar. Neil was with his parents. Alone.

He walked in and his heart sank as he heard Neil talking ten to the dozen. But when he got to the kitchen door, he was shocked to see his mother and father not appalled by whatever he was saying, but rapt.

'Charles is a sore loser,' he was saying, 'but Anne's a pearl. Ton of fun.' Graham shifted against the doorframe, and all three turned to him. 'There you are. I was regaling your parents about playing gin rummy at Windsor Castle with the other kids.' Graham blinked. Neil was telling his mother he knew the royal family. Barbara looked up at Graham, able to meet his eye properly for the first time.

'Your friend told us your – the company,' Barbara said.

'Record company,' Neil helped her.

'That they forced you to do it. On this show. Whatever you did.' Neil swirled off his chair, coming to Graham.

'I couldn't help spilling the beans about the album,' he said. 'And how much we're getting paid.'

'Couldn't be less interested in anything in the world,' Barbara said to no one. Paul cleared his throat. 'But if you're making your way. Lord's a mystery. Not for me to understand his works.'

'I wanted to tell your ma and pa how grateful I was,' Neil said. 'For the sacrifices they've made. None of our success, the television, acclaim from the papers, the money,' he raised an eyebrow at Graham, trying to stifle a smile at the insincerity, 'could have happened without them.' Neil went back to the table, poured Graham tea from the pristine china set they'd had since he was a boy but never used.

Graham sat with his parents for the first time as an adult and it was strangely normal. Neil continued on about the album, selling it as a biblical allegory, his knowledge of the Good Book greater than Graham could have imagined. He marvelled how Neil knew how to win over his parents with religion, name-dropping their type of celebrities, exclusive locales and promises of wealth.

At one point Neil mentioned a bootleg Muddy Waters track Graham had described to him and Paul looked at his son with a warmth he'd never seen, realising he could only have heard it on one of the records he kept in the garden shed.

'I'm glad he knew it was him who got me into the music,' Graham says, voice cracking for a moment on the tapes. 'He didn't have much to be proud of.'

As night fell, Neil got carried away hinting at some rumour he'd heard about Princess Margaret's sexual escapades so Graham made their excuses to leave.

'All this money, this great success,' Barbara said to her son in the narrow hall after Neil had made his exuberant goodbyes. 'Don't forget who got you up in front of people. I know you didn't want to. But look where you are now.' Graham clenched his jaw, the bonhomie of the previous hour extinguished. He looked at his mother, no urge to hug her, touch her at all.

'Alright.' Then he left.

Neil had gone and bought a bottle of gin from a nearby pub and insisted they run up the hundred and ninety-nine steps towards the ruined Whitby Abbey – a famous setting from *Dracula*. At the top they climbed onto a rampart facing out to sea and smoked.

'Did you believe all of what you said, about the success, all the money, us being big stars?' Neil watched the waves pounding the black desolation of the East Yorkshire coast before turning to Graham.

'Does it matter, if we're having fun?' They returned to the station and hunkered inside a waiting room until the first train back to London came the next morning.

My mother hadn't heard about the trip until she heard the tapes.

'Opportunism was Neil's real talent,' she said after listening.

'What do you mean?'

'Going to Whitby, getting Barbara onside? He knew Graham was on the fence about the album. What better way to convince him.'

I hadn't seen it but of course Sadie was right. Graham and the boys signed the record contract the day after they got back from Whitby. They became the Satyrs. The Marshalls were no more.

18.

Aside from clipped conversations about when he'd pick me up for our weekends together, Sadie and Graham were barely talking in the months leading up to Neil's death. She had no idea why Graham might have visited Neil a few weeks before.

'Do you think the two of them could have had feelings for each other?' I asked outright one afternoon, having skirted around it to little effect.

'God, you're a romantic,' Sadie said. As a response it wasn't untypical. She gave many such non-answers, seeming exhausted any time I tried to interrogate anything from their past for some deeper meaning. Though my mother wouldn't entertain it, I'd come to think Graham and Neil's meeting had to be the key moment leading to his death. Graham had concealed it from Lincoln Trevick. The same had to be true for Nereus, as it's not mentioned anywhere, despite the various biographies spending thousands of words on the last months of his life. Though I couldn't work out what happened between them that night, I wondered if I could figure out *why* Graham had gone to see him.

Neil never kept diaries. But he did continue to sketch. Thanks to Yin Li, the senior curator at the V&A, I managed to have some time with his notebooks. I soon saw that, without the access I had to Graham or Sadie's thoughts, these drawings and the annotations around them might be the closest I would ever get to what was going on for Nereus throughout his rise and eventual demise. So I began making elaborate demands of Yin and her archive in an attempt to buy time alone to photograph the pages on my phone. Though this was a clear violation of the kindness and trust the V&A had extended me, given I was aiming to uncover the true history of their subject, I reasoned they would eventually forgive me. Yin was always very patient with me and nothing I asked ever seemed too much. So I'd like to apologise to her for the infraction and hope she will agree that the ends have justified the means.

I began with the last sketches he made while on the US tour. They were dark, all charcoals and a little disturbing. There was a skull motif which kept appearing, like Edvard Munch's 'Scream'. Some with bloodshot eyes in open sockets. There were wider scenes featuring piles of bodies. Sometimes corpses stood like a crowd at a ceremony; in some they held flaming torches. In others they lay on top of each other, the figures interwoven, perhaps the remnants of a bloody battlefield. There aren't many notes amongst the pictures, but in some of the final ones, Neil's written 'Apollo. Apollo. Apollo' in frantic lettering. The word appears often. Sometimes underlined.

The obvious inference was Otis de Kock's Apollo Records with whom Neil had parted ways a year or so before, perhaps a statement of regret. But as I cross-referenced these last sketches with photos of Nereus at the time, looking more cadaverous and out of it than ever, with my classics-brain buzzing, I wondered whether Apollo was some kind of message to himself – in mythology, Apollo is seen as the symbol of rational thinking. Perhaps Neil was telling himself to get it together. To use his head. To reject the Dionysian, hedonistic path he'd been following. I started wondering whether his seeing Graham was his own form of doing 'the steps' towards recovery. Perhaps an apology, or trying to work out where it had all gone wrong. Following the US tour, his drug addiction was the worst it had been.

When I put it to the group chat they wholeheartedly agreed. Whether disagreeing or agreeing I found they tended to do it wholeheartedly. I'd shared some of the covert photos I'd taken of the notebooks and my group went mad looking for other allusions which might indicate why Graham went to see Nereus that night, and further back for clues to who killed their hero.

They had many, many suggestions. Most were vaguely sensible, though Andor66 thought one sketch looked like a *Star Wars* stormtrooper – the film didn't come out until two years after Neil's death. I got a message from Dr Hailee about a small drawing she'd found in the top corner of one page, a many-armed, urchin-like creature attached to a huge cliff.

'Scylla?' Dr Hailee said. In the *Odyssey*, Scylla was a former sea nymph who'd been transformed into a monster who ate sailors. She sent back another zoomed-in picture of one of the sketches from around the same time of half-women, half-birds on jagged rocks in the middle of the sea. The Sirens, also from the *Odyssey*, a more overt symbol of female temptation. 'Woman trouble?' Dr Hailee suggested.

Though there were always women in his orbit, until Neil met Greta Handverk, there was never any hint he had strong feelings towards any of them. Groupies who'd slept with Neil talk about how fun, casual and profoundly unserious their interactions were.

'Sex for Nereus was a jolly old thing we did to pass the time,' infamous West-Hollywood groupie Gaynor Gable wrote in her book. So I couldn't make sense of what he might be referring to by drawing such archetypal descriptions of women as dangerous man-eaters. Until I checked the dates and saw both drawings were from the late summer of 1970, around the time Sadie became a central figure in the band's life.

19.

Graham was the last one to arrive at Phantom Studios on Baker Street on the first morning of the writing sessions for what would become *Dance of the Satyrs*. He walked through the doors of the studio Otis had booked them and was bowled over by the scale of the huge room, felt weightless with excitement as dozens of bearded engineers angled mic-stands around their equipment, troops of assistants plonking sheafs of paper, trays of tea and toast on back tables. It felt like when he'd visited school friends working at factories, a slick machine all there to do one thing: the thing Graham wanted more than anything, to write great songs.

'I'd never been anywhere like it before, but it felt like home.'

He burst into laughter when Danny and Fraz emerged from a back room wearing new threads bought with their first record deal money. Fraz was in a white fur stole while Danny had adopted a rolled bandana and a shirt so low-cut, you could practically see his belly-button.

'Lots of people told me to do a couple of buttons up,' Danny writes. 'But it was my USP. Like an arrow pointing down if you get me.' Unfortunately, I got him.

Graham spotted Sadie Blakely tinkering by a costume rail.

'I was pleased to see her,' Graham recalls. 'Everyone was so young but she seemed like a grown-up. Someone you could rely on.'

What he hadn't relied on was Sadie stepping behind the

organ next to Danny's drum kit when producer Garret Billson clapped his hands to begin the session.

'Think we're getting started now,' Graham said, after walking over and putting his hands on the top of the instrument.

'I know,' she said, batting her long eyelashes.

'Might be needing that,' he said, going for charming. Failing.

'Has no one told you?' Sadie smiled, smoothing out a string of quick jazz chords on the keys.

'Told me what?'

'I've joined the band.' Graham was about to respond when he saw Neil drifting in wearing bronze fish-scale leggings. He crossed the room to head him off.

'What have you done?' he said, indicating Sadie.

'We needed a girl, don't you think?' Neil said.

'What? No. Why?'

'The look. Got you for the ladies, her for the gents. I'm there for the weirdos.'

'I play piano, organ parts, anything on a keyboard.' He stopped short of reminding Neil he'd spent his early years feted like a tiny Mozart for it.

'You can't play two instruments at once.' Neil had a point. On tour Graham would play guitar.

'We could get any number of musos for a tour,' he said. 'Getting some dressmaker in because she's nice-looking.'

'Look at her,' Neil said, turning Graham to look at Sadie. 'For what we're trying to do, can't you see it? Isn't she perfection?' Though Graham assumed Neil had done it to try to sleep with Sadie, or possibly that he already had, with her chic hair and home-made couture, he couldn't deny how great she looked with the others. And however frustrating it was to be blindsided again, Neil changing the direction of the band had landed them in the big room at Phantom Studios.

'I made it happen,' Sadie said when I asked how it came

about. 'Neil asked me to be his stylist but I said I wanted to be in the band.'

'Why? You never seemed that bothered by music.'

'By 1970 "free love" was just a free pass for men to sleep with as many of us as they could. A girl who chose to spend her time around rock stars was seen as nothing more than prey. No one knew what a stylist was. I'd have been lower down the food chain than a groupie. I thought if I was in the band, I'd be protected.'

Graham would discover Sadie was much better than he'd expected, learning she'd had Saturday classes at the Royal Academy of Music, a place he'd been forbidden to attend as a child, until she was sixteen. He talked to her as little as possible at first.

'Thought I was after Neil,' she told me. 'Dramatic, men, aren't they?' Graham would take Neil off into corners to work on the songs while Sadie, Danny and Fraz would play cards, drink and smoke countless cigarettes.

'Neil and Graham were like mum and dad. We were their naughty kids.'

Like Graham, I assumed Neil putting Sadie in the band had nothing to do with his musicianship. But then I read a 1975 interview from a Japanese magazine I had translated in which Neil was asked about the decision; this was after the two men had stopped working together.

'Graham on keys . . . was always trying to show Mummy he was her little virtuoso,' Nereus tells the interviewer. 'Desperation in every chord.' Graham wouldn't have known that at the time, but I thought of Bryn's idea of him as a brooding alpha male and could see him looking back at such moments later as defining a pattern of behaviour, of emotional manipulation, and how, after he'd been sidelined permanently, that might drive a man like him to seek revenge.

20.

Two weeks into the sessions, Otis announced a UK tour at the beginning of November to coincide with the release of their first album. At the news, Penny procured a huge house in Streatham nicknamed Hatful House for them to rehearse in from a nearly dead aristocratic ex-lover of hers. All the band's best work happened at night, so within days the decision was made for all of them to move in.

'Streatham was a shithole,' Danny writes. 'But three of us had grown up in shoeboxes. Clapped out as it was, that place was like the Disney castle.' Danny and Fraz, along with models Julie Stark, Zara Vico and any of Neil's Soho set dived into day-and-night hedonism as if to that manor born. And when Neil wasn't upstairs in bed writing, post-coital, or annotating his ever-increasing piles of obscure books, he led the raucousness like the estate's own lord of misrule. I expected to find accounts about that time grim reading, *Saltburn* with amplifier stacks, but it sounded surprisingly wholesome.

'People went to bed together but it was mostly picnic rugs on the lawn,' Sadie said. 'Messy dinners, messier ideas. Dancing. Graham struggled.'

'We had an album to write,' he recalls. 'A tour to prepare. It was like I was the only one who knew it,' Graham remembers.

'He didn't know how to let go,' Sadie told me. 'But he wanted to. So much. It ate him up.'

'Is that what you were drawn to?' I asked. 'His vulnerability.'

She rolled her eyes, but I gave her a warning look, reminding her of our deal regarding her relationship with her granddaughters.

'He was tall,' she said, defiant. 'And, with Neil and his acolytes, when you're surrounded by children, the most grown-up looking one becomes more appealing.'

Whatever it was Sadie really saw in Graham, within a couple of weeks at Hatful House, she found herself wanting to spend more time with him, which was a challenge as Graham was never alone. Constantly hustling Danny to work up drum parts, trying to get more out of Fraz, chasing Neil around the grounds to finalise his songs. Taking matters into her own hands one wet afternoon, she escaped the rabble and sought Graham out, eventually finding him on the floor, ear to an amp, in the main banquet hall they'd co-opted as their rehearsal space.

Pretending she hadn't seen him, she sat at the Hammond organ and began playing her part of 'Cormorant Sun', intentionally badly.

'Oh, hi,' she said, stopping when he stood up.

'You alright?' he said, eyeing the organ, brow knitted at what he'd just heard.

'Not great. Can you help?' Graham looked round the room, looked back at her like he was staring down a great white shark. 'Have you got a minute?' Graham smiled, picked up a Rhodes piano and plonked it down opposite Sadie. He nodded for her to play the part, listened, giving nothing away.

'Could you maybe –' He began playing incredibly complex motifs between her chords. Sadie laughed as they came to the end.

'I'll never be able to play that,' she said.

'You will,' he said. 'Wouldn't have suggested it otherwise. Here.' He joined her on the organ seat and, phrase by phrase, went through it with her.

She tutted at herself as she made error after error. Graham would go back, patient, wait for them to settle their fingers on the keys as they'd play it again. They'd make progress, then she'd bludgeon the next section.

'Sorry,' she said, lifting her hands away from the organ.

'Hey,' he said, taking one of her hands. 'This is how we make it.' He let go of her hand. She had to look away, not used to Graham's earnest kindness.

As the days went by, the two of them would find reasons to linger alone in the banquet hall, hoping the other might turn up. When they did, they'd play together. Between songs she learnt who he was. She wanted to know about the fishing boats, laughed at the thought of him in his bow tie at concert grand pianos. They talked of absent fathers. She wanted to understand what it must have felt like to live in a house fogged with Jesus and the thousand deaths of nameless young men in the war. In turn she told him how she begged her mother to leave her father after he'd brought national scandal on their family, how it broke her heart she wouldn't.

'I was always up early so mornings became our time,' Graham says.

'We'd pour the others huge drinks, egg them on to stay up later, party harder so we'd have more time together the next day.'

'Did anyone notice?' I asked Sadie.

'A rock band together in a stately home,' she said. 'People barely noticed whether it was day or night.'

After dinner one night, a week before their first gig, someone put Crosby, Stills and Nash on and Neil jumped up onto the window seat in the kitchen and started a game, bringing people up to sing harmonies with him, pushing them off if they missed a note. When Sadie was foisted up, he put an arm around her bare waist, pulled her into his body, nuzzled into her neck. Graham noticed him staring at her with a sort of adulation, different to the hunger he looked at most of his would-be conquests with.

'She looked dead at me, scared,' Graham says.

'Before I knew it the record scratched and the music stopped,' Sadie said. 'Graham was over at the turntable. My White Knight.' Neil turned around with his back to his audience below, looked at her pointedly and fell back, only just caught by the crowd. Sadie stepped down, ran out into the garden. Graham followed but when he got out onto the lawn, she seemed to have disappeared. He scanned the grounds through the dawn light looking for her. Something landed on his face, a sandal. He looked up to see Sadie in a makeshift treehouse, a pallet hammered into a branch, in the beech tree next to the house. He climbed up in three swift bounds, sat opposite her. She laughed at the cross-legged giant in a place made for children.

'You laughing at me?' he said.

'I am, yeah.' She leant forward and kissed him.

'What was that for?' he asked.

'You're an idiot,' she said. 'I like you.'

'Oh,' he said. He was like a rabbit in headlights, barely able to look at her, staring back into the glow from inside the house.

'I thought I'd made a huge mistake,' she said. But then Graham took her face in his hands and kissed her back.

'He really meant it,' she told me. 'I hadn't been sure whether he would.'

21.

Whenever I've talked to friends about Nereus's death the first thing which comes up to refute the idea he was murdered is the locked door.

Nereus's top-floor bedroom was locked from the inside. A simple Victorian turnkey lock, original to the house. It wasn't something which was announced by police at the time of his death, nor mentioned in press reports once the autopsy leaked.

'You mention a locked room,' Detective Bryn told me, 'the whole world thinks they're Miss Marple.' Having spent many years going over it in his head, Bryn believed that if someone else had been involved, the only logical explanation is that the person who'd administered the heroin left and Nereus, having not succumbed to the drug's effects, locked himself in. But I was never happy with that.

And while listening to Graham talk about my parents' first kiss in the treehouse, a different possibility occurred. The murderer could have escaped the top-floor room out the window and climbed down in some way. I took the train to Victoria station and walked over to Cheyne Walk. I'd visited Nereus's old house before, imagining my father parking up that night, putting myself in the shoes of the red-headed woman, the parade of fans and press who had walked the street, hoping answers may filter in by osmosis. But I saw my new theory fall down when I arrived at number one. The top floor was thirty metres up. There was a drainpipe which went down to a balcony two floors below, but none of the people on my list of suspects would have been able to make the climb, least of all fifteen-stone Graham.

I went down to Hatful House shortly after my visit to Chelsea, wondering if the ghosts there may lead me somewhere but I couldn't get past the metal fencing surrounding the property. Despite plans to revivify it as an arts space or shrine to Nereus, it stands derelict now, sheet metal for windows, razor wire, warnings of prosecutions for intruders, trespassers, squatters. But from outside, you can make out the murals drawn by Nereus fans over the years, the submarine worlds he invented, slogans graffitied on its stone walls. The facade is covered in song lyrics, professions of undying love, and over the arch above the front door, someone has sprayed 'Poiseidon lives' in pink paint. (I looked into the niche theory that Nereus faked his death in order to escape the limelight and is still, in fact, alive. I can say with great confidence it isn't true. There have been sightings all over the world but, like UFOs, Bigfoot or mermen themselves, none have been backed up by concrete evidence.)

All that remained of my parents' 'treehouse' were two planks nailed to the trunk at right angles. I thought it symbolic of their relationship – together but always somehow at odds.

'I never thought, not for a moment, that someone like Sadie would be interested in me,' Graham told Lincoln Trevick about that first kiss, genuinely blindsided by it. It could be his humility, but the hesitation before they kissed, the reticence, I wondered if Graham hadn't seen it coming because of what he thought of as Neil's prior claim. He had assumed he and Sadie were already together. Why was that? I thought about what he said about Neil looking at Sadie with something greater than just his usual lust that same evening, how Sadie had described Neil seeming unusually shy with her the first time they met, how he'd brought her into the band just because she asked.

I couldn't see into Neil Forbes' head so I went back to the pictures I'd taken of his sketchbooks which I'd printed and pinned on the wall chronologically. I cross-referenced that night, the fourth of November, and found a picture he'd drawn of a man holding a chisel looking at a statue of a woman. More Greeks. Ovid's myth of Pygmalion. The artist who fell in love with his creation. In plucking her from her design course and putting her in the band, I could imagine Neil thinking of Sadie like that. But following on from the other woman-fearing sketches he'd drawn at the time, was he, like the mythical sculptor, worried he was falling in love with what he'd made?

When I put it to her, Sadie dismissed the idea out of hand. 'There was only one person on the planet for Neil,' she said. 'Neil.'

22.

The tour kicked off with a gig at the Half Moon in Herne Hill, which sold out within minutes of being announced. There's a photo in the exhibition catalogue of the band before they went on. Sadie iridescent in figure-hugging, petrol-coloured plastic tiles, the sides of Neil's head newly shaved, the rose-gold cape which would evolve into the iconic Bronze Stingray look, Graham in his skin-tight jumpsuit, fish-scale clips in his hair, eyes half-closed like he's hoping it'd stop anyone noticing him.

'He would have refused point-blank if I hadn't made the costumes.'

The crowd was like nothing any of them had seen. Between fifteen and twenty years old, wearing shimmering jumpsuits, home-made shell costumes, in some cases very little at all, hair braided on the tops of their heads like Nereus.

'Lads holding hands, girls sticking their tongues down each other's throats,' Danny Greig writes in his memoir. 'Could barely keep time it was so distracting.' The fans surged forward when they started playing, hands grabbing at the band's legs. Graham dodged them off but Neil went further in, letting them touch him. 'Somehow the costumes and make-up made us ten time sexier,' Danny continued of their new look. 'We didn't understand it but we didn't care.'

Near the end of the show they went into 'Platinum Scales', Graham turned to Sadie and they shared a bold, unapologetic smile. Rehearsing almost all hours, they'd barely spoken since their kiss in the treehouse, though its half-life lingered between them in smirks and eyerolls at Neil across the banquet hall.

Neil saw the two of them, came over and thrust his arms through Graham's, holding him in an intimate embrace. A few months before, he would have pushed Neil away. But meeting Sadie had changed him. He hugged back, pushed him towards the mic and the two of them stared into each other's eyes as they belted out the last chorus, sending two hundred bright souls berserk.

There's a picture of this moment in the archives too. Graham wasn't a natural smiler, creases of concern forever etched in his forehead. I wondered if he'd have been diagnosed with anxiety now. But in that moment, there was an unadulterated joy on his face as he sings with Neil while fans yank at their legs. I showed the picture to Sadie. She looked at it for some time, a whisper of something in her eyes, before handing it back with a shrug and going off to her kitchen to make tea. Despite the front, I think she'd seen what I had. In all the images I'd unearthed of my mother and father together, Graham had never looked at her like that.

The more I learnt about their relationships, the more knotty, nuanced and unresolved the triangle which had formed between them appeared. Neil seemed to be grappling with feelings for Sadie. I knew Sadie was falling for Graham and possibly he her. But how he looked at Neil, the two of them spending the night together a month before his death. And how Neil was with Sadie. And they were young. Drunk a lot of the time. Exhausted, excited, dreamers. I felt in my bones if I could unpick these entanglements, it would lead me to the truth about the night Nereus died. But at that point, I was as confused as they all must have been.

23.

The band played gigs to more adoring crowds for the next eight nights while trying to finish the album at Hatful House during the days. The audience's love liberated something in Graham. He began seeking Sadie out, hands finding each other on the corners of sofas, chaste kisses in their treehouse, slow dances behind the foliage curtain of the huge weeping willow at the far end of the estate. Though Graham wasn't ready to tell the rest of the band.

'Did you mind?' I asked Sadie.

'We were flying, all was harmonious. I wasn't about to be Yoko,' she said.

On their first day off, a rainy Sunday in late November, Graham took Sadie to the cinema to see *The Out-of-Towners*, a Jack Lemmon comedy about Midwesterners moving to New York.

'Is that how you see me?' Graham said afterwards over ice cream at Ferraro's on Walworth Road. 'A provincial hick?'

'It is, yeah,' she said. 'Why I like you.' She blew whipped cream into his beard. They sat on the top deck of the bus back to Streatham. Sadie put her hand in Graham's, leant her head on his shoulder.

'I looked at the top of her head, the follicles beneath her always perfect hair. The other lads were frightened of her, but I wasn't. She didn't want me to be.'

Hatful House was silent when they returned. It was never

silent, never unoccupied. It was a rare opportunity. Sadie stopped at the bottom of the stairs, took Graham by the hand and gave him that kind of look. But before he could follow, there was the crash of broken glass above them.

'Stay here,' Graham said, first thinking that they were being burgled. As he got up to the landing he heard someone cry out near Neil's bedroom. He bounded down the corridor, opened Neil's door and was taken aback by what he saw inside. A mass of naked and semi-clothed flesh writhing on the four-poster bed and rugs around it like one expanding organism. Neil, in the middle of it all, staring at Graham with a wide-eyed grin. He disentangled himself and walked over, fully naked.

'Want to come join?' he said, as if inviting him to join a game of cards. 'Wonderful scene in here.' Graham half-closed the door, looked inside again, snapped away like he'd just seen a mutilated body. He blinked, about to say something, though what could he say, before turning round and walking back down the stairs to Sadie.

'Like he'd seen a ghost when he came down,' Sadie said.

'He didn't tell you?' She shook her head, though didn't seem surprised.

It struck me for the first time how difficult it must have been for Graham, a twenty-one-year-old, Christian-raised virgin, living in a house with Neil and his taboo-busting sexual appetites. And of course there was the elephant in the room, which if Graham hadn't encountered it before, he must have done that night – Neil was famously well endowed. Tiffany Almond, the leader of the collection of groupies known as the Knightsbridge nymphs, said his appendage 'swung around his skinny body like a medieval mace', so big she often expected it to make him topple over. It's something which is often brought up by my fellow fanatics to support the idea that Graham's feelings of inadequacy drove him to murder. I've always dismissed this as simplistic sensationalism. It's surprising how often men's problems are thought to be related to penis size. But if they will keep measuring them.

Despite how shocked Graham may have been seeing Neil in flagrante, it seemed to spark something because he and Sadie went on to spend their first night together afterwards. I was loath to ask my mother for too much detail, but it must have been a meaningful night because the following morning Graham wrote a song as he watched the sun lighting his sleeping girlfriend.

'I wrote something,' he told her as soon as she opened her eyes. She blinked herself awake, propping herself up. She'd heard demos of The Marshalls' early songs, but Graham had never talked about working on his own stuff since they'd met.

'Play it to me,' she said. He smiled, took in the sunny morning through the trees outside and did as she asked.

'I love it,' she said when he came to the end. She put her hand on his heart.

'I can hear this,' she said, 'trying to get out. Play it to Neil.'

'That's not how we've done things.'

'Worst he can say is no.'

The song, 'Untitled 11 (Heaven's Exile)', appears on a bootleg of Graham Harris recordings Insurance Stan bought from a Japanese collector. It's sentimental but there's a compelling purity of emotion in the lyrics about the sun calling an angel back to heaven which you can't find anywhere in his earlier songs.

In the following days, Graham tried to get Neil alone to play him the song but found him entrenched with a new international crowd he had dragged down from London Fashion Week. Worried he'd lose his nerve, Sadie took the matter into her own hands, stopping the band from disbanding for a dinner-break one evening.

'Graham wants to play you something he's written,' she said.

'Oh,' Neil said, turning from gossiping with Zara and Anton by the ad-hoc cocktail bar in the corner. 'Very good.'

'The temperature changed,' Danny remembers. 'No one had suggested their own stuff to Neil before.' Graham moved into the middle as a dozen onlookers seemed to light cigarettes at exactly the same time. He cleared his throat and began to play. Halfway through, Sadie added organ, sung a harmony on the last chorus.

The vast room was pin-drop silent when they finished. Graham looked to Neil, who was still staring at the side wall as he had throughout. Thomas Tee, a recent addition to Neil's retinue at that point, in wife-beater vest with his trademark pencil moustache, started humming the tune of 'Mary had a little lamb', bringing the rest of their crew to burst into hyena-giggles, collapsing on each other on the sofa.

'Neil,' Sadie said, furious. 'Can you not –' But Neil didn't silence his friends. He made the long walk across and knelt down next to Graham, who was turning off his buzzing amp.

'Not sure how it fits,' Neil said. Graham took off his guitar, held it in front of him.

'Right,' he said. 'Sure, that's right.'

'Oh, come on,' Sadie said, slamming down the lid of the organ. Neil glared at her, something reptilian in his eyes.

'That was the moment, I think,' Sadie told me. 'He knew about us.'

'He knew it was about you, the song?' I said. 'So he was jealous?' She rolled her eyes.

'He knew us both first,' she said. 'In his mind that meant he owned us. He felt left out and humiliated Graham for it. He was a child.' Sadie saw it as a sign of Neil's vindictiveness, but when my husband Bobby heard the song, he agreed with Nereus.

'It wouldn't have fit with the other songs on *Satyrs*,' he said. 'Because it wasn't as good.' But Neil must have been aware of the effect it might have on Graham's confidence because the same night, he proclaimed him a genius after he played what would become the legendary solo from 'Found Them There' in front of the same hangers-on who'd laughed at him hours before.

'Playing *his* song,' Sadie said. 'People who sacrificed themselves on the altar of Nereus Forbes. There you have Neil's definition of genius.'

24.

Based on Sadie's assessment, another person Neil might have thought a genius was Thomas Tee. A lot has been written about the longstanding chair of the Nereus Forbes Estate over the years, though very few have read it because Tee is famously litigious. So I was surprised he responded to an email I sent asking if he had any information which might help me find my father, saying he'd like to meet.

It was almost six months after Sara received the threatening poster when I sat down across the desk from Thomas in the top-floor office of the Bond Street building he stood outside to announce Nereus's death fifty years before. He was eighty-one when we met but looked ten years older, face wrinkled as a scrunched paper bag making his nose job nose seem all the more innocuous. In an expensive charcoal blazer over a black polo neck, the only hint at his sordid, hedonistic past was his ever-present pencil moustache. Born in 1943 to bank manager's daughter Valerie and Covent Garden market trader Herby, Thomas left school at sixteen to work with his father on the stalls before being drawn to the lascivious lights of late-sixties Soho where he would meet Nereus near the end of 1970.

At that point, he was the only person I'd met who had been with Nereus the day he died. Which, after lattes were delivered by an exceptionally blonde assistant, is where I steered our conversation, asking why Thomas went to see Nereus that morning.

'Had to see him about something every day,' he said.

'Do you remember what the "something" was that day?' He took a deep breath, chest sounding like there were rocks in it.

'The Turkish disaster,' he said, referring to the concert at the sunken city of Kekova. 'Insurance wasn't going to pay.'

'How did Nereus react?'

'I didn't mention it. He was in a good mood and hated money talk. But, ah –' He dragged his vowels like he was laying tarmac. 'Johnson and Johnson had offered me a hundred K to use a track off *Poiseidon* for talcum powder ads. I needed his sign-off.'

'Really? Talcum powder?' Nereus was famously opposed to his music being used for commercial purposes. To this day, none of his songs feature in adverts, nor in TV shows or films. 'Let them make their own magic,' he said to Michael Parkinson when asked about it.

'Didn't even tell him about that stuff normally. But the situation wasn't normal. We were stuffed,' he said. 'Bankrupt.'

'You were bankrupt?'

'And then some. Silly bugger still said no to the ads.'

'Were you angry?'

'Wasn't happy,' he said. 'I'd said that concert would kill us but he never listened to me.' As we'll see, this can't be true as Neil listening to Thomas was one of the factors which would bring on his rupture with Graham.

'Did you argue?' I asked. 'Was there a confrontation?' Thomas cocked his head, raised an eyebrow.

'We never did,' he said, eyes on the iPhone recording our conversation. 'I went in the kitchen, made us a fix.'

'Heroin?'

'We were partial to the stuff. Greta appeared from upstairs a little later and I took that as a good cue to sling the proverbial.'

I tallied it in my head with the police and eyewitness reports on the comings and goings of that day – it checked out.

I asked about Greta, about the party she'd organised the day before. He said he didn't stay long as it was Greta's crowd.

'Things with her lot always got a bit strange for my constitution.'

'In what way?'

'Seances, spirits. She thought she could talk to the dead. Convinced Neil she was in communion with his forefathers in Atlantis. Raging junky of course, worst of the lot of us.'

'Is that what they were doing at the party, a seance?'

'Neil wanted to know why the storm had come in at the concert so she stuck some crabs from the wet-fish man in the pub opposite on the fire. The smell! Made myself scarce.'

'Do you think he got any kind of answer?' Thomas's eyes sparked with incredulity.

'From the crabs?'

I explained I was trying to understand why, if he was there at all, Graham might have visited Cheyne Walk later that day. Thinking that if Neil's head was in a place he thought burning shellfish might give him answers, perhaps his old friend Graham might have also been summoned as part of his inquiry.

'Because of the crabs?' he said again, losing respect for me by the second.

'How about the month before?' I said. 'When Graham went to see Neil. Do you have any idea why that might have been?'

'A month before?'

'A neighbour saw Graham visiting Neil in early September. He stayed the night.'

'Didn't know that,' Thomas said. I asked if he knew why they might have reunited, why Neil might have kept it from him. Thomas shrugged, said something hackneyed about Neil being an enigma.

'You said he was in a good mood that morning,' I said, not letting it go. 'Greta Handverk told a journalist he'd had an idea for "a new direction". Do you think that could have had something to do with Graham?' Thomas swivelled in his chair, mouth creasing into the beginning of a snarl.

'You said you wanted to find your father,' he said, voice low as a panther. 'Why all the questions about that day?'

'Because it had to be why Graham left,' I said. 'Why he never came back.'

'You think he killed him?' Thomas stared at me, eyes glassy with dispassion. I didn't know at that point what I thought. Part of me wanted him to have killed Neil, part of me was appalled he might have. Thomas saw me flailing, sat back, eyes softening again.

'I identified Neil's body,' he said. 'It stayed with me, the sight of him, cold, alone on the bed. He wasn't always a ray of light, but he was my closest friend. And brilliant, like a miracle when he was flying. Overwhelming being with him from time to time. I didn't want to believe that that life, his life, could be snuffed out in such a banal way. I wanted there to have been foul play too, Winter. Thought it would make sense of it. But after a couple of days giving the police hell, I had to accept it. After many years, I've realised it was the way it had to be. He died a secret. Young, radical, perfect.' I took in Thomas's Saville Row tailoring, the Rothko on the wall behind him, the troop of pristine blonde women tapping on iMacs in the open-plan office behind us and wondered whether Neil would have seen his dying a penniless addict at twenty-five to have been as perfect as Thomas did.

He ended our conversation soon after.

'If there's anything you need,' he said, walking me to the lift. 'I'm little more than a relic here. Won't be too busy to pick up the phone.' We passed a frosted-glass boardroom, five men in suits sat behind huge binders inside. When we came to the end of the office, Thomas looked at me and something caught in his throat.

'You remind me of your mother,' he said. 'Lucky thing.' He gave a little wave as I stepped inside the lift. As the doors closed, I saw him pause outside the boardroom full of suits. Later that night I found myself wondering why someone who was 'little more than a relic' would be walking into what looked like a top-level meeting at a multimillion-pound business.

25.

On 2 December 1970 *Dance of the Satyrs*, the album which would kick-start the accumulation of those millions, was released, whisking the band into a whirlwind of acclaim none of them could have anticipated. They were suddenly being rushed in to do radio recordings with John Peel, back on *Top of the Pops* and, in the weeks up to Christmas, seemed to spend every other day posing for either a newspaper or magazine photographer, in between tour dates around the country.

'Journalists didn't want to hear much from anyone but Neil,' Graham recalls on the tapes. I read some of the articles from the time. Neil talks of impending nuclear Armageddon, civilisation collapse, how people responded to their album because they were looking for a new world to 'harbour their hopes'. I can imagine Graham sitting behind him wondering when they might actually talk about the music.

'Did it bother him at all?' I asked Sadie. 'Neil being the main attraction.'

'The journos were all private school, Oxbridge,' she said. 'Graham never lost his veneration for the well educated, so was happy to let Neil go into battle.'

'All that attention,' Graham says at one point on the recordings, 'wasn't real. I'd had it as a kid. I had Sadie then. She didn't care what I thought about music. She wanted to know me.'

It was the happiest time for the band. A bunch of beautiful young people high on stratospheric success. As their UK tour came to an end they all forsook their families to spend Christmas together at Hatful House. Every drink, every dance, every new guest an excuse to shake their heads in disbelief at their dizzying triumph. Penny came to stay, demanding cocktails and impromptu performances, hostess and lauded guest of honour in one. On Christmas Eve night, Penny took Graham's hand and led him to the garden.

'I see the two of you,' Penny said when she was alone with him under the tree he and Sadie had first kissed in. 'You and Sadie, fluttering.'

'What do you mean?' he said, caught out.

'You're in love.'

'We're not, we're only –'

'I can smell it,' she said. A silence spread between them. Graham swallowed a lump in his throat, feeling like he had been hauled up in front of the headmistress. She linked her arm through his. 'The two of you deserve to be happy.' Graham huffed out a smoky breath; getting Penny's blessing meant everything to him. 'You should know, though,' she continued, holding out a cigar for him to light. 'My son's sweetness is boundless when he has everything he wants.' Bottles smashed inside. Penny got up to go back inside, leaving Graham blinking in the moonlight.

Christmas Day didn't start until three o'clock the next day.

'Let's just say the turkey didn't get cooked.' It seemed there was very little eaten because by this point cocaine had entered the equation, prescribed like medicine by Thomas for their exhausting schedule. Graham didn't touch it.

'Something about kneeling down like saying prayers, then snorting like that.'

'It made me grind my teeth,' Sadie told me. 'I'd had orthodontics as a child.'

Neil, however, dived into whatever coke they had like it was the last on earth. 'Nereus's biggest addiction was to newness,' a childhood friend wrote in one of his biographies. I could imagine how the cocaine might have made everything sparkle that little bit brighter. And because Thomas Tee always had it, he became more of a fixture around then, never leaving Neil's side from the moment they came off stage. With his alligator laugh and the impressions he did of their accents, the rest of the band couldn't see why he wanted Thomas around, thinking it could be because Neil needed hours of drinking to wind down from the euphoria of performing and Thomas had extraordinary stamina.

On New Year's Eve, however, Graham witnessed something which would rock him to the core and fully explain the hold Thomas seemed to have over Neil. He left Sadie's room around one o'clock in the morning to retrieve a Galette des Rois Penny had brought for the festivities. But when he got to the bottom of the stairs he saw a light on in the boot-room. As he moved closer he heard grunting noises and as he peeped through the crack in the door he saw Thomas in a robe clutching a wine-rack against the stone wall, Neil behind, thrusting into him.

Graham span away, deep breaths from his nose, blinking the image away, as shocked as if he'd seen a car crash. He went back upstairs, skirted Sadie's room and locked himself in his own bedroom. He could barely sleep that night, trying to make sense of what he'd seen. Neil was camp, effeminate but he'd seen him with dozens of women, sex workers, in the middle of an orgy. But seeing him having sex with a man? This was the man he thought of as his best friend, his closest collaborator, and he had no idea who he was anymore.

Graham's need to clarify Neil's sexuality might seem bigoted to modern eyes, but in the 1970s, bisexuality was seen as a form of fence-sitting and wasn't acknowledged as an identity at all. On top of his confusion about Neil's sexuality, it was who he'd caught him with. Thomas and Graham didn't like each other and both knew it. What could the ramifications be on the band's hierarchy if he and Neil were involved in some illicit affair?

But what of the act itself. He doesn't reflect on it on the recordings, but it's fair to assume Graham would never have seen two men having sex before, not considered the mechanics of it, what that act might have actually been like. He might have been disgusted, conditioned by his upbringing to see it as grievously sinful. Perhaps jealous, even if not romantically, but that someone else was closer to Neil than he was. Or perhaps he was curious. Aroused even by what he saw.

Might he have lain in bed that night questioning whether the admiration he had for Neil, the strength of feeling he had for their collaboration might be something deeper. And if Neil liked men, it opened up the possibility it was something which could actually happen.

Much to my frustrations, it was impossible to know. But the one thing I did know was that a month before Neil's death, Graham had spent a night at his house which he wasn't willing to admit to his own biographer, that Neil hadn't told Thomas, his then-manager and closest confidant, about. And if something had happened that night, if it was the culmination of years of longing which might have started the night Graham witnessed Neil with another man, what could that have done to Christian-raised Graham? Love, lust, loathing. Three out of four.

26.

In the weeks after meeting Neil's former lover Thomas Tee, I puzzled over how someone who'd had the dazzling success of Nereus Forbes could have been in such dire financial straits at the time of his death. I decided to try to 'follow the money', enlisting Iris Derbyshire, the bookkeeping wife of Insurance Stan, to try to work out whether he really could have been bankrupt.

Iris managed to acquire the financial information for Pacifica Holdings from Companies House and the last set of accounts revealed a surplus of six hundred and fifty thousand pounds – roughly ten million in today's money. Far from bankrupt. These figures, however, only took the company's balance sheets up to April 1976, twenty months before Nereus's death.

Iris and I spent several evenings over supermarket-brand kettle crisps, trying to work out if there was any way Nereus could have spent that much in a year and a half. The losses from the Sunken City concert had been reported, as had estimates of the US tour revenue, which took around a hundred and fifty thousand pounds off the 1976 figure. With the help of the forums, we discovered several extravagant purchases made in his last year – two lesser-known Roy Lichtensteins, a Mumbai railway carriage he bought and sold at a huge loss, twenty thousand pounds on a fossil of a small plesiosaur – but even after we deducted all of that, and took off another seventy grand for drugs, booze and miscellaneous rock-star excess, we couldn't see how he'd spent even half of the company's six hundred and fifty thousand. He couldn't have been bankrupt. Which meant Thomas had lied to me.

When I dug deeper into the Nereus Forbes Estate which Thomas had stewarded since its inception, I was bemused to find almost nothing about it available in the public domain. No website. No phone number. Nothing. I wouldn't have known the address if I hadn't been there. The only mentions online come in news articles and posts on social media about charitable donations, or as being patrons of various arts bodies and addiction charities – usually put out by the charitable venture itself. The Estate didn't seem to put any time into trumpeting its own good works. I was struggling to think what the blondes on the iMacs were doing to fill their days.

I clicked on its entry in Companies House where I discovered the Estate, as separate from Pacifica Holdings, was incorporated on 19 November 1977 – three weeks after Nereus's death. On one hand, this could be seen to support what Thomas said about their financial difficulties. It's common to dissolve a company and set up a new one to circumvent bankruptcy. But, coming in the direct aftermath of his death, it raised questions. I phoned former detective Bryn. It was 11.45 at night. On Good Friday. He wasn't over the moon to hear from me.

The new company was something he had questioned at the time.

'But there were legal documents for the foundation of the Estate from many months before his death,' he told me. 'I didn't see them but higher-ups did. It was all at Nereus's behest, all signed and above board, Thomas Tee the named director.'

'But what if Nereus had plans to change that?' I countered. The perception had always been that the 'new direction' Nereus had been excited about the day he died was musical, perhaps his next reinvention. But what if it had been a business decision. His split with Apollo Records had come out of nowhere, it wasn't inconceivable he wanted to take things away from Thomas Tee's control following the disastrous year they'd had together. And I remembered it was when I asked Thomas about this new idea in his office that he suddenly turned frosty.

'You said you couldn't find a motive for anyone in Nereus's milieu to want him dead,' I said to Bryn. 'But getting kicked off the gravy train is one of the oldest ones in the book.' Bryn said little after that which I knew meant he'd look into it.

A couple of weeks later, after I'd met with Insurance Stan, Iris and Candi at the Crown Tavern, I saw a man in a flat cap, who could have been the person I'd thought was following me before, sitting behind the wheel of a black Vauxhall Corsa outside the pub.

I had seen this car already, parked on my street a week or so earlier, thought it was my neighbour's son back from university. But then I saw it several nights after that and now it was in a completely different part of London where I happened to be. When I got back home, my husband Bobby was engaged in what sounded like a stressful call with his business partner, live music being one of the hardest hit post-Brexit and Covid, so I didn't mention the Corsa.

But I went to bed that night feeling for the first time I might have been scratching the surface of something bigger than the murder of a rock star nearly five decades before. I knew the rational thing would be to walk away. I was floundering in the dark anyway, no closer to solutions than I had been nine months before. But this man in the flat cap, the glitching phone – maybe I was onto something. What it was, how dangerous it might end up being didn't concern me then. Stopping didn't seem to be an option.

27.

The European tour Nereus and the Satyrs embarked on at the beginning of 1971 was a four-month roller coaster of emotional euphoria and claustrophobic exhaustion. The album hadn't made huge waves abroad but by the middle of the year, the whole continent knew about Nereus Forbes.

'We were happy to get away,' Graham says. 'Things at Hatful had got nasty.'

'Julie Stark hated me from the off,' Sadie said. 'When grass gave way to coke, she and her acolytes got worse at hiding it.'

The band were packing up their gear in the banquet hall the day they were due to leave when they heard a deep car-horn honking off in the distance. They rushed out to see Neil hanging off the side of a huge American Greyhound bus pulling into their driveway. The vehicle was painted aquamarine and adorned with psychedelic sea-serpent designs and Atlantean imagery – tridents, mermaids, bearded mermen. This was what would come to be known as the 'Teal Eel', inspired by the school bus from Ken Kesey's *Electric Kool-Aid Acid Tests*.

Danny, Fraz and the others rushed on to check out Neil's handiwork while Graham took a deep breath and walked back inside.

'I got it that the more ridiculous it all was, the more attention we got,' he says to Trevick. 'But music wasn't a joke to me. I was never in a band to be laughed at.'

Despite Graham's reservations, the band got on the Teal

Eel and crossed the Channel. Away from the melodramas of the Hatful House hangers-on, they fell into a rhythm, nights playing gigs to increasingly rapturous fans, afternoons playing cards in plush green rooms or breakfasting together in grand hotel brasseries. They became comfortable with each other, closer than they'd ever been.

'We all fell for Neil again the first few weeks,' Sadie said. Europe was still exotic to most Brits then but everywhere they went, Neil knew where to have the most enlightening, inspiring and ludicrous time. In Normandy he convinced Graham, Sadie and Fraz to cross to the island castle at Mont Saint Michel at two in the morning, where they built a fire, singing songs round it till dawn. In Brussels he had Otis arrange an overnight stay at the space-age Atomium building as a kind of method-acting exercise for how he saw the people of Pacifica living. He dragged them to a bullfight in Spain, explaining its primal grace as they polished off two crates of red wine in the stands.

'I knocked dead a hundred fish on the boats as a kid,' Graham says on the tapes. 'But watching them kill this beast, making a show of it, for nothing else but our entertainment. Something so debauched about it, so profane. I just wanted more. Seeing the world through Neil's eyes was like a dream. Didn't know what I'd done to deserve it.' He sounds infatuated, intoxicated by Neil at times but I could understand it. Graham's world had been so small, so enclosed. Every day Neil seemed to open a new world, a new dimension he'd never imagined.

Despite the thrills of their European adventure there was one hanger-on they couldn't seem to shake. And within a few days, the whole band understood why Thomas had joined them when he and Neil began kissing and groping in full view of them, arms draped around each other's waists like newlyweds.

'There were raised eyebrows,' Sadie said. 'A few giggles when they left the room. But I'd seen it coming and from the boys' point of view, it just meant more girls for them.'

'And Graham?'

'I'm sure he had thoughts, but never said a word.' She blinked impassively. I was certain he had more than just thoughts but my mother seemed determined not to indulge my tragic love story theory.

'Wasn't my business,' is all Graham says to Lincoln when he asks what he thought of seeing Neil and Thomas together. But midway through the tour, Thomas did become his business when he became the person handing out the band's per diem payments, travelling ahead of them to talk to venue managers and reprimanding him and Sadie one night in Hamburg when they turned up late for a soundcheck.

Sadie wanted to bring up Thomas's growing influence with Neil after the show that night but Graham, still glowing from the show, persuaded her not to rock the boat. The tour was going well. Graham was having the time of his life, embracing his on-stage chemistry with Neil.

"That connection we'd first had back in Archway just got stronger,' Graham recalls. 'It was like we could read each other's minds. Not just on stage but any time we played. Music seemed to flow out of the two of us like we were one person.'

'It was magical to watch,' Sadie said. 'When they were locked in that moment, like everything buried in them exploding in the sky. You couldn't make sense of it, it wasn't rational.'

'I suppose it was spiritual what we had,' Graham agrees with Lincoln at one point. But Graham was finding his inner performer too, connecting with the crowds in a way he wouldn't have thought possible when he was an anxious child-pianist in a starched collar.

During a show in Rotterdam, he broke away to climb a

huge rack of amplifier stacks during a break in 'TransFusion'. Once at the top, he kicked into a solo so majestic, Neil stopped in his tracks, fell to his knees below Graham and threw his arms up in prayer. The crowd followed him, two thousand souls dropping down and bowing to praise him. Graham blinked, overwhelmed, Sunday School lessons of golden bulls swimming into his head, ashamed at how much he loved it.

After the show Neil found Graham in his dressing room. He'd shed the Bronze Stingray robe so was just in a loincloth and body paint.

'It's happened,' Neil said, leaning over the back of his chair. 'You're a star.' Graham stared at himself in the mirror, his costume, eyeliner, typhoon hair. He hadn't started a band to be a star. But up on that amp stack, he felt he might have finally found why God had blessed him with his talent. He turned to Neil, took his hand.

'It's down to you,' he said. 'I never would have –'

'Bollocks, it's symbiosis. Like an anemone and those fish.' Neil put his head to Graham's and began plaiting their hair together.

'What you doing?' Graham laughed, batting Neil's hand away, but he wasn't to be put off. And before Graham knew what he was doing, Neil had tied up the braid he'd made and cut it off using a pair of Sadie's scissors. He held it in front of Graham's face and they both stared at their different-coloured hair entwined.

'There,' Neil said. 'We're together.'

28.

In the various Reddit posts proclaiming Graham killed Nereus, the braid comes up more often than anything else. After their relationship deteriorated, Nereus never mentioned Graham in any publicity. But in 1974 on American broadcaster Sally Neilson's ABC breakfast show *Rise and Shine*, he did bring up the braid. Movie star Kurt Reeder was talking about the outlandish props he'd stolen from movies over the years and Sally put a question to Nereus.

'You're not in the gills today, but with all your sets and costumes,' she said, 'what's the craziest thing you've held onto?'

'I have a lock of hair, two people's hair, mine and an old bandmate,' he said. 'We'd done a magical gig in the Netherlands which needed commemorating. So I braided our hair together and cut it off. It lives in an aquamarine jewellery box.'

'Was he happy with the haircut?' Sally said with a guffaw.

'Some people are never happy, Sally,' Neil said. Everyone on the sofa laughed.

The interview came to light twenty years later when a crime scene photo from Nereus's bedroom emerged showing an aquamarine-encrusted jewellery box sat on top of a midcentury sideboard in Nereus's bedroom – its lid open.

'There was nothing in the box,' Bryn said. 'We didn't know about the hair. It was surrounded by powders, pills, a tourniquet. We assumed it was for storing drugs. Hundreds of prints on that stuff. Nothing we could do with it.'

For those looking for evidence to support their theories, the missing braid was a smoking gun. The thinking was that Graham had found the braid of his and Neil's hair and taken it, fearing leaving anything containing his DNA at the scene. These people, however, were granting Graham an incredible gift of foresight, because DNA profiling wasn't used in criminal proceedings until 1986, nine years after Nereus Forbes's death.

Despite it proving straightforward to debunk, I was interested in what it might mean if Graham, who we know had been at the house a month before and could have been there the day of Neil's death, *had* taken it.

'Murderers and mementoes,' Wisconsin attorney Lennox told me. 'Doesn't happen as often as it does on TV.'

'When you listen to *Satyrs*, how Graham talks on the tapes,' Dr Hailee said when I asked her. 'He saw them as musical soulmates. It was a moment in time when they were as one. He could have wanted to keep it to remember it, or I have wondered if it could have been the thing that provoked him.'

I hadn't thought of this. That Graham could have found this physical manifestation of when they were together, whether a love story or just relating to their collaboration, and it could have been the regret, the sense of injustice at how he'd been cast aside which drove him to do something unthinkable.

'DNA or not,' activist Candi thought, 'taking the hair is creepy as. It's not the action of a well person.' I didn't point out that Neil had made the braid in the first place, cut Graham's hair off against his will, as I'd learnt Candi, as with many Nereus fanatics, was myopic when it came to their hero, something I came up against multiple times when trying to find my way out of the murky forest of half-facts and opinions.

Anyone could have taken the braid of hair that day, even the day before when there were upwards of twenty people at the house. If the wheels were falling off the Nereus train, there's no reason to think his entourage wouldn't want to grab mementoes while they could. Neil and Greta had burnt crustaceans the night before, who's to say the lock of hair didn't make it onto the pyre?

But the braid was a symbol. Perhaps the last moment Nereus and the Satyrs saw their future as an endless rainbow road of joy, artistry and success. Because after their return from Europe, things would never feel as good again.

29.

On 20 April 1971, the Teal Eel rolled off the boat at Newhaven, bringing Nereus and the Satyrs back to England. Neil had Otis put word out they'd be playing a homecoming concert at Hatful House the very same night which his band only discovered when they found rigging crew walking staging through their front door.

'We've just got back,' Sadie told Neil when she realised what was going on. 'Are you mad? There's no way we're playing tonight. Not here, not anywhere.' She looked at Graham for support and when none came, stormed out into the garden. Neil glared at Graham before flouncing upstairs.

'The two of them were at each other's throats in the last month on the road,' Graham recalls. 'Neil was burnt-out, we all were. I kept my head down, didn't want to make it worse.' There had been a marked change in Neil near the end of the tour as the novelty of the adulation wore off. He drank more, stopped going to bed, began questioning why they were playing concerts, seemed disgusted at their becoming 'mere entertainers'. He read constantly, his fascination with Atlantis tipping him towards Foucault, Nietzsche, the Russian mystic Helen Blavatsky with her dubious ideas of a lost master-race. He'd have strange political tracts sent from England and began drunkenly lecturing the band about their overconsumption, the end of the world, how they needed to transcend the masses with him to overthrow Capitalism.

The boys managed to ignore him, but Sadie couldn't help calling out his entitlement and hypocrisy.

'Women's rights were, unsurprisingly, absent from his new ideology.' Graham tried to calm things down, but that made it worse.

'Try not to rise to it?' he suggested after a flare-up which had their driver Joe pull up at a truck-stop so the band could cool off.

'That's what he wants!' she said. 'For us to say nothing while he tells us to our faces how inferior he thinks we are.'

'That's not what he's saying.'

'Do you know what the fish do to the anemone,' she said, bringing up the example of symbiosis Graham had recounted to her so proudly. 'Clean the crap off them. That's what he thinks of us, little fishies lucky to eat his shit.'

'We weren't in a good place,' Sadie told me. 'I wanted to tell the others about us but once Neil's mood went off the cliff, Graham was on eggshells.'

'We still had weeks living on a bus together,' he said. 'What was I supposed to do?' All of which makes Sadie's reaction to being told she had to play a gig, in her house, the same night she'd got off the bus, seem fairly reasonable.

Thomas Tee sent for Otis who told them it was too late to cancel and convinced Graham to go and talk Sadie down.

'Don't you get sick of living in his world?' she asked him when he found her in their treehouse.

'It's one short set,' he said. 'Ten songs.' A loud hailer called them to soundcheck. 'Then we can rest. A proper rest. I'll make sure of it.' She looked at him, scared, before throwing her arms around him like she was holding on for her life. He squeezed her into him, guilt-ridden at forcing her to play that night. But still he helped her down the tree and led her into the banquet hall.

Four hundred and ninety people turned up for a concert in a room which even in the old lord's heyday held at most two hundred. As soon as Sadie came on and saw emaciated girls spilling over each other, topless boys crushing into the barriers circling the small stage, she felt sure something bad was coming.

'I spent the entire gig trying to catch Graham's eye to get me out of there,' Sadie said. 'But his attention was elsewhere.' Neil was like a man possessed, climbing up on the fencing like Henry V at the barricades, whipping the crowd up into a bouncing frenzy until chunks of plaster rained down from the ceiling.

A few songs in, the audience began squeezing through gaps in the fencing, climbing over, invading the stage. Danny and Fraz grabbed drinks and cigarettes from the kids before they were hauled off by security. Neil made a burly man limbo his mic stand. But then, during 'Platinum Scales', three men with Viking braids and shaved undercuts suddenly swarmed Sadie's organ.

'They were hopped up on something,' Sadie remembers. 'And you could see what they wanted to do.' She tried to bolt from behind the keyboard, but the men blocked her way, leaving nowhere to go. One of them grabbed at her breasts, another began ripping her top off. The ringleader stuck his tongue in her mouth. A horrified Neil saw what was happening, stopped singing and shoved Graham to turn and help.

Graham threw his guitar behind him with a clang of feedback and reached through the invaders to grab Sadie away from the men, handing her off to Neil. Once she was safe he turned, ignoring Sadie's pleas to let security handle it, and stormed back amongst the men. He launched one of them at the metal barricades, punched another, breaking his nose with a shower of blood, before lifting the one who'd forced himself on Sadie high above his head. The man smashed a bottle on Graham's head but he barely flinched as he threw him to the crowd who swarmed round, kicking, punching until bouncers broke them up. Sadie screamed, distraught through the whole thing, Neil trying to shield her from the violence.

Graham walked to the front of the stage, blood pouring from his head, adrenaline through his body and swung his guitar back into his hands. Neil, Sadie still shaking in his arms, tried to grab him, tell him they were stopping the show, but he went straight back into the song and the crowd burst back into life. Neil had security guards escort Sadie upstairs to his room and sleepwalked through two more songs before walking off. After he'd come off stage, Graham went to find Sadie in Neil's room. Julie Stark, of all people, came to the door and told him she didn't want to see him.

A while later, Sadie went looking for Graham but when she got to his bedroom, she found him sitting on the bed having his head bandaged by a beautiful woman. She watched the two of them talking in hushed voices, Graham more relaxed than he had been with her for some time and left, jealous, hurt and confused.

'Harriet Tausig came that night,' Graham told Trevick, referring to the sex worker he'd met with Neil. Graham and Harriet had become friends of a sort. After they met he'd sometimes go with Neil to chat to her on the sofa in the anteroom while his friend went about his business. Graham didn't know Sadie had seen them together, nor what she may have thought seeing him with Harriet, but when he went looking for her soon afterwards, he couldn't find her anywhere.

'I shouldn't have let the show happen,' Graham tells Trevick. 'I was the bad guy who'd put her in harm's way. How she saw it.' But there was more nuance to Sadie's reaction to the incident than Graham thought.

'My father was a weak man,' Sadie told me. 'I had really thought Graham was different. But not standing up to Neil that night, only showing strength when it was too late, because of how what happened to me made him look, I saw perhaps I'd been wrong.'

Graham saw Sadie spilling out of Neil's room hours later, watched her walk through dawn sunbeams down the staircase. He looked at Neil's closed bedroom door, heard Middle-Eastern music inside, wondering how it was he'd been shut out of the inner sanctum, wishing he didn't care. He watched Sadie disappear out of the house.

'I should have gone after her, told her I was sorry. But I was fed up. Beyond it. Managing them all, stopping it combusting, keeping all those threads together all the time. I was exhausted.' The band had played an incredible set that night. Graham didn't understand why that wasn't enough.

30.

Investigating a mysterious death you're personally invested in requires you to live on a hyper-rational plane while simultaneously throwing all rational thoughts out the cognitive window. One has to take enormous leaps, truly believe in tenuous links between disparate details, only to strip all those assumptions you've made down to the bone until there's nothing but dust and disappointment. It puts you in a world where everything seems meaningful: the light, colours, people's tone of voice, hand movements, animals that cross your path in the street, all of it becomes shockingly significant. Before you have to dismiss everything as the nothing you always knew it to be.

All of this is to say, I didn't tell my husband about the man I'd seen following me, even after I saw him parked in his car on our street, because I was sure I was being ridiculous. The *nereusforever* group didn't help me dispel my paranoia.

'Security services,' Candi said when I let 'flat-cap chap' slip to her over coffee at her house. 'Has to be.'

'In a Vauxhall Corsa?' I countered.

'You think they drive invisible Aston Martins? Think about your phone, now Jason Statham?'

'It was just the hat, he didn't look like Jason Statham.'

'You're getting close to something.' But Candi couldn't tell me what it was I might be getting close to. If Nereus was threatening to expose some powerful person's dirty laundry, through Harriet Tausig's brothel or any other means, I'd found no evidence of it. If the 'Deep State' did it to bring down a powerful countercultural figure for corrupting the youth, why wait until his career was on the slide, when the 'youth' who'd adored him were looking to punk for their anti-establishment chutzpah. None of it made any sense.

But the man in the Corsa continued to bother me. Knowing it was pointless reporting something so innocuous to the police, and not sure what else I could do, I decided to ramp up my own investigations by engaging Dale Harrahan, a former police forensic investigator I found on the internet who sold himself as a 'crime scene consultant'. I sent Dale pictures detective Bryn had saved with his files of notes from the case. I wasn't sure it was strictly legal that Bryn had kept them, and suspected it was definitely not legal for him to give them to me. But Dale didn't seem a stickler for the law and had some interesting insights.

He was in his late forties, sideburns, short hair, and wore one of the hats people who like cycling wear. He looked like Bradley Wiggins, though that could have just been the hat. Across a Caffè Nero table, he took me through enhanced pictures of the sideboard with the jewel-encrusted box and drug paraphernalia. He pointed out that all the vials of cocaine and wraps of heroin were open.

'There's an awful lot there,' he said. 'Most half-full, why open more than one?' He showed me how some had been knocked, how much was spilt. He moved onto the fox-fur coverlet, the way it had been folded, demonstrating with origami on a paper napkin. I remained baffled.

'What exactly is it you're telling me?' I asked.

'It looks like an accident,' he said, which, having spent the previous nine months working on the assumption it wasn't, I felt a little crestfallen to hear before Dale clarified what he meant. 'In the sense that it looks too much like one. I believe someone wanted it to look like an accident.' I blinked, butterflies in my stomach. It might seem odd to have felt pleased to hear Nereus was murdered, possibly implicating my own father, but the world believed it an accident, as did my husband, my daughters, any rational voice on the internet, my own mother who knew Nereus. So I felt vindicated at finally having someone tell me I might be right. The investigation which had come to dominate my thoughts, which I'd been neglecting my students to work on, which I had in my head as I barely listened to my youngest telling me about college over dinner, which I managed to divert almost every bedtime conversation with my husband towards, might not just be the tragic search for meaning of a menopausal woman 'going through something'.

'But who?' I said, assuming if Dale could be so certain about someone tampering with the scene, he might whip out an envelope revealing the identity of the killer.

'Well,' he said, 'anyone who wants to get away with it.'

'With murder?'

'Maybe,' he said, pulling his cap off his head to reveal peroxided hair. 'But then you add in the alcohol on his hair, in his lungs. Mess the scene up, make it like general debauchery killed him, not an overdose. Might be what I'd do if I'd been the one who supplied the drugs.'

31.

Matthew Salvini would be the man who brought Nereus Forbes into contact with Dominik Szlonik and the international hard drugs trade, but before the unsung pioneer of electronic music joins the story, someone had to leave the Satyrs to make space.

Graham found Sadie in a hotel in Putney the day after the concert at Hatful House. He brought them tea from the hall downstairs. She asked him to sit beside her on the plasticised floral bedspread.

'I'm leaving the band,' she said. Graham blinked, blindsided.

'It got out of hand last night –'

'It's not about last night,' she said. 'It's the chaos. The constant chaos. People, normal people, aren't meant to live like this.'

'Is that what you want,' he asked, 'to be normal?'

'I really think I do.' She grabbed Graham's hands into hers, tears pricking. 'I know you don't see it, but Neil, he's a black hole. Draws you in but when you get to the heart of him, it's empty.'

'What does that mean?'

'You can give him everything you have but he'll always want more.' The floodgates burst and she collapsed into Graham's chest. He looked out the window at a blackened brick wall opposite.

'If you leave, though,' he said, 'what about us?'

'We won't survive if I stay,' she said gripping his arms, tear-streaked cheeks desperate to reach him. Graham couldn't see how their relationship could continue without being together every day, couldn't see how he'd deal with Neil, with Fraz and the increasingly irascible Danny without her.

'I can fix it,' he said. 'Get Otis to step in, get rid of Thomas. The drugs. I don't know, but I can talk to Neil, look at how we're doing things —'

'Neil won't change!' she near-screeched at him. 'When will you see that? He'll never change.'

'I don't want to lose you.'

'If I stay in the band you will.' She took his face in her hands. 'I want us to last. I do. This is the only way.' There was nothing he could say to that. Sadie left the band.

'How could you be so sure,' I asked her, 'that Neil couldn't change?'

'Because that night,' she said, 'hours after the show, the fighting. He told me about his father.'

Nereus's biographies barely mention his father. Only that Neil and his mother moved to Britain when he was young to further Penny's academic career. Most suggest she and his father either weren't together by the time Neil was born, or that they split in his early years. The truth, as my mother told it, is somewhat different.

Penny was twenty-six when she met Nearchos Kanelides, who was three years her senior. He was a chef with designs on opening his own restaurant in Patras, a musician with ambitions of moving to Athens with his band and a cliff-diver intent on one day winning the Peloponnese championships at Kalogria Beach. He'd been an engaged father, caring for little Neil, who was also named Nearchos before moving to the UK, while his mother sought teaching work to support their young family. The toddler Neil idolised him.

But when he was about five years old his father changed. He had always drunk; Neil's memories of Greece consist of buzzing around tables of grown-ups playing rebetika music, growing sloppier as the retsina went down with the sun. What Neil didn't realise was his father's roll-up cigarettes were increasingly spiced with opium. As Nearchos's addiction worsened, he stopped working in kitchens, playing his bouzouki around local tavernas, forcing Penny to take Neil out to work with her.

Nearchos smoked more to cope with his depression at not being able to provide for his family, which led to him injecting. Penny and Neil returned one day to find Nearchos passed out, syringe still sticking from his wrist, while a woman and two men Penny had never met had sex on the bed the family shared in the back room of their small seaside house. Neil saw everything. Penny screamed at the people to get out, grabbed things from all around the room, hit them with plates, candlesticks. 'Neil said she was so angry he was waiting for her hair to turn into snakes,' Sadie said.

Penny packed clothes and a huge wedge of banknotes from a box at the back of their wardrobe. She grabbed Neil's hand to leave but he wouldn't, seeming to know their walking out that afternoon would be definitive. By the time she eventually dragged him to the door, Nearchos was there, standing in their way.

His father tore at the bag, grabbed it from his mother, their clothes and money bursting into the air around them. Penny got down on the floor and packed the banknotes back into her bag. Nearchos pulled her up, tried to reason with her, beg her, pleading, grabbing her roughly, spitting his words into the side of her head as she kept her body lifeless. Neil watched in stunned fascination as his previously gentle father shook his mother violently, shoving her into the wall, and holding a clenched fist inches from her face, before collapsing on his haunches and bursting into tears, rending his shirt like a mourner.

Neil tried to go to him, but Penny held him back. She packed further books from a shelf, ignoring the weeping Nearchos, and when Neil refused to leave his father, she grabbed the little boy into her arms and walked out of the only home he'd ever known. The only thing Neil remembers his father saying as they left was, 'You're killing me. If you go I'll die.'

A year and a half after Penny and Neil left Greece, Nearchos's body was found washed up on the shores of Lake Vouliagmeni, south of Athens. His bouzouki, the traditional Greek lute-like instrument, was found on the cliffs a hundred feet above. No one knew whether he jumped, fell or if it was a dive gone wrong. But he had been right. Penny had left with their son when he had needed them. And he had died.

'He told you that night?' I asked Sadie.

'Seeing Graham switch like that with the men on stage,' she said. 'I think it brought it back. That moment he realised there was violence in his father, in everyone perhaps.' I had never thought of Graham as a father figure to Neil, but it made sense he might equate them. Graham was three years older, and when they met in Neil's late teens, that would have seemed like decades. He was gentle, grounded and, like his father, played beautiful music. Nearchos was a dreamer who, perhaps like Graham, didn't know he had a right to dream. To see someone he'd only ever thought of as benign snap like that, realising that big, strong men could destroy as well as protect, must have had a profound effect.

However, I doubted it was happenstance he decided to unburden this secret childhood trauma to Sadie that night. Neil must have known he was responsible for what happened to her on stage. He knew about Sadie and Graham's relationship and however much she repeatedly denied it, despite his relationship with Thomas, I was certain he had feelings for her. His story deflected from what he'd done and painted Graham as a brute. I thought it odd at the time Sadie couldn't see how manipulative it was, which jarred with how cynical she was about him. Nor could I make sense of what Neil's dad had to do with Sadie leaving the band.

'It told me two things,' she said. 'The first was that the chaos in Neil was hard-wired from a young age, maybe in his DNA. At that point it was just coke, booze, sex and Nietzsche, but he was tiring of it. We could see it. Whatever he found next wasn't going to make things better.'

'What was the second thing?'

'I realised Neil wasn't the circus clown he seemed. He was driven by guilt, by the guilt at leaving his father behind, at letting him die like that,' she said. 'I knew he could never fill that chasm in him. But that he'd destroy everything around him trying.'

32.

Graham stayed with Sadie in the hotel for two more days before returning to Hatful House to break the news to Neil.

'It's for the best,' Neil said in the hallway after Graham told him, hand shaking a little round a tumbler of Scotch. 'New horizons in sight and that's not for the faint-hearted. And –' He bit his lip, sliding the glass onto an occasional table. 'Better for the two of you.'

'Oh, right.' Graham swallowed. He and Sadie knew Neil knew, but no one had acknowledged it until then. Silence fell like a cloud between them, neither wanting to talk further. Neil smiled, gave Graham an uncharacteristic brotherly punch on the shoulder and made his way upstairs.

Sadie leaving felt like a watershed moment for them all. The band moved out of Hatful House in the following weeks. Neil took up the top two floors of a house in Cheyne Walk, four along from number 1 which he'd go on to buy. Thomas squatted in one of his Soho sugar-daddy's Covent Garden townhouses. Danny and Fraz rented a place overlooking Hyde Park they couldn't afford from a friend of Julie Stark.

Graham and Sadie moved into a third-floor flat in an art-deco block on Prince Albert Road overlooking Regent's Park, together at last.

'Come on then,' Graham said, holding his arms out to Sadie as they stood outside the front door, having just got the keys.

'What are you doing?'

'Got to carry you over the threshold.'

'Isn't that after a wedding?' she said. He shook his head, not wanting to think about the fact they were moving in together unmarried before grabbing her up and taking her inside.

'It was a good place,' he says on the tapes. 'Could see the giraffes in London Zoo from the window. We'd walk up to Primrose Hill, watch the sunset with a Newcastle Brown.' It was bliss. Sadie had been right. With her out of the band, away from the whirlwind of Neil's ever-changing whims, they were finally free to be together. They could breathe.

Back at work, Neil enlisted Graham to find Sadie's replacement, auditioning more than thirty musicians to be the Satyrs' new keyboard player. They listened to concert pianists, Nashville veterans and even a blind seventeen-year-old percussionist who was adamant every Nereus song could be improved with a glockenspiel. Matthew Salvini, who'd moved to New York from his native Anglesey at fourteen to study jazz in Brooklyn, blew them all out of the park with a mind-bending improvisation which was as frightening to listen to as it was beautiful. When Matthew finished, he slammed the piano shut, told them he hated rock music and wandered off 'for a shit'.

Neil wanted him on the spot. Otis really didn't. With his near-baldness and thick-framed glasses, Matthew didn't look right. He was awkward, had no stage presence, smelled, and was anything but personable. Sadie hadn't been the greatest musician but the balance had been right. Otis didn't want to overrule Neil, his golden goose, which left Graham with the casting vote. It wasn't an easy decision. He was the best musician in the band. Apart from a few festivals and competitions he'd played as a child, Graham had barely been in a room with anyone who was his musical equal. It was possible Matthew was better.

'If it was about the person, I wouldn't have had him within a hundred miles of my band. But though *Dance of the Satyrs* was good, I still hadn't done it, that song, music that could live in people's hearts. Neil and I wanted the same. And he wanted Salvini.' Matthew was invited to join the band.

When Graham walked into the lobby of Trident Studios for the first writing session for the next album the following Monday, he was amazed to hear the sound of an orchestra's entire brass section, blasting a fanfare in the main space. He found himself laughing, amazed at Neil's ability to surprise him yet again. But when he walked into the cavernous studio and saw the sound was only being made by Matthew at the keyboard of a machine which looked like a three-storey telephone exchange, he got a titanic sinking feeling. Matthew moved wires around, changing a horn sound to create something Graham describes as 'inter-dimensional'.

'Sounds like the end of the world,' Neil shouted across the room, possessed with excitement. Graham frowned, wondering how that was a good thing.

He had heard synthesisers before, an entrepreneurial Denmark Street shop-owner had shown him a Moog, and thought them a gimmick. But hearing the technology in Matthew's hands, Graham felt instant existential panic. I can only think of it in terms of a graphic designer having seen the first AI designs, copywriters messing around with ChatGPT. To Graham, guitarist, musical director and powerhouse of Nereus and the Satyrs, it did start to sound like the end the world.

'Those first few weeks making a home together were wonderful,' Sadie told me. 'But after hearing Matthew's machine, the honeymoon was over.' Graham came home every night in despair at how little progress they were making on the record.

'Every time we'd try to shape Neil's initial melody, Matthew would overwhelm it all with some completely inaccessible soundscape.'

'Which Neil would always *love*,' she said.

'Salvini's machine was scrambling our heads,' Danny writes. 'It was round then, Neil went fully off the reservation.'

'He became obsessed with the "Music of the Spheres",' Graham says. 'Showing us these five-hundred-year-old medieval diagrams. Got Matthew trying to create some divine harmony, the omnichord. Thought it could move planets.'

The only thing worse than Matthew's world-ending machine was his personality.

'Matthew was always a bit of an arsehole,' says Danny Greig. 'But when he was drunk, which was most of the time, he was a complete one.' Matthew went on to work with some incredible artists over his career, none of whom had anything nice to say about him. As a lifelong people-pleaser, I was almost impressed reading of his total refusal to acknowledge any social niceties, people's feelings or decorum.

Neil seemed to encourage Matthew's unpleasantness, believing it created the right tension for the challenging work he wanted to make and took his new bandmate's drinking habits as license to follow suit.

'They had a cocktail. Brandy, cherry liqueur, ginger wine. Black Forest Fiasco. Spent five weeks working on a song named after it. Which he then binned.'

'They were like eight-year-olds who'd raided the drinks cabinet, but much less fun,' Sadie said. ''Course by that point, the skag had arrived.'

The band didn't know Neil had started using heroin. But they did notice the square-shouldered man in the finest linens, with sunglasses always perched in his nest of sandy hair, who began drifting in and out of the studio, pub sessions and their planning meetings – Hungarian aristocrat and international drug trafficker, Dominik Szlonik.

'He didn't say a word to any of us,' Graham recalls of the man who had people call him 'The Count' despite never holding the title. 'Didn't know he could speak English for months. Would turn up and stand in the corner, at the back of the control room, give Thomas or Matthew a nod, then disappear.'

By all accounts, Nereus Forbes took his first hit of heroin the morning after that last night at Hatful House. He's said to have told people who were there that he found the whole thing a disappointing anti-climax.

'If he'd liked it off the bat, he would have moved on,' Sadie said. 'It was always about the chase for Neil.'

33.

Matthew Salvini took me to a summerhouse at the end of his large, unkempt garden outside the village of Audley End, twenty minutes from Cambridge. He opened the door to reveal a semi-circle of ancient cabinet-like machines. Dials twitched, lights flickered, reels of tape whirred.

He pointed me to a seat, the only recognisable object in the cramped space. Seventy-nine years old when we met, with yellowing skin and redness round the eyes which reminded me of a basset hound, Matthew took his place at a control desk. There was a smell of yeast. He twisted knobs, fiddled with tangled wires and from nowhere, speakers either side of me produced the most extraordinary noise I'd ever heard. Like a Middle-Eastern orchestra produced in the throat of a robot, surprisingly beautiful. Energised amongst his machines, with his tufty grey hair he looked like a crazed scientist, as obsessed as he must have been in the summer of 1971.

I found myself emotional thinking about him and my father working together. As Matthew fiddled like a virtuoso electrician, I imagined Graham adjusting guitar pedals, moving mics, honing and tinkering the ancient equipment – like I'd seen my husband do in studios so many times. In our early days, I loved tagging along to his work so I could watch. I realised I might have been trying to connect to a vision of Graham. The men who made the artists sound good. There's a humble nobility in the sacrifice of it, the knowledge it's perhaps the closest they could get to greatness.

Matthew Salvini was 'on his way out', he had told me when he'd responded to my many phone calls – his liver due to 'pack up any minute'. He hadn't wanted to talk to me but when I mentioned I'd spoken to Thomas about the day Neil died, Matthew said I could visit him. Which was suspicious.

He stopped the machines, told me to get up so he could sit down and slurped a mug of what I could smell was rum. I didn't want to be there any longer than I needed to, so cut straight to asking why he went to see Nereus the day he died.

'Needed money,' he said. His Welsh accent sounded like it had been dropped in hot tarmac. 'Owed people.'

'Did you think Nereus would help you out?'

'Always had.'

'What did you spend it all on?'

'Hardware,' he said, nodding his head at the machines behind. 'Out my own pocket.' I found it hard to believe drugs, booze and various other vices might not also have generated some of Matthew's debts but I wasn't about to press him.

'You were with Dominik Szlonik that day.'

'Horrible prick,' Matthew said, hacking a cough into his mug.

'I heard you were friends?' Matthew looked at me with a cruel glimmer.

'Szlonik always had gear. Better than friendship.' Matthew met Dominik Szlonik in a smack den in New York and brought him to London. Through Matthew, Dominik met Thomas and Neil who introduced him to their wider circle. By the time Nereus died, Dominik was supplying heroin to the vast majority of the Soho, Chelsea and Carnaby Street users.

Born into a minor line of the Hapsburg family in 1956, Dominik was the third-born son of Baron Szlonik, a leading light in Hungary's diplomatic circles following the

Austro-Hungarian Empire's collapse in 1918. A legendary operator in Africa and the Middle East as the various countries reconciled their futures following the Second World War, the baron made a huge fortune he refused to share with any of his children. Although he didn't approve of his son's lifestyle choices, there's little doubt Dominik's network of suppliers, mostly in Tunisia and Afghanistan, came through his father's little black book.

Sadie knew Dominik a little. He was at Harrow so they'd occasionally mope around the lawns of diplomatic high teas together.

'Charmless, underbite,' she said when I asked what he was like. 'Complete entitlement. Paralysed what to do with it. Took plates of cakes round the corners of buildings, not wanting to be seen eating them.'

'Who was it you owed money to?' I asked Matthew. He coughed up phlegm, spat into the corner of his shed.

'Dominik owed the people he bought from. Needed the money that day. He called in my bill but I didn't have it.'

'How much money was it?'

'Sixty, seventy.'

'Thousand?' Matthew shrugged. I tried to play it out in my head. Thomas Tee had just left Nereus, having told him there was no money left. Then the two most problematic men in his circle turned up and asked for tens of thousands of pounds which they needed that day.

'How was Nereus?'

'Cock-a-hoop when we turned up. Never seen him happier. Until we demanded the cash.'

'Neighbours heard arguing, raised voices?'

'I helped myself to a fix when Neil said he couldn't help. The Count though, he was scared.'

'Scared of what?'

'People he owed were serious.' Matthew drained the mug of rum. 'That's why we went to Neil, why the Count was throwing threats around.'

'What sort of threats?'

'Arsehole wanted to keep the use of his legs, so who knew what he would have done.' My breath caught. Dale Harrahan thought Nereus's drugs supplier might have manipulated the scene to escape censure following an accidental overdose, but if he needed his money, was scared for his safety, perhaps Dominik Szlonik might have had a more active role in the death.

'Did Neil actually owe Dominik?' I asked.

'It would have been news to him. The guy had a suitcase full of gear at all times. We took what we wanted. No one paid him.'

'So Neil did owe him then, you all did?' Matthew coughed, cleared phlegm from deep in his lungs.

'Either way, Neil told us he couldn't get the money.' Which made sense if he was bankrupt. 'So we pissed off.'

'Where did you go?'

'Oxford way, I think. Cottage on some great aunt's estate.'

'You were hiding out?'

'I wasn't in a state to make an escape.' Matthew went into a cupboard on the floor next to him to top up his drink. I wasn't sure how much longer I'd have him lucid for.

'Was Dominik with you?' I said. 'That night in the cottage?' Matthew slurped his drink. I worried he was going to spit again and wasn't sure I'd be able to keep down the sandwich I'd eaten on the train.

'He left a couple of hours after we arrived.'

'Where did he go?'

'He was always jetting off. Didn't see him again. Wasn't bothered when I heard the news that he'd popped it.'

'Do you think he could have been involved?' Matthew shrugged, one eye beginning to close. 'With Nereus's death.'

'Junkies are like vermin. They look weak, but they're capable of anything.'

'So you think he was?'

'Could be. Or whoever he owed.' I was losing him and wasn't sure how much longer he'd be alive for me to come back, or if I wanted to. He drank deeper. 'Why didn't you tell the police?' Matthew's half-closed eye opened. 'Your bandmate was murdered and you did nothing.'

'Didn't want to be in his poxy band,' he said. 'Man was caustic.'

'What does that mean?'

'Ask your old man,' he said, turning to a keyboard and starting to play.

'This isn't about Graham Harris,' I said.

'You sure?' he said, smiling cruelly. 'His fault Neil was bankrupt.' I snapped back to him as the tune swelled around me. I shouted to ask what he meant but I was in the middle of two monolith speakers so Matthew couldn't hear. Or didn't want to. I approached, thought about shaking him and asking what the hell he meant, but by the time I got there, I realised he'd fallen asleep. The music looped, again and again.

I marched back up his muddy path, rolling through the facts, trying to see if Dominik Szlonik fitted, trying to make sense of Graham having had something to do with Nereus's money problems. A tune I recognised but couldn't place swelled out of the decrepit summerhouse, blooming into the Cambridgeshire dusk.

34.

Dominik Szlonik was never questioned by police. They didn't find him at any of his various properties and it was assumed he'd left the country on one of his father's planes, most probably to North Africa. From the various secondary accounts, it seemed people in Nereus's circle were also in the dark over his whereabouts until the end of 1978, when he was discovered hanging dead in the wet room of a seaside villa in Santorini.

When I put Szlonik forward to the WhatsApp group as a person of interest having discovered he'd gone to Nereus the day he died asking for money to pay off drug-runners, I was surprised to get a muted response. The same questions emerged. Why did no one see him come back? How did he get out? And, questioning my logic entirely, if he wanted Neil's money, how would he get it if he was dead?

When I put what Matthew had hinted about Graham and Neil's finances on the group chat, however, I could tell I'd caught the imagination.

'Hush money,' Candi wrote. 'Has to be.'

'Fees in lieu,' wrote lawyer Lennox Dixon from Wisconsin. 'Industry notorious for withholding earnings.'

'Penance,' wrote cultural academic Dr Hailee, 'for what happened with the band.'

'He knew where the bodies were buried.' Candi wasn't to be deterred. 'Has to be blackmail.' Someone put a laughing emoji face on her message, prompting her to write back 'Piss off.' Which several people put more laughing emojis on.

'NO EVIDENCE NO REASON TO ASSUME SALVINI TELLING THE TRUTH,' former detective Bryn Halleran wrote, in caps and without punctuation. None of us could agree, none who had strong opinions could back up their instincts. There was no logic as to why Neil would have given Graham the sort of money that would bankrupt a healthy financial position just a year later.

I put it to IP lawyer Helen Grady who I'd first spoken to about the documents Lennox found implying Graham made a legal challenge to Nereus in 1974. I wanted to know whether she thought the money could be related to it.

'Can't see how,' she said. 'Even if Graham had been entitled to a share of publishing on top of mechanical rights, it would never run to hundreds of thousands back then.' Publishing is the term used for songwriting royalties, mechanical rights are split between those playing on the original recordings. The money for a song is normally split equally between these two, which is why the songwriters in bands, usually one person, generally make much more in the long term than the other band members who have to split the mechanical rights between them. If that seems boring to you, imagine how it must sound to a musician. Which makes sense of how they've been consistently exploited by executives since man first invented fire then sang around it.

I didn't want Helen to be right, but thought she probably was. It was too much money. I found myself in my summerhouse staring blankly at the mess I'd made of its walls, wishing I could go back ten months and react to my daughter receiving a weird bit of post like a fully realised adult would have, by ignoring it. My head of department at university had noticed my increasing absences and the papers I wasn't delivering.

Delphi, still at home, was in some teenage funk with me which, to my shame, I was pleased about because it gave me an excuse to avoid her in my little den. I could tell my husband's work was stressful but likewise, I avoided getting into the weeds of it with him. As for Sara herself, I hadn't spoken to her in weeks. On top of which I thought I was being stalked.

I was no closer to the answers to the fifty-year-old questions I was looking for. Everything in my present seemed to be screaming at me to stop looking.

But then Dr Hailee called my iPhone 5 and said, 'Methuselah.'

Methuselah was the name of Graham's beautiful Georgian house in the heart of Sussex's South Downs. I didn't follow her meaning but Dr Hailee was used to talking to people less intelligent than her. 'He bought Methuselah in 1975, a few weeks after your mother bought the flat in Marylebone. How?'

'How what?'

'How could he afford it?'

'Holy shit,' I said, collapsing back in the spinny chair which had grown mouldy in the damp summerhouse. I looked at the picture of Methusaleh I had pinned up, kicking myself I hadn't thought of it. Graham had been in a wildly successful rock band, I'd assumed buying a country pile was just standard practice. I'd never considered what share he'd have made of the band's earnings, nor his having to pay for my mother's house after they separated, for my upkeep, the money he sent home to his parents and that he was only actually in said wildly successful rock band for just over two years. Dr Hailee was right, there was no way he would have been able to afford a place like Methusaleh. The money had to have come from Neil. Where else could Graham have got it?

'It has to be what Matthew Salvini meant,' Dr Hailee said. 'Nereus hated money, gave it away to whoever asked.'

'But that much money,' I said. 'Why give him that much?' Dr Hailee didn't know.

But I wanted her to be right. I wondered whether some kind of loan might explain their meeting a month before his death or, more pertinently, the night he died. Nereus's big concert extravaganza had been a massive failure, Thomas had told him they were bankrupt, Matthew Salvini and Dominik Szlonik had come demanding tens of thousands of pounds to get international drug barons off their backs. Is it possible Nereus was calling in Graham's debt to him that night? And if so, depending on the terms they'd agreed, could it be enough to drive Graham to murder?

35.

On 3 June 1971, six weeks after Sadie left the band, Nereus Forbes' Poseidon character would have its first unveiling.

A week before, Otis called Graham for a secret lunch at Soho's Quo Vadis.

'I didn't want to go,' Graham says, 'but we'd been in the studio a month and had nothing anyone would think was actual music.' They'd expected the songs from Neil's concept album about Poseidon to still be about falling in love, sex, the rock and roll lifestyle. Not about colonialism, climate disaster and the apocalypse.

'He's always like this at the start,' Graham told Otis. 'We'll get there. Have faith.'

'Faith doesn't pay the six grand a week for the studio.' Otis ordered more wine. 'You need to get me something I can actually listen to,' he said. 'Or I'm getting someone in.' Otis de Kock doesn't mention this meeting in his memoir, preferring to paint himself as the serene voice of reason amidst the tornadoes he tangled with during his career.

'Graham has songs if you want something you can listen to?' Sadie said. She'd joined them for lunch. They didn't leave each other's side when Graham wasn't working back then.

'That so?' Otis said, curious. Graham swallowed, nervous. Inspired by his new conjugal bliss, he'd been writing again. He and Sadie would work on the songs together. They were good. But he hadn't dreamed of telling anyone about them.

'They're just sketches.' He put his hand on Sadie's, fearing the suggestion might get back to Neil. 'Listen, I'll sort it out. Get things back on track.' Otis paid the bill, told them to finish their meal and left.

The next day, Graham found Neil on a plinth in the middle of the studio being sewn into a salmon-scaled ballgown by a troop of fashionistas. Thomas, who was drawing something on the shaved sides of Neil's head, eyed Graham as he came in before whispering something in his ear.

'What's this?' Graham asked, trying at jovial.

'The Aeon of Horus, of the child, of self-actualisation, is upon us,' Neil said. The women attached a huge stingray-like cloak to him as he stepped down. 'I am reborn Poiseidon.' Neil glared at Graham, daring him to object.

'I could tell straight away they knew I'd met with Otis.' I wasn't sure how but Dr Hailee and Bryn didn't seem to think it surprising. There were only about five restaurants London scenesters went to. Graham tried to explain the lunch, make sure they knew he wasn't siding with the suits, but Neil waved him away, falling back in with the designers and dressmakers bustling round him like a forcefield.

If Graham thought Neil's transformation into the Poiseidon persona was a statement against Otis de Kock's attempts to rein him in, it was nothing compared to the hurricane which would barge into the studio a few hours later in the form of a very angry Danny Greig and Fraz.

Danny stormed over and began yanking cables out of Matthew's machine. A drunk Matthew, who'd been asleep somewhere, jumped up onto his back and began throwing impotent punches before Fraz entered the fray, grabbing the pianist off Danny's back and throwing him to the floor.

'Did you know?' Danny said when Graham arrived. 'That he was getting paid six times what we are?' Graham turned to

Thomas, skulking in from a back room, and asked if it was true. Thomas didn't answer, shivering.

'Annie showed me the payslip,' Danny said, referring to the Apollo Records receptionist he'd been seeing.

'Bastard's on three hundred a week,' Fraz said.

'I was speechless,' Graham tells Trevick. 'The boys were on fifty, I was on seventy, extra for the arrangements. It was a monumental piss-take.' Someone must have pressed the recording studio equivalent of the panic button because Otis arrived within the hour to defuse the situation. He explained Matthew was conservatoire trained, had been mentored by John Cage and had joined the band once it was already successful, so his pay was commensurate with that.

'We're being punished for being here from the start,' Fraz said.

'When Neil was nothing,' Danny added. Otis cocked his head, stifling a smile.

'I am a businessman working for a company that, in turn, works for its shareholders,' Otis said, not even looking at them. 'If my staff are happy to be paid at a lower level, my job is to do exactly that.'

'Well, now we're not happy,' Danny said. 'We want more, don't we?' The boys looked at Graham, who'd remained quiet.

'It's only fair,' Graham said, voice tentative, caught between deference to their boss and loyalty to his friends.

'You signed an agreement and won't get a penny more,' he said. Danny went berserk.

'I ran and kicked a hole in the kick-drum, pushed the whole thing over, cymbals crashing everywhere, and stormed out,' Danny Greig writes. 'I'd made my point.' A bewildered Fraz stood like a dog without its owner.

'I'm going to sort this,' Graham said to him, ushering him out to deal with Danny.

'Even throwing loyalty in the bin, we're the backbone, the sound,' Graham said when the boys had left the room. 'We walk away and everything changes, everything.' Otis sat on the back of a sofa, scratching the back of his head. He sighed, seeming genuinely upset.

'Just them,' he said.

'What?'

'Not you Graham, just them.'

'You can't though,' Graham said to him. 'You can't do this.'

'It's done,' he said. 'I'm sorry but it's done.' Graham took a stuttering breath in, chest tight, overwhelmed as he understood what was happening. Otis was a genius for diplomacy. He could have smoothed things over, offered the boys a little more, made them feel valued. He pointedly didn't. The two of them had had lunch the day before with no mention of anything this rash. It wasn't coming from Otis. Graham grabbed his coat.

'Graham, wait.'

'I can't stay,' he said. 'If you're slinging them out like this – you know I can't stay.'

'One fifty a week.'

'Those boys are like brothers.'

'I can go to two hundred.' Graham swallowed. It was less than Salvini was getting but fifty times what anyone on the boats at home could even dream of. He had royalties due as well, who knows what would happen to those if he left the band. Graham put down his guitar case, turned to Otis.

'Thanks for everything you've done,' he said. 'I don't hold you responsible.' He picked up his guitar case and marched out of the studio.

Like many other unpleasant moments in his storied career, Otis skirts that day in his autobiography. Instead focusing on his first encounter with Poiseidon.

'As soon as I saw him, my concerns about the new musical

direction evaporated,' he wrote. He conflates the two things, implying the former Marshalls leaving the band was linked to Nereus's reinvention, as if they were somehow nothing more than the chrysalis he needed to leave behind to become the beautiful butterfly the world needed. He never says the directive came from Neil, nor that it was perhaps a response to his own attempts to try to control his star asset.

After he left, Graham should have joined the lads at The Coach and Cart two streets away, but instead he went home, needing to be with Sadie. He felt numb walking from Chalk Farm station. The animals in London Zoo watched as he rubbed his eyes to stem tears as it sank in that he was walking away from Neil for good.

He walked through the front door of their flat and through to the kitchen, where he found Sadie in nothing but one of his shirts, cradling a huge mug of tea. He took her in his arms, deep, heaving breaths into her shoulder.

'Gray, what's wrong?' she asked.

'He threw them out,' he said.

'What?'

'Dan and Fraz.'

'Neil? Why?'

'I don't know why,' he said, pulling away from her. 'Why does he do anything he does?' Sadie leant on the sink behind her. Graham stood stranded in the middle of their lino floor.

'I have to leave,' he said. 'I have to leave the band.' Sadie looked to the side, out the window at leaves brushing the panes of their lattice window. 'I have to leave, don't I?' She nodded, looking outside still.

'You should,' she said but then she stopped, swallowed, looked at the floor, mouth open, before swinging round to the sink and being violently sick. Graham ran to her, held her hair away from her face, rubbing her back. Sadie spat, ran the tap, and washed the vomit out of her mouth. After a few breaths to recover herself, she turned to him, water dripping from her lips.

'You should leave, Gray,' she said. 'But the thing is, you're going to be a dad.'

The Apotheosis of Poseidon

Nereus's masterpiece, 'Lady Theia', encapsulates everything the wider album seeks to achieve. Matthew Salvini's computer-sounds dance round the phase-heavy guitar before embarking on a full-scale battle between good and evil, future and past, life and very death. And in the middle of it all is Nereus singing an elegy to a Mother Earth figure he fluctuates between wanting to worship and destroy. And that melody. That melody. 'You can work on every other element of the song,' musicologist Ani Grabhosi once wrote, 'build it up using knowledge, craft, musicianship. But the top line of a great song, for that you have to look to heaven and hope.'

From *The Hundred Greatest Albums of All Time*, ed. Jasper Naylor.

36.

Nereus died on a Friday. I had been due to be down in Sussex with Graham that weekend before the Jordanians invited him to Monaco earlier that week. He had been giving Princess Bismah piano lessons on and off for a year, her Aunt Khalifa for several months before, always at their residence in Mayfair. When Lincoln Trevick asks how this came about, Graham says he was contacted by the family as they were fans of his work on Nereus's first two albums. But reading of Neil's friendship with the Crown Prince from 1974, it seemed more likely he recommended Graham. Though with the two men at odds, I'm not sure why he would. Regardless, the residential visit was to be Graham's first to the royal family's European seat. I was five so I have few memories from that time, but I can remember that Friday because no one was there to pick me up at the end of the school day.

I held it together for the three or four hours I had to wait with the school receptionist but when my mother turned up at sixish, explaining the mix-up was down to Graham's last-minute work trip, I had a full-on meltdown. Sadie took me to an ice-cream parlour nearby and bought me a huge sundae.

I used to love weekends with Graham in the country. The flat I lived in with my mother was beautifully styled, warm, cosy, but almost everything in it was functional, befitting its size. Methuselah was a warren of cubbyholes and passages, haunted-house paintings and lattice-work windows. The place was a wreck when Graham bought it so I'd spend hours sitting on the bottom of his ladder as he repaired ceilings and replastered walls. I thought he could fix anything.

He'd play a song to me at night instead of reading a story and it would put me in a trance like I was a snake in a basket. When I later read about Orpheus calming monstrous beasts with his lyre, I'd hear the sound of Graham's guitar those nights. The house was in a valley, huge walls of green on each side punctuated by little gatherings of sheep. There was a paddock and small stables where he had two ponies and a miniature donkey.

There were no donkeys there when my daughter Delphi and I went to visit Methuselah one afternoon in January. As the family's only unabashed Nereus fan, Delphi was fascinated with my investigation from the moment Sara received the poster and I'd often catch her sneaking into the summerhouse, rifling through notes, taking photos of various papers. As an extraordinary musician herself, she always had a romantic view of some lineage between her and Graham and was desperate to help but I didn't want my obsession to be the reason she flunked her last year at college. However, having never learnt to drive and not daring to ask Bobby to take a day off work to take me down to see the house in Sussex, I had no choice but to ask her.

Methuselah was sold on Graham's behalf in 1999 to one of the neighbouring farmers who siphoned off the land for grazing and, much later, planted it with solar panels. The house itself, which had been left abandoned just as Graham finished his refurbishment, was bought by a hotelier in 2018 as a wedding venue before his plans were iced by the pandemic. When we pulled up outside, the grounds were surrounded by metal construction fencing. I found myself pinioned with emotion as I looked through to see the facade smothered in scaffolding, the fountain in the middle of the driveway filled with bags of hardcore. But then Delphi started squeezing through one of the gaps in the fencing.

'What the hell are you doing?' I said.

'I did not endure two hours of Radio 2 to turn back because of a bit of fence.'

'You can't, there's –' I pointed up at signs warning there were guardians watching, that we were under strict CCTV surveillance. 'We'll get in trouble.'

'Anyone can get a sign printed, Mum.' She continued through and walked up to the house. Despite what she said making no sense, I found myself following her in.

I've tried to think about 28 October from Graham's perspective. His flight was late afternoon, so he would have left for Heathrow around midday. I've never been able to find a record of it but as the car wasn't on the driveway when the police arrived, if he didn't go to Cheyne Walk, I assumed he drove to the airport, parked at one of the many airport park-and-ride garages and took some sort of transfer bus to the terminal. Which would explain the car never having resurfaced.

When we got to the porch, we found the house's front door very locked. Bolts, metal boarding, more threatening signs. We walked round to peer through one of the ground-floor windows which I remembered leading into a dining hall. Large wooden tables stood, some on their sides, stacks of those terrible wedding chairs in the corner. Delphi knocked on the thin glass window embedded with metal diamonds. She bent down and picked up a rock.

'What? No!'

'We can say it was the wind.' I pointed above us at a camera attached to a pole, blinking at us like an insect.

'It won't have tape in,' she said. I wanted to ask how the hell she's always so sure of everything and if she knows, to share the secret. I grabbed the rock from her and tossed it on the floor, where it clanged heavily against an old piece of piping. The wind shook the trees surrounding the estate. I swung round, looked at the rustling foliage, convinced I was being watched and, I'm not proud, I took Delphi's hand and ran away. It wasn't dignified. I'm not a runner. I comforted myself that if whoever seemed to be keeping an eye on me ever watched the video, they would at least see I was no physical threat. Once Delphi had calmed me down, we walked around the property and drove into the nearby village, trying to work out why the conservative Graham would have chosen to buy such a lavish property, but both drew a blank.

When we returned home that night, a little over a year since I'd first tiptoed through the looking-glass of Nereus's death, I found a lovingly made dinner gone cold and the husband who'd cooked it, very annoyed with me.

'She missed an assessment today,' he said after I admitted where we'd been. He was a visiting tutor at her college so Delphi's teacher had messaged him to tell him she hadn't been in.

'She told me she didn't have anything.'

'Wonder if you'd have been so trusting if it didn't help you do what you wanted. I can't stop you losing your mind with all this stuff, but please don't drag the kids into it.'

I retired to my den in the garden, the nearest we had to a doghouse. Bobby was annoyed with me, Delphi had got in trouble at college and I didn't even think to go and visit Sara in Brighton. On top of which the trip had yielded nothing. I had thought seeing it might bring forth some eureka moment. Methusaleh always had such a fairy-tale quality to me I had never thought to ask why Graham bought it. If Dr Hailee was right, if Nereus had loaned Graham the money for it, there had to be some reason he wanted it so much.

I spent a few hours listening to the recordings looking for clues about the house, but aside from some talk of Graham's renovations, they barely mentioned it. But around midnight, Delphi marched into the summerhouse wielding an iPad.

She'd been digging around on the internet and discovered that at the end of the nineteenth century, Methusaleh was rented from its owner by someone called Julian L. Baker. A chemist who had made some advances in brewing techniques.

'Most famously, Baker was pals with Aleister Crowley,' she said. The 'satanist' Aleister Crowley was Britain's most influential occultist, known at one time as 'the most evil man in the world'. Delphi had found an article from the Horsham Historical Society saying Crowley had convalesced from pneumonia at Methuselah with Baker in 1901. They had letters from people in the community which suggested the two men were attempting alchemical experiments in one of the outbuildings. Alchemy, as in trying to turn base metals into gold. In the twentieth century.

I was baffled. Graham's feelings towards his Christian upbringing would have been complicated by 1975, but he still went to church from time to time. I couldn't see the slightest reason why he would have wanted to buy a house because it had once hosted the world's most celebrated devil-worshipper. I thanked Delphi for the lead but asked her to focus on college and made her a promise I wouldn't lead her astray again.

I dismissed the Crowley angle as a dead end, but a few days later I remembered a book Bobby had bought me about Nereus and the occult, when he still thought this was a fun little side project. Inside I found a picture from the Apotheosis tour – Nereus as some Meso-American god, the Eye of Horus symbol in gold on his shaved head. The section following the picture explained that the concept of the Aeon of Horus which Nereus told Graham about back at

Trident Studios, came directly from the extensive writings of a certain well-known occultist named Aleister Crowley. So it wasn't Graham who was a fan of Crowley, it was Neil. I found an academic paper on satanism and the seventies music scene which described Nereus's interest in Crowley as a 'borderline obsession'.

I'd read that in 1975, before he went to the US, Nereus was looking to get out of London and escape the grip of his addiction, perhaps take an extended break from music. If he was obsessed with Crowley and a house he was connected to came up for sale, it seemed safe to assume he might want to buy it. Graham was so pragmatic, buying a money-pit country pile had never made sense to me. But buying it under the nose of someone who'd cast him aside, abandoned at the height of their powers? I couldn't find any other reason why Graham would have bought Methuselah. But if it were the case, why the hell would Nereus have lent him hundreds of thousands of pounds for it and not bought it himself?

Iris, Stan and I went over it again and again. Graham couldn't have got that sort of money anywhere else but from Neil, or at least from Neil's company. But there was no logical explanation for a loan. Surely not even Nereus could be as mercurial as to lend someone money to buy a house he wanted. There had to be some reason he'd handed the money over. A big reason for him to undermine his own interests so directly. I didn't want Nereus to have died over money. His whole persona was too out of this world to have been brought to earth over something so grubby, so superficial. But as Bryn told me when we first met, the most obvious answer is usually the correct one. I was being watched, surveilled; if someone still had something to protect fifty years after Neil's death, was it more likely to relate to professional jealousy, shame, unrequited love, or base, human greed?

37.

Three and a half years before Graham bought the house, it wasn't greed dictating his path but survival.

'I had no family money, nothing in reserve,' he says. 'No one else was going to be the provider. Hands were tied.' Sadie's pregnancy gave Graham no choice but to stay in the band with Nereus.

At least, Sadie told me, that was how Graham saw it.

'There's always a choice, isn't there?' she said. 'It was the best excuse he could have hoped for. He *felt* he should walk after what they did to the boys, out of loyalty, but he didn't want to leave Neil behind in a million years.' It seemed my being conceived saved Graham from having to.

Sadie was torn about the decision.

'I saw when we were in Europe,' she said. 'Nothing with Neil could ever end well. But the other option was moving our lives up North, to Whitby . . .' On Sadie's only visit to the town, she told Graham she was surprised Dracula didn't turn the boat round when he saw the place.

Though my conception had saved him from having to leave Neil behind, he still had to break the news to Danny and Fraz, meeting them at a greasy-spoon café near Victoria Station.

'What we going to do then?' Fraz asked after Graham told them he'd failed to sway Otis on their behalf.

'Back home,' Danny said. 'Never should have left.' Graham pushed congealed egg yolk around his plate. He'd not eaten a morsel. 'Going back, aren't we, Gray?' Graham shook his head.

'I can't.'

'What?'

'I can't leave.' Danny looked at Fraz, murder in his eyes.

'Can't leave the band or you can't leave him?'

'Listen, Dan –' Danny shoved the table forward, standing up.

'Makes me sick,' he said.

'Sadie's pregnant. We've a little one on the way.' Danny stopped, swallowed spit.

'Well, I hope,' he said, leaning down over the table, 'it doesn't come out as much of a coward as its old man.' He grabbed at Fraz's shoulder and walked out. Fraz stood up, glanced back at Danny eyeballing him furiously through the window.

'Congratulations,' Fraz said before joining Danny outside. Graham didn't know it in that moment, but it would be the last time he would see his two oldest friends.

However difficult the conversation had been, Graham felt more nervous going into the studio the following day to face Neil after he'd kicked his old school friends out of the band.

'I was angry, wanted an explanation,' he said. 'But with them gone, my position felt precarious. And the baby too. I just had no idea how he'd react to something like that.'

Graham walked into Studio 1 to find Thomas, Otis, Matthew and Neil in full Poseidon regalia, huddled together, drinking martinis. They all stopped, turned, like something from a Western. Graham went to sit on the bench in front of the organ. Neil walked over, sat down next to him.

'Since we met,' Neil said, 'you've been like the iron core of the earth. Keeping the trees pointing up, the soil from flying into the sky.'

'Can you just say –'

'You pull in the mountains. Thank you. For staying. To achieve what I know we both want, it had to happen.'

'No it didn't.'

'Enthusiasm and a hairdo can only take you so far.' Graham clenched his jaw, furious at how he could dismiss his friends, angrier still that he knew what Neil meant. 'We had to move on. You wouldn't stay if you didn't agree.'

'Sadie's pregnant,' he said. 'Only reason I'm still here.' Neil looked up at the ceiling, played a diminished chord on the organ. Then launched himself on Graham, embracing his huge shoulders.

'You,' he whispered into Graham's hair, 'will be the most wonderful, wonderful father. And if it is the only reason you're here I'm doubly grateful to the little creature, because I can't imagine doing this without you.' Something caught in Graham's throat. He felt the same way. He pushed Neil away, tried to hide his elation at his reaction, at being able to stay, continuing their journey towards something great together with the mad, silly boy he'd first got to know.

Graham, Neil and Matthew got to work immediately. Despite the lingering guilt over Danny and Fraz, the following months turned out to be the most creatively exhilarating of Graham's life. Without the parochial musicianship of the former Marshalls they began working in an open, experimental way they never could before.

'He was still obsessed with the music of the spheres, the omnichord,' Graham says. 'But somehow, without the lads there, I could see it was a metaphor. An aspiration almost.' Neil talked of the resonance of earth minerals, the microscopic life around underwater chimneys, the echoes of stalagmites in ancient caves, and Matthew and Graham would endeavour to create those soundscapes.

One afternoon when Neil wasn't there, Graham played his

guitar into one of Matthew's machines, the Welshman looping and manipulating it. They stepped away and looked at the top of the studio as the melange of virtuosity and technology seemed to be raining down on them from the vaulted ceiling. They hugged, ecstatic like they'd split the atom, before catching themselves and pushing each other away. As Matthew wandered off, arsehole demeanour returning having let the mask slip, Graham continued looking around in wonder. This wasn't four-hundred-year-old cantatas to stuck-up members of the St Saviour's Church committee. This was Little Richard screaming into his psyche. This music could change the world. And, whether or not Graham ever knew it, it did. They used the effect from that session at the end of 'Tide of War', a song which would come to be an anthem of resistance during the Siege of Sarajevo in the nineties.

Although the deadline for the album was looming, Neil refused to be rushed so the recording sessions kept being put back.

'Who was I to get in the way of the creation of a masterpiece?' Otis de Kock wrote. But although things were going brilliantly in the studio, things at home had become more difficult for Sadie.

'I was puking my guts up morning and night.' She was suffering from hyperemesis, a condition during pregnancy which causes constant vomiting. On top of which, Sadie's formerly slim body became huge by the middle of her second trimester. The cosy flat she and Graham had loved now stank of sick and felt far too small for a family of three.

'We needed a bigger place,' Graham says.

'He wasn't due money until they'd delivered the album.'

'The delays became a problem.'

'He refused to talk to Neil. Point-blank.' Instead Graham went to Otis, suggesting they tour some of the new material but he didn't think Neil was up to it – Otis was already concerned about his prize asset's drug use. But, as December tipped into the New Year, with Sadie's due date a few weeks away, Graham's money worries must have passed around the camp because Thomas approached him one Friday night in the kitchenette of Trident Studios as he ate his pie and chips.

'Word is Sadie's found a house,' he said. Sadie had told Erica Walker, the band's stylist, that she'd found their dream home, a four-bed a stone's throw from Lord's cricket ground.

'What's it to you?' Graham had long given up on courtesy with Thomas.

'Can you afford St John's Wood?' Graham speared chips with his wooden fork, said nothing. 'I was with Otis yesterday,' Thomas said. 'Said he might give you an advance.'

'Why would he do that?'

'Damned if I know. Perhaps he feels bad about your old pals. Fact is, I'd say you could push him for a grand a week.'

'Bollocks.'

'Your hand has never been stronger.' Ten to twelve weeks of sessions of a thousand pounds would have covered their deposit and whole first year's rent.

It seemed almost too perfect, but what had gone down with Danny and Fraz had been brutal and Graham had remained loyal. If anyone deserved a favour from Otis de Kock it was him. Desperate to bring good news home to an increasingly frantic Sadie, he went to Otis at the Apollo offices, agreed eight hundred a week and amended his previous agreement that same day.

'I was over the moon when he told me,' Sadie said. 'Though if I had known it had come through Thomas Tee, I never would have let it happen.'

38.

Dale Harrahan WhatsApped me some zoomed-in photos one afternoon with the shocked eyes emoji. Pulse racing, I glared at my phone, looking for the breakthrough in what looked like pixelated mud. My husband went to put his mug away in the dishwasher far more loudly than was necessary. An understandable reaction given we had been mid-conversation when I picked up my phone and immediately stopped listening to him. At that point all I talked about, thought about and, to be honest, was even remotely interested in, was Nereus's murder.

I couldn't see anything shocking in the photos so I called Dale who instructed me to meet him at Cheyne Walk. We met at the green space opposite where he handed me hard copies of the pictures, explaining that they showed the ground of the front garden of 1 Cheyne Walk the morning after Nereus's death. I peered at the garden in front of me, the layout more or less unchanged. Two small strips of grass bisected by a paving stone pathway that led to the door, framed by large box hedges which made it difficult to see in. The picture from 1977 showed many sets of footprints imprinted on a flower bed under the window to what would have been Nereus's front room. I'd seen these pictures before.

'Is it the red-headed woman?' I asked, referring to the footprints from a pair of stiletto heels which stood out amongst the larger male prints of what Bryn had told me were most likely police.

'Those,' Dale said, circling one of the men's footprints with a sharpie. 'They're deeper.' I saw what he meant. One pair of very large shoe prints, size eleven or twelve at least, looked to be pressed further into the ground. I still couldn't figure out why he was excited.

'I'd normally think it was someone stood there for a long time,' he said. 'Deep imprints by windows, often a sign of someone snooping. But look up there?' I looked above the window and saw the balcony he was pointing at.

'Could be someone jumped down.' He brought out an annotated picture of the print. 'There's a smear at the back, here, as if it wasn't a smooth landing.' My eyes travelled from the brick-fronted, first-floor balcony all the way to the top floor, a further two levels above, at least twenty feet. Was Dale seriously suggesting someone Spiderman-climbed down to the first-floor balcony and jumped down?

'You don't think there are people who can climb down that?' he said when I suggested it seemed unlikely.

I realised I'd never questioned Dale's credentials or checked his history working with police. This sort of reaching had me wondering how reliable this man from the internet was. As I got the Tube home, I began reconsidering many of the avenues I'd walked down. When I started looking into the night Nereus died, I was trying to be the voice of reason, seeking to dismantle the myriad theories I'd read to try to find the definitive truth. I realised, more than a year in, no closer to a solution, that perhaps I had become like Dale, like the subredditors, like asperryman3 and all the other weirdos online.

I'd turned fifty the year before Sara received the poster at her house. Rather than being driven by a sense of wanting to protect my child, with that milestone behind me, had I used it as an excuse to go on some wild goose chase to make some sense of my life, a life I've always felt I was drifting in rather than living?

The room was locked from the inside. Nereus had had a terrible day, off the back of a terrible year. He took too many drugs. We don't want life to be random, unpredictable, cruel, but sometimes accidents happen and people, even seemingly superhuman ones like Nereus Forbes, just die.

39.

After I met Dale at Cheyne Walk and began questioning my motivations for investigating Nereus's death, I lost hope. My whole body was tired from clutching at so many straws. There's a good chance that would have been it for the story, if Delphi hadn't crashed into our bedroom in the middle of the night about a month later, shoving a too-bright laptop into my face like an instrument of torture. Once I'd sufficiently roused myself, I saw she was showing me a guitar listed for sale on a website called Reverb.com. I looked at the price.

'Absolutely not,' I said. 'You have a guitar and neither you nor I have a spare eight thousand pounds knocking about.'

'It's his, Mum,' she said.

'What?'

'Graham's.' I recognised the orangey-yellow instrument. It wasn't one of the normal three or four guitars he played, but I was sure I'd seen him holding one like it in several of the archive photos.

'How do you know it's his?'

'It's a D'Aquisto New Yorker,' she said. 'Only made about four, five hundred. And look –' She zoomed in on a translucent green knob on one of the guitar's two dials, then brought up a google image of a concert picture from Zurich. The green dial matched, along with what looked like a thin crack which had been sealed with something just below it. I looked at the guitar-seller's profile. A man called Nicolò from Milan who was mixed race and about thirty years too young to be Graham.

'Even if it is his, it doesn't prove anything.'

'He says he bought it in 2022, originally came from a professional guitar restorer.'

'How does that help?'

'The guitar restorer. It could be Graham!' I closed the laptop, shaking my head and dismissing my daughter as I settled down to go back to sleep. I'd passed my elastic limit for such wild speculation. I was done.

A week later, Delphi came to show me a response she'd had from a message to the Milanese guitar-seller.

'Hi Delphi,' it began. 'I bought the guitar from a vintage guitar shop here. The owner told me he got it from this old guy, a guitar restorer. I don't know much about this person, but I was told he was looking to sell other instruments. A black CBS Stratocaster, a burgundy Norlin era Les Paul, a '73 twelve-string Rickenbacker and one or two others I can't remember.'

Delphi didn't have to, but she showed me a slideshow of pictures on her phone of Graham playing all of the guitars Nicolò listed.

'Find the shop,' I asked Delphi.

'Already done,' she said. An old guy who restored guitars was in possession of Graham Harris's exact guitar collection. If Delphi hadn't found the guitar online, I might have just joined Ancestry.com and done my family tree like a better-adjusted middle-aged woman would. But, although it wasn't incontrovertible, it seemed that, in 2022 at least, my father was still alive.

40.

Perhaps it was my dramatic birth which led me into seeking some rich, unknown meaning to my existence. I was born ten days late, on 5 February 1972 at St Mary's but was immediately taken to Great Ormond Street Children's Hospital because I was barely breathing. Sadie suffered massive haemorrhaging and was rushed to intensive care at St Mary's.

'On the drive to the kids' hospital, I had my mother's voice in my head saying I had it coming, turning my back on the Lord.' Graham was a few days away from turning twenty-three, stalking the hospital corridors in purgatory, his wife and newborn's lives in the balance. 'I was certain they were going to die.'

A few hours in, Neil arrived. Graham almost didn't recognise him in jeans and a sweatshirt. He handed Graham a mug of tea and sat next to him.

'I asked the dear in the canteen for lapsang souchong,' he said. 'No dice.' He nudged shoulders with Graham. 'I'm here. Whatever you need.' A doctor emerged an hour or so later.

'Your daughter's stable,' he said. Neil jumped on the chair, put his hands on Graham's shoulders. 'Come see her.'

Graham and Neil went through to the emergency care room and found me in an incubator, breathing through a tube.

'Gosh,' Neil said, kneeling to look at me. 'No bigger than two balled hands.' Graham stood back, swallowed, overcome with relief.

'Looks like they've put a snorkel on a piglet,' he said. Neil laughed his high laugh, tears in his eyes. Graham left and rushed back to Sadie who was in an operating theatre having part of her uterus removed. He had another two excruciating hours, imagining raising a child without Sadie, before doctors told him she too would pull through. It would only be later they would understand the operation would make it impossible for Sadie to have another child.

Against all medical advice Sadie demanded to be taken to her baby.

'You know,' she said. 'It's like being stabbed between your ribs, not being with your baby.' They took a town car Neil had waiting for them. Sadie lay on a bed next to my incubator because of the pain, contorting her body so she could get as much of her arm in the glass box with me as she could. Graham watched, understanding the depth of life in a way he hadn't thought possible. His girls had made it. When I heard Graham describe our first morning as a family, I cried. For the loss of him, for decades of grief I didn't know was there.

Sadie slept but Graham couldn't. He crouched beside the incubator and watched his daughter.

'You could see the blood pumping round her tiny body,' he said. 'I know it sounds mad but I felt it. Each beat. I felt it in my veins.' Graham found himself singing, something he made up there and then. After a few minutes he added words. His eyes sprung open. It was a song.

'I looked round for something to write on,' he said.

'He wanted to use my medical notes, so I tore a page out the back of my diary.'

'I wrote it on this scrunched up piece of paper with a bookmaker's pencil I had in my coat.'

Graham went into the studio the next day to a rapturous reception. Neil had someone festoon the room with bunting and streamers. Party bangers and champagne bottles popped. Otis was there with a case of cigars. Matthew, Neil, Thomas and many other drawn-looking Soho reprobates had been up all night toasting their bandmate's child, and were in various states of worse for wear.

'I've written something,' Graham said, eyes glimmering. There was silence for a moment, everyone looking to Neil. But he roared in delight.

'Yes!' he said. 'Wonder. Great wonder!' He had them all turn and make an audience for Graham. Though the last time he'd played a song for Neil had been a disaster, it felt different, this song was different.

He played the song, unable to look at his crowd for the first verse about the life flowing through a baby, but when he did look up he saw shining faces, glistening eyes. Neil was stood behind Thomas and a girl he didn't know, but he could feel the rest of the room liking it. Really liking it. At the chorus, he threw back his head and belted out the song he wrote for his daughter. Twenty years of musical training. A childhood touring the North under his mother's unforgiving hand. Years with The Marshalls playing anywhere that would have them. Months with Neil, Penny, Matthew. Weeks sharing his life with Sadie, finally starting to know himself. His whole life, the emotion he'd kept ratcheted in, he ploughed all of it into this incredible piece of work. It was the best song he'd ever written.

'It was the music I'd been dreaming of.'

But as he came to the end of the chorus, Neil jumped up, knocking a mic stand to the floor, before blazing towards the door, and knocking over a table as he left, sending reams of sheet music whirling amongst the decorations.

Graham stopped dead, his last chord ringing through the air. He looked at Thomas who shrugged. Otis got up and went back to the control room. Graham returned to the hospital, distracted himself learning from the matron how best to feed me. Sadie forgot to ask how it went with his song. Graham would have had no idea how to answer if she had.

The next morning he turned up at Trident Studios at the normal time, determined to put the song behind him, to act like it didn't happen. Neil didn't like it, didn't like Graham writing anything which didn't fit his vision, but he had to accept it. They were there to make an album. That was Graham's job. Whatever Neil thought, he knew it was a great song. He could work out what to do with it later.

Graham stood by the huge doors to the main studio, took a deep breath, pushed them open and walked in. The room was empty. Their equipment was gone. Their engineer, their team, Matthew, Thomas, all of them were gone. Neil had gone.

41.

After I discovered Nereus's interest in Aleister Crowley had some part in Graham purchasing Methuselah, I decided to look into Neil's fascination with the occult which was supercharged when he got together with Greta Handverk.

The more I learnt about the German muse, mystic and generally one of the hottest and coolest women in history, the more I fell a little bit in love with her. She couldn't sing, couldn't act, barely spoke English and was notoriously difficult to work with, yet there were three or four years in the mid-seventies when everyone wanted a piece of her. What was it about her? She had a breathtaking Teutonic beauty, blistering warmth in her brown eyes and, with her leather-fringed clothes and trademark honey-gold boho bangs, a unique style which would influence designers for years. But it seemed from all the accounts I read that her appeal was mostly down to her tumescent energy of not giving a single shit.

She had an interest in mysticism through her mother's Romany heritage, but it was seeing *Rosemary's Baby* in 1968 which cemented her love of all things pagan. After arriving in London as French cinematographer Alain Giverne's girlfriend in 1972, she swiftly became the pin-up priestess for the Soho set's drug-fuelled fascination with the esoteric, becoming a much sought-after medium and psychic adviser to bigwigs in the higher echelons of the art and music world.

She met Dominik Szlonik in 1974 and the two struck up an

unlikely partnership. He provided drugs on tap, she unrivalled access to the in-crowd. One night in October 1975, Dominik invited Greta to a party on a Covent Garden rooftop. The roof was heaving with people, ivy strewn along wooden walls, huge bowls of fire dotted amongst the crowds. Exhausted from Milan Fashion Week, the last of the season, she didn't plan to stay long. But at the far end, she saw a crowd round what looked like some kind of whirling dervish. As she got closer, she saw the dervish was a man spinning, giggling, his long cape flying out behind him.

When he turned he caught her eye and stopped as if someone had cut the power. He shook his head, blinking himself into reality, before stepping through his entourage and bending towards Greta in a sort of arabesque, taking her wrist and kissing the inside of it.

'There you are,' he said, as if he'd been waiting his whole life for them to meet. She looked down, saw he was wearing nothing but a metallic loincloth under his cape.

'You're not cold?' she said.

'Not any more.' Greta was thrilled to see the desperate hunger of a fellow junky in his sunken eyes. A thin man with a pencil moustache, Thomas, pushed through the crowd. He glared at Greta, knowing who she was, having seen the way Neil was looking at her.

'We're expected at the Garrick,' he said to Neil, trying to get him away from her. But Neil was deaf to him, enraptured. Dominik Szlonik burst into the circle, throwing fur-clad arms around the three, inviting them downstairs for a fix. Even Thomas couldn't say no to that.

After that night, the two became an item. No one expected it to last two weeks let alone two years, but somehow it did. In pictures, Neil's arm is always wrapped around Greta's waist. He told reporters they bathed each other nightly and she'd massage his temples with essential oils to ward off the migraines which had come to torture him. Regardless of her esoteric beliefs, it seems she was a genuine empath which, riven by addiction, with looming financial problems and the beginnings of a critical backlash, Nereus sorely needed.

There have been two biographies written of Greta, and both talk at length about her being with Nereus the day he died, focusing on the ceremonies she held the night before. One implies she was trying to raise the dead but wasn't clear who it was they were trying to reincarnate. The same book claims Greta cured someone's blindness in Djibouti which she definitely didn't, so I'm not sure how much store we can set by it. But nothing I read told me anything concrete about her part in Nereus Forbes's final day. Which is what led me to fly to Berlin in March of last year to meet with her niece, Judith, at the Reichstag, the German parliament, where she worked as an administrator.

It was a sunny morning. I was excited to be in a different country, to have some time away from home. Bobby and I had had an argument when I told him I was going.

'You're going to see Greta Handverk's niece?' he said. 'Isn't that a bit –'

'A bit what?' I said, defensive.

'Well, mad.' He didn't even know I was being followed at this point.

'Are you actually saying I'm mad?'

'No, I just. People are talking about it at work.' He sat at our breakfast bar.

'What people?'

'You went to see Thomas Tee. Asking him all sorts of questions. Making accusations.'

'Is that what they said? Exactly? That I made accusations?'

'Why do you need to know?'

'Because I didn't accuse anyone. Which tells you something, don't you think?' Bobby put a hand to his head, sighed. 'That maybe I'm onto something.'

'Or that you're irritating people for no reason. The Nereus Estate has influence with the labels. The labels, my clients. The ones who pay the mortgage.' I nodded, pretending I was taking his point. Thomas Tee had been speaking about me, had put word out he wasn't happy. Why would he do that if there wasn't more to Nereus's death than the accepted story? I told Bobby I was sorry, that I'd wrap things up but that the flight was already booked.

I felt liberated from the spinning plates at home as I walked up the grand stone steps into the German parliament building, breezing through security and metal detectors before taking the lift up to the restaurant. Judith, a reserved woman in her late thirties, was waiting for me at a table when I emerged onto the balcony with its views over Berlin. We ordered coffee. Judith encouraged me to order a cake in perfect if accented English, telling me proudly she got a discount.

'My aunt died before I was born,' she said as soon as our drinks and discounted cake arrived. Her father Jacob was six years younger than Greta. 'I didn't know her. There is not so much I can tell you.'

I told her what I'd learnt about her aunt. Judith admitted her family only talked about Greta as a cautionary tale for the youngsters to work hard, choose the conventional path. With my tales of drugs, occult ceremonies and talking to ghosts, she didn't think her family's appraisal was too wide of the mark.

'Did your father never wonder why Greta came home after Nereus died?' I asked. 'She hadn't been back for six, seven years, but flew to Germany the morning after.' As with Graham having left the country, people online held Greta's return home as evidence she may have been involved with

Nereus's death. Their theory being that she wasn't just providing access to Dominik Szlonik, but that she was more directly involved in his drug operation.

'I had a girlfriend at university,' Judith said. 'Asked about this stuff with Nereus all the time. She would bring it up with my parents. It came between us. I don't know. I never liked the music so much.' I nodded. 'One night, I think my father, Greta's brother, he was having chemotherapy, on many painkillers. It was my birthday so maybe there was alcohol. He said something to my friend but, I don't know.'

'What did he say?' I leant forward as officials did government business on tables surrounding us.

'He said my aunt blamed herself for what happened.'

'Do you mean because of the drugs?' In photographer Jay Mansfield's autobiography he talks about Greta always wanting stronger drugs, that they never quite 'hit the G-spot'. I wondered if it was Greta who insisted on the potent new strain which they discovered in Nereus's system. But Judith shook her head.

'My aunt was unapologetic about her drug use. Thought of them as carrots in the ground. No, it was for something she said, before she left.'

'Do you know what it was?'

'I think maybe he proposed and it was something in response to that.' I blinked, mind tripping a moment.

'What he – Nereus proposed to her, to Greta? You mean marriage?'

'I think so yes, a few times maybe.' I traced back to see if I'd read this before, heard it from anyone. I didn't think I had.

'People proposed to her all of the time,' Judith added when I sat back baffled. I would later read about seven different men from that milieu who'd written about trying to get Greta Handverk to marry them.

'I suppose she said no,' I said.

'He'd asked a lot. It was a joke with them I think.' I checked this later with Thomas by email, hamming up that I needed it as context for a book about my father, trying not to get Bobby in trouble. Thomas didn't know about that day but said marriage had always been a big joke to Nereus. Neil had proposed to Greta, to Thomas even though gay marriage was illegal. He remembered resolving a situation where Neil proposed to an exotic dancer in Houston who wouldn't accept it wasn't real. 'And once to a mangrove tree in Louisiana,' he wrote by email.

'So what was different that time,' I asked Judith. 'If it was a joke between them, what could she have said that day which made her feel responsible for his death?'

'I really have no idea.' Judith pushed her cream cake onto its side with her fork. Soon after she made excuses about getting back to work and said she 'hoped I found what I was looking for'. Which made me feel like a gap year student going to India to find myself.

As I walked through the famous glass dome on my way back outside, I tried to imagine Neil and Greta's conversation that morning. The night before they'd partied to obliterate the memory of a disastrous concert, engaged in some sort of seance, drunk too much, taken a lot of heroin together. They'd woken up, presumably feeling dreadful, before getting visits from Thomas Tee trying to get Nereus to sell out to Big Talcum Powder as they were bankrupt, before Matthew and Dominik Szlonik, who Greta relied on for drugs, arrived demanding money to pay off debts to drug traffickers who they'd told Nereus would pay off. Then he proposes.

The proposals are normally a joke, but perhaps, after the concert, the money problems, more hangers-on making demands, he has the sense his life is a sinking ship and sees a life with Greta as a sort of life raft. So he proposes. But this time he makes it clear he's serious. And she says no. For her to have blamed herself afterwards perhaps goes further than no. Perhaps tells him exactly *why* she won't marry him. Then she leaves, joins friends at the Colony Room. Where does that leave Nereus? He's made himself vulnerable, expects her to say yes, possibly doesn't even imagine she would have said anything else. It wasn't love he was asking her for in that moment, it was safety, a guarantee she wouldn't leave him when everything good in his life seemed to have. But he didn't get it. He wasn't just facing lost friends, financial ruin and public backlash, he was having to wrangle with the fact he couldn't make the world bend to his needs.

'Neil wasn't good alone,' Graham had said on the tapes. He would have been terrified.

I stepped into the Berlin daylight, everything I'd learnt from Judith seeming to support the idea that a self-destructive blowout led to Neil's death, when I noticed a man looking at me from a silver SUV across the street. I looked down, walked away from the Reichstag like I hadn't noticed. It wasn't the flat-cap man. He was pale. This man was swarthy, tanned. I wasn't sure what to do. I had time to kill and had planned on some sight-seeing before my flight. But when I glanced over and saw the man still looking in my direction, I walked to the U-Bahn and got a train straight to the airport.

Once in the terminal, with several hours to wait, I felt stupid, blaming the strong coffee, a sugar rush from the cake for my overreaction. I did the airport things, Toblerone, souvenirs, etc, but just as I got through security, I looked back at the queue and saw the same man, standing in the main departures building half-looking at his phone. Like he wasn't there to keep tabs on me.

42.

In the days after my birth, Graham would have the opposite problem to the one I seemed to have brought on myself. No one cared where he was. In the days after finding Trident Studios empty, he discovered Neil, Thomas, Matthew, and half their engineering staff had decamped to a farmhouse owned by a friend of Count Szlonik, in the town of Applecross on the Scottish mainland opposite the Isle of Skye. Though he was unusually present in the first candlelit weeks of my life amidst the disruption of the blackouts of the winter of 1972, his mind was in the Highlands.

'Didn't know what I'd done to be frozen out.' Graham called their record company every day to try to get in touch with Neil, but Otis said he couldn't get hold of Neil either.

'We'd just moved in,' Sadie said. 'Boxes needed unpacking. He just paced around mumbling to himself. Then there was the money.'

'After two weeks my pay checks stopped arriving.'

'It had to be a mistake. I sent him in to sort it.'

Graham met with Otis in the top-floor office at Apollo Records where he found out it was no mistake.

'It was an advance,' Otis explained. 'On the recording sessions. Which you're no longer involved in.' Otis had an assistant bring in the new working agreement Graham signed just weeks earlier, turned to the third page, indicating paragraphs for him to read.

'He'd agreed to be a session player,' Sadie told me. 'He was paid well for the sessions he did. But it meant he'd waived any rights to future earnings off the album.' Otis made noises about getting Graham some of the money he would have made if he'd continued recording the album, which he never did, but even if he had, it was a pittance compared with what he would have been paid when the album sold as well as it seemed obvious it would.

'You did what?' Sadie said when he told her, whispering as I was asleep on her shoulder.

'I didn't know what it was I was signing,' he said.

'The future,' she said, blood rising in her cheeks. 'You've destroyed our future.' She took me upstairs. They didn't speak for almost two weeks.

'Angrier at myself,' Sadie said. 'Knew how he was. Should have been across it.'

The rent on the St John's Wood house was extortionate so once they were speaking again, money became the only topic of conversation. Sadie was offered styling jobs but Graham wouldn't hear of her leaving the baby. In turn, he found himself rejecting offers of session work.

'Graham thought Neil would come back cap in hand. Convinced the whole thing was a misunderstanding,' Sadie said.

'If I'd gone to work for other bands, it would be like I'd closed the door myself,' he said.

After a month without anything coming in, Graham agreed to go and work with a band called Scimitar in secret.

'I ordered him to, more or less,' Sadie said. As soon as Graham arrived, the young band asked about Nereus's legendary manhood, what Julie Stark was like in bed, and asked him to give them the riff he played on 'Found Them There'.

'They wanted Nereus songs,' Graham said. 'Felt dirty after what we'd been doing on the new album.'

'God, he felt worse about that than anything,' Sadie said. 'Like he'd cheated on his wife.' Graham refused all other offers and found himself stuck at home most of the time. 'Hands-on dads didn't exist,' she said. 'I wanted to be a mother, enjoy time with you. He wanted to be at the studio. Neither of us was happy.'

Sadie encouraged him to use the time to work on his music, try to get his own deal. He tried writing Nereus-lite songs about gods and mythology but it felt ridiculous, so went back to writing about love. But with Sadie sleep deprived and consistently furious at him for throwing away their financial security, there wasn't a lot of love to draw on.

Things came to a head one morning when Sadie was out buying groceries. Graham was with me in the garden when the phone rang and without thinking he ran to their first-floor bedroom to answer it. On returning home, Sadie came out to the garden to find her baby alone on the grass, with a tabby cat licking my face. She ran over, yelling the animal away which set me off screaming. Sadie brought her bawling baby upstairs to the bedroom where she found Graham sat on the bed.

'What the hell were you thinking?' she said. Graham looked up, confused. 'She's eight weeks old.'

'The phone rang,' he said.

'Neil's moved on,' she said, not needing to ask who Graham hoped would be calling. 'You need to do the same.'

Graham spent several weeks trying to move on. He took me to the park, walked me round the house at night singing me to sleep and got a few days' work a week at a big construction site in Camden.

'Felt good to use my body again,' he said. Sadie put feelers out for dressmaking jobs, and reached out to people she'd known from the scene. A calm settled on the house.

'Didn't take much,' she said. 'Sharing stories of the stuck-up mums I'd see at the swings, the Irish lads at the building site. Smoking on our terrace, drinking wine when you'd gone to sleep. We found each other again.'

But one sun-dappled afternoon as he and Sadie were blowing on my bare tummy after a bath, the phone rang again. Graham tensed. Sadie put her hand on his, willing him to ignore it, to stay with the two of us in the bubble they'd worked hard to rebuild. He stood up, went to the bedroom and picked up the phone.

'Otis de Kock,' Otis said, like the two men had never met. 'We need you up in the Highlands as soon as you can.' Graham swallowed. 'Neil's gone off track.'

Sadie arrived at the doorway, holding me wrapped in a huge towel.

'Is it him?' she said. Graham put his hand on the receiver.

'Otis,' he said. 'Wants me to go up.' Sadie crossed the room and hung up the phone. 'What are you doing?'

'Please don't go,' she said.

'I have to.'

'Look at her,' she said, handing me into his chest. 'Look at her and tell me you have to go up to Scotland to help some junky who doesn't give a damn about you.' Graham looked at me, I pawed at his bearded face. 'I can't go through it all again, and it will happen again. We're here,' she said. 'We're here and we want you to stay with us.' Graham looked up at her, took my hand away from his face and handed me back to my mother.

'Neil needed me,' Graham says on the tapes. 'What choice did I have?'

43.

I didn't mention the man at the airport to Bobby, who was still upset with me for going in the first place. Bryn said I could report it to the police but we both knew they'd dismiss me as a paranoid, possibly menopausal woman.

When I returned to work the following Monday I was immediately called into a meeting with the head of my department who informed me the university had been made aware of multiple complaints about me on the website ratemyprofessors.com. I'd been given twenty-eight separate one-star reviews, all written in the previous six months. Most were to do with my non-attendance, many students mentioned not having seen me for many weeks and their dissatisfaction with the graduate students I had recruited to teach my seminars. I skimmed the pages and saw the words distracted, disinterested, one theorised I might have a drink problem, another saying I came across 'a bit tragic'.

My boss, the Herodotus scholar Davis French, wanted to know more about the 'side project' I'd been working on which had been dragging me away from my teaching responsibilities. I wasn't sure he'd see the links between ancient Greek poets and solving the murder of Nereus Forbes so I kept my answer vague.

'Though we encourage further studies,' he said. 'We can't ignore student feedback. We need you back, re-engaged. Perhaps whatever you're working on can take a back seat.'

I wanted to tell Herodotus scholar Davis French where he could stick his advice, but I needed a job and, before all this madness had consumed me, I had mostly enjoyed the tranquil life of academia. Without the hours of weekday seminars I had been skipping in my office, my investigation was forced home. Having to sneak down to my summerhouse late at night to avoid Delphi trying to involve herself further and Bobby's disapproval, I started thinking about Nereus and marriage.

People often mentioned the new project or reinvention Nereus was excited about the day he died. I started to wonder whether his new persona could have been something as simple as 'husband'. It's possible his joke proposals had hidden a backbone of truth. Although a serious proposal seemed to have taken Greta by surprise, it's possible it's something Nereus had been considering for some time – some stability amidst all the turmoil. I started working out what the implications would have been if Greta had said yes.

'Successful acts delineate everything in contracts now,' lawyer Helen Grady told me over shakshuka at her house. 'Prenups, NDAs and the like. Back then it was far less commonplace. Because IP-wise, with works of art, recorded media, etc, marriage is an absolute nightmare.' It's impossible to know exactly what would have happened if Greta and Nereus had married, but it seems unlikely from his slapdash and impulsive attitude to other elements of his business affairs that he'd have made Greta sign anything. Which, in just a couple of signatures on a registry, could give her half of a body of work that would go on to be worth tens of millions.

As it was, unmarried at the time of his death, all his assets passed straight into Pacifica Holdings, which would be transformed into the charitable Nereus Estate a few weeks after his death – 'to avoid the whopping eighty per cent tax driving the other rock stars out the country,' Helen suggested.

Thomas set up this new company, Thomas who would possibly stand to lose control of the valuable assets of Nereus's work if he married. Thomas who was with Nereus just hours before his proposal on the day he was talking about his 'new direction'. The exact subject he grew hostile about when I asked him about it, and which he conveniently couldn't remember. Love, lust, loathing, loot. If Greta was likely to marry Nereus Forbes, perhaps Thomas Tee was driven to do something by all four.

44.

The idea of marriage and Nereus's legacy were a long way from everyone's minds at Troweldun Farm in the Arctic late-March of 1972. By all accounts their minds were a long way from anywhere. In his memoir, Otis de Kock describes the clapped-out estate Neil had moved the recording of *Apotheosis* to, as 'the Manson Family ranch in kilts'.

Troweldun is still privately owned but they do a tour every twelve weeks, which I couldn't get on because they're booked for the next seven years. Pictures show the symbols, pentagrams, Eyes of Horus, painted on the various outbuildings in that insane few months. Those there described it as near-constant partying, endless drugs, picking pieces of smashed wine glasses out of bare feet.

No one met Graham when he arrived after the four-hour taxi ride from Edinburgh Waverley station. He walked up a long farm track to the main house, looking out for anyone he might know.

'Random people everywhere,' Graham said. 'All had heads shaved, girls too, tattoos, cuts on them, dark under their eyes like they'd not slept for years.' When he asked for Nereus he was met with giggles. He searched several outbuildings. 'Saw a few things I didn't want to see,' before hearing one of Matthew's sonic hurricanes pulsing through the slats of an old cowshed.

He went inside and saw instruments strewn across the

floor, a mess of wires, speakers, the occasional sleeping body. Graham studied the faces of the ghoulish boys to see if any of them were musicians he knew to see if he'd been replaced. Most of them could barely open their eyes let alone play a guitar.

'After a few times round asking people for Otis, Neil, anyone I knew, Annie,' the Apollo Records receptionist who'd gone out with Danny Greig, 'told me to take a seat while she went to fetch someone.' Graham waited for an hour and a half. 'I didn't want to touch anything, case whatever was going on with them all was catching.'

Finally, the huge barn doors opened and Neil was there, dressed in a development of the Poiseidon costume, a dark cape with a ridiculously long train, lines shaved into the tufts of hair at the top of his head.

Graham bounced up, delighted to see Neil despite everything, after such a long journey and the hours amidst the madness at the farm. He had decided not to be bitter, told himself Neil's behaviour had to be the drugs. He would never have abandoned him in his right mind. Graham crossed the floor, opened his arms to embrace his old friend, desperate to show him there were no hard feelings. But Neil walked right past as if Graham wasn't there.

Graham was winded, suckerpunched. He swung round.

'Neil,' he said, voice cracking. Neil turned, looked at Graham. He took off his sunglasses, eyes blank, trying to work out who Graham was. Then he seemed to relax.

'Stevie,' he said. 'Stevie Sands from the, the Brawn,' he slurred, gave a thumbs-up, then mumbled to someone who whisked him off towards the far end of the barn. Graham opened his mouth but no words came. He leant on an amplifier stack in the middle of the room, drugged-up zombies fixing him with cruel smiles. He'd travelled fourteen hours, waited for a further two, left his baby daughter, a loving partner who'd pleaded with him not to go.

'And he didn't recognise me.'

His eye was drawn by a flame, a girl heating a spoon over a camping stove, a boy tying a tourniquet round his upper arm. He went and sat next to them, watched the girl hold the syringe up to the light, flicking the needle.

'You want?' she said, noticing Graham. He bit his bottom lip, considered for a moment before shaking his head, standing and stumbling away where he bumped into Clive Dors, their long-term engineer, a friendly face.

'Come out back,' he said, 'they'll eat you alive in here.' Clive put an arm round Graham and led him into the control room at the back of the shed.

'Want to hear it,' he said in his thick Birmingham accent, pouring Graham a slug of brandy, 'the album?' Graham thought about saying no, fearing how it had ended up if the grotesquerie he'd seen at the farm was anything to go by. But of course he wanted to hear it. Clive pushed up the faders.

Graham heard a pulsing synth like the blades of a helicopter, marching feet, a political speech in a foreign language. It was shocking, upsetting, enthralling. His own guitar part came in.

'I couldn't breathe,' Graham told Trevick. 'Couldn't get a breath out.' It sounded incredible and he was on it, his playing. Not only had Graham not been cut out of the album, his riff was central to the song. 'When Neil's vocal came in, the overwhelming impact it had. The song was everything I'd ever wanted to do.' Clive was playing 'Missed Abyss', which would end up the fourth track on the album. With the land of Pacifica on the verge of being invaded, the album's central character Poiseidon has hidden himself at the bottom of the Mariana Trench to escape the pressure of leading his people.

There he reflects on how his cowardice lost him a childhood love and now threatens the lives of his people. It's about sliding doors moments, wrong turns, the vagaries of fate.

Graham drained his drink, closed his eyes, head bowed. As he listened he realised something he'd been in denial about from the first night he'd met Neil. Despite Graham's extraordinary skill, his talent, Neil and he were not musical equals. They never had been, they never would be.

'But it was liberating,' he tells a surprised Lincoln Trevick. 'My whole life I'd been called a prodigy, a genius. It meant nothing to me. I'd never felt like one. Hearing Neil's album, because it was his, even if I was on it. I was listening to genius. I realised what I'd been looking for my whole life, that music, that thing I was trying to find. Well, I already had it. It was Neil. Working with him, playing some part in what he could do, however small, that was what I had been put on the planet to do.' Graham was furious at himself for bringing one of his songs, however good he thought it was, in front of Nereus Forbes, the man who'd produced this masterpiece. Neil had been right to abandon him in London for his presumptuousness.

'All I ever had to do was get out of his way.'

'Where's Neil?' he asked Clive, standing up. He was going to apologise, throw his pride on the pyre and prostrate himself in front of Neil. He'd do whatever it took to be back in the fold.

'He'll be in the woods,' Clive said, pointing out a back door. Graham was on the album, he hadn't been fired, he still had a chance to be at the right hand of a genius, a unique talent. He finally knew it was all he really wanted. Graham had his hand on the door handle that would lead him to Nereus when the next song started playing.

45.

Ever since I opened the box of tapes sent from Sweden, I'd been trying to get in touch with the man Graham was talking to, journalist Lincoln Trevick. He proved a difficult man to find. Although there were pieces he wrote for the *Hull Daily Mail* in their archives and other articles clipped up and posted online, none of them helped me track him down. I gave up after the first couple of months of looking but, having become convinced he was the only person who might know the truth behind Graham's story, I was driven to become resourceful. I went online and bought Hull phone books from the fifties and early sixties.

In the 1954 edition, amongst one or two other Trevicks, I found a Margery. Lincoln mentions his mother, 'Margy', in his October 1959 review of heavy rock band, The Panda Bears. Margery's name led me to Hull Town Council's archive – I went to Hull to do this, much nicer than people say – where I found out why it had been so hard to find him. The birth registry had Margery Trevick's son's name as 'Lionel'. He'd given himself the name Lincoln as a pen name. Fair enough, I thought. He never got round to changing his name in official records, so it didn't take long until I found Lionel Trevick. And that he'd died in 2002. I felt ready to flip my laptop through the window, before I saw a link to an old church website still showing the details of his funeral. Which is where I found he was survived by a son, Paul Trevick.

I met Paul in Betty's Teahouse, a local institution in the Yorkshire town of Harrogate. Paul was in his forties, dressed like a stagehand all in black, with a small ponytail and David Brent beard. He works as a drum teacher in various schools in the area and wears his love of music like a halo.

'That all came from Dad,' he told me. He was so thrilled to meet the daughter of Graham Harris and Sadie Blakely, there were times I thought he'd topple off his chair. Of all the people I met, Paul Trevick was by far the most enthusiastic.

I'd read several glowing reviews of The Marshalls his father wrote and asked Paul whether Lincoln ever talked about what Graham was like as a kid.

'They didn't know each other that well,' he said.

'Oh – I thought, because Graham got him in for his memoir . . .'

'Dad approached Graham,' Paul said. 'He'd seen the concerts Graham gave as a child, then with his band later. I think Graham's success, someone from his crappy part of the world doing what he did with Nereus gave him hope. When it all went sour, Dad said it broke him up.' Paul and I had gone for a walk around Valley Gardens after our tea; we took a seat on a bench.

'Lincoln was trying to help Graham get his version of events out there?'

'God no, he'd sniffed out a story.' Paul raised his eyebrows. 'A bloody good one.' He stood up and said he had something to show me at his place. Despite feeling paranoid that anyone wearing a blazer might be tailing me after seeing the man in Berlin, I was oddly guileless in going to Paul's place. I figured someone so happy couldn't be capable of bad intentions.

When we arrived, Paul went into a messy bureau in the corner of his ground-floor flat and handed me a yellowing scrap of paper with faded writing on it. It was song lyrics. I read them. Certain lines reminded me of something.

'Life ticking through paper-skin', 'more life than dream, you're part of me', 'you're our tomorrow'. My breath caught as I realised it was the song Graham wrote about me the day I was born.

'I should have found you,' Paul said, voice quivering with emotion. 'You deserved to have it.' I shook my head, absolving him, read Graham's words again. It hurt reading such love for me was in the world that I never got to receive.

'But, um –' Paul shuffled off to another corner of the room. He began playing an old upright piano. I recognised the chords, the melody he'd begun to hum along with it. It was the same Matthew Salvini had played as I'd left his shed. Paul beckoned me over, took the sheet of lyrics and began mumbling them to the song. He smiled up, encouraging, and I found myself joining in with my uncertain voice. I knew the tune. How did I know the tune? Paul stopped, let me lose myself singing the song my father wrote for me for a moment.

We came to the end. Paul turned, beaming smile almost radioactive. And all at once so many things made sense to me, I had to sit down on the stool next to him. I knew the melody of Graham's song because it was exactly the same as one of the most famous pop songs in the world – 'Lady Theia'.

The good story Lincoln had sniffed out was that Nereus Forbes had stolen it.

46.

After Graham heard his melody in 'Lady Theia' that first time in the control room, he stormed into the night looking for Neil. He eventually found him in the bed of a Romany caravan, half-naked and curled asleep next to Thomas. He was shocked at the state Neil was in, arms lined with track marks, dark bruises inside his elbows, under his arms. Police would find him dead in the exact same position at Cheyne Walk five years later.

Thomas rolled with a phlegmy snort towards the window. Neil blinked, waking, bloodshot eyes landing on Graham. Neil took a moment to make sense of who it was before almost falling off the bed to get outside to him. He threw his arms around Graham, buried his face in his chest. He was crying.

'It's so, so wonderful to see you,' Neil said. He pulled away, covered his face a little, ashamed but unable to stop the tears. 'I don't know who any of these gremlins *are*.' He laughed, tried to blink tears away. Graham looked away, the fury at the song sizzling but with no idea how to bring it up with Neil in that state. Suddenly festoon lights strung between the outbuildings behind them went black, the music in the barn fell silent.

'Ah ha, you're needed,' Neil said, unusually practical. He pulled a length of hosepipe out of the toilet of the caravan and handed it to Graham.

'What's this?'

'Secret mission,' Neil said, bouncing past him.

Ten minutes later, having trudged through several fields, the two of them were crouched in the dark siphoning fuel out of a tractor. They'd filled two of their three jerry cans before Neil accidentally swallowed some diesel, coughing it up all over himself. He collapsed down next to the tractor wheel.

'You need to see a doctor,' Graham said.

'Oh, it's fine. Most nutritious thing I've had in weeks.' Neil got a cigarette out, Graham wrenched it from his hand.

'You're not well. You're sick.' Neil looked away, overcome with emotion for a moment.

'Doctors,' he said, sarcastic. 'Miracle workers all.' Graham had never seen him so stripped of his boundless enthusiasm. There was something deeper to his misery than the drugs. Part of him wanted to haul Neil onto his back and hitchhike back to civilisation. But he had abandoned him, it wasn't Graham's job to save him anymore.

Neil patted the mud next to him for Graham to sit.

'I've been lost without you,' he said. Graham sat, crossed his hands over his knees and stared into the night. 'Just you being here, I feel I might be able to climb out of the well I seem to have fallen down.' Graham looked away, stifling a smile. Having spent the weeks before thinking he meant nothing to Neil, he was flooded with relief to hear how much he missed him. 'It's been so terribly hard, getting anyone to actually record anything. You made all that so effortless. I never appreciated it.' Graham shook his head, shrugging off his sincerity. 'No I'm serious. I never realised how fucking impossible I am.'

'It's no picnic, that's for sure.'

'And having a friend in the room. They're all wolves here. I could only see that once I didn't have you to hide behind. Matthew's a psychopath.'

'Could have told you that when we hired him,' Graham said. 'But what we did together, back at Trident . . .'

'If he was less of a cunt I'm sure it wouldn't be half as good. Imagine it,' Neil said, suddenly painting a scene. 'Him at the back, locked behind his big monoliths, we could handcuff him, while you and me are at the front of the stage, thrilling thousands. Changing them with our songs. Like you said back at Mother's.' His words seemed to catch, he stared down at the ground.

Graham pictured it. An elaborate stage set from Neil's book, the two of them, brothers in arms, a huge band behind them, touching the lives of hundreds of thousands throughout the world. And the music he'd heard in the barn hours before could do that. He'd never been more sure of anything. This was music which would last, which would live in people's hearts for decades, centuries, longer.

Neil shivered, he shuffled closer to Graham, dragged his big arm around him to keep him warm. He was back in. That seemed to be what Neil was saying in his own way. That he'd made a mistake leaving Graham in London. That he wanted him back, back by his side. And when he'd dropped everything, his young family, to travel up to the Highlands, that was all he wanted. Graham was on the album. On every song. He hadn't been replaced. Things were going to be OK again. Better. Their collaboration was going to soar to heights no one could ever have imagined.

But then Neil asked how I was and Graham remembered the song he'd written the day I was born. The song Neil had taken.

'Clive played me some of the album in there,' Graham said, ignoring Neil's enquiry about his daughter.

'Oh, right. Wonderful. Did you like it?' Graham looked at him, eyes wide, incredulous he didn't even seem to know what he'd done.

'You stole my song,' he said.

Neil took a deep breath, said nothing. He got out a cigarette.

This time Graham didn't stop him as he went to light it. He didn't go up in flames.

'Graham Harris, you have no idea,' Neil said, dragging out the words, hard as the jagged edge of a broken bottle. It was a voice Graham had never heard before and it scared him. 'You never have. Never had a single bloody idea.'

Neil stood up and walked off into the night. Graham didn't follow. Thomas Tee found him in the kitchen a few hours later drowning in gin and self-pity. He said there was a car at the bottom of the track waiting to take him back to wherever he'd come from.

47.

Graham had always wanted to write a song which stayed with people, which would mean something, perhaps change them a little. For five decades 'Lady Theia' has remained one of the top ten most-played songs at weddings, funerals, christenings, the most significant moments in people's lives. If his best friend, the man he'd wanted to dedicate his working life to moments before hearing it, stole that song from him, would that be enough to drive someone to murder?

At first I couldn't believe Neil could have done it, but it made sense of certain questions I'd had on hearing the tapes. I'd never understood why, if the song Graham had written was so good, he never tried to release it, never got it in front of anyone to restart his own career. But of course if Nereus had already released it as his, he couldn't. It also explained why Graham's attitude to the man he'd thought of as his best friend, perhaps someone he had romantic feelings for, transformed so quickly into hatred. Stealing a song Graham had written about his newborn, repurposing his sincerity with make-believe mythology to slot into his comic-book album would have been a betrayal of unforgivable proportions.

'Your dad approached Graham about it?' I asked Paul once I'd recovered from the shock with sweet tea at his kitchen table. He nodded. 'How did he know?'

'He first played me *Apotheosis* when I was seven or eight. He asked what I thought about "Lady Theia" compared with the others. I said it sounded different. He was delighted. Because he felt the same. That it was *too* different. He was like a Shakespeare scholar with that stuff.'

'In what way different?'

'It's grounded somehow, the tune. Nothing else Nereus did had that quality. But the band Dad heard on Hull bandstands did.' I hadn't listened to 'Lady Theia' for many years. I'd stopped listening to Nereus in my mid-twenties after an obsessive phase after falling out with my mother over the birthday cards. I had heard it on the radio in the interim. Bobby played it sometimes when he thought I was out. I'd never spotted the discrepancy Lincoln Trevick had, but once Paul said it, I saw what he meant. Later I went through the countless breakdowns of the song's brilliance: words like 'pastoral', 'solidity', 'folkloric' are often mentioned. There seemed to be critical credence to Lincoln's theory.

'Why didn't he write the story?' I asked Paul. 'It's a big scoop.'

'No evidence. He tried to get access to Nereus, Apollo Records, anyone around him at the time. By that point he was a freelance music journo. Northerner to boot. No one important was interested.' Except Graham.

'Then why isn't it on the recordings?' Paul opened his mouth, closed it again. Although he knew his father approached Graham Harris, he'd never heard the tapes, nor known they were for anything as extensive as a memoir.

'Perhaps it was too difficult to talk about,' Paul suggested but I didn't buy it. This was Graham's memoir, his right to reply, he could have overcome how hurt he was to expose a man who'd ruined his life.

I thought it could be Neil, how he felt about him. Graham always seemed ready to make excuses for Neil's behaviour. Perhaps he didn't have it in him to bring Neil down in public. Or possibly, having lost so much, he simply didn't have the will to fight anymore. I didn't want to think my father was weak, but with the force of Nereus's celebrity, the industry machinery around him, could you blame him?

As I watched rain cascade down the train window back from Harrogate, I thought about what it might feel like to have to see the man who stole the pinnacle of your creative career broadcast across the world like a god for it. What knowing you'd let it happen, said nothing, done nothing, might do to a man's psyche? I still had no idea what the catalyst might have been near the end of 1977, five years later, but for the first time since I'd begun all of this, Graham had a motive I could understand. More than that, reading his lyrics, the era-defining melody, I felt a burning, irrational rage at the injustice. And for the first time thought Nereus might have had it coming.

Two weeks after I met Paul, he sent me a huge box of notebooks he found amongst his father's things. He couldn't read the shorthand, so wasn't sure if they were pertinent to his interviews with Graham Harris. I narrowed down the sixty-eight notebooks to three or four which corresponded to the time Lincoln would have been with Graham. I scanned the pages and sent them to a Ben Franklin, no really, a sixty-five-year-old freelance journalist who, based on a sample page I sent, was confident he could translate them. For a lot more money than I would have expected. I didn't tell Bobby.

It seemed Lincoln made the notes without Graham's knowledge, perhaps after their sessions, and covered topics which must have been discussed when the tape recorder was off. Literally off the record. The information is fragmentary, but confirms Graham believed Neil stole 'Lady Theia' from him. I took this to my mother. She sighed longer than I'd ever heard anyone sighing.

'I hoped I'd not have to think about that again,' she said.

48.

In January 1973, ten days before my first birthday, 'Lady Theia' came out and was hailed as an instant classic. Radio DJs played it twice an hour. Critics reviewed it like it was a whole album. Fans dissected the lyrics as if it was the Rosetta Stone. Theories as to which of Nereus's conquests could have been the inspiration for Theia, the enigmatic Queen of Pacifica, became the talk of every pub and hair salon. If the internet had been around, the speculation would have broken it.

Eighteen days after its release the world had an answer of sorts when news broke that Penny Kanelides had died after a long battle with pancreatic cancer. Her funeral was to be held a week later. Graham refused to go.

'You loved her,' Sadie said to Graham in their kitchen on the day of the service. 'We met because of her, Winter wouldn't be here.'

'How though?' Graham said, possessed with rage since returning from Scotland. 'How can I look him in the eye and say "there, there", after what he did?'

'Penny was everything to him,' she said. Graham faced the wall, she took his hand in hers. 'You can do something incredible today.'

'I can't.'

'It's just a song.' He looked at her with cracked-mirror eyes before leaving the kitchen. I challenged Sadie, did she really see Graham's greatest work, about the daughter sitting opposite her, as 'just a song'?

'I was angry with Neil too but I wasn't surprised. He couldn't stand how we, you and me, we'd taken Graham away from him.' I hadn't thought of it but it began to explain Neil's reaction in Trident Studio when Graham played his new composition. Penny was diagnosed nearly a year before her death. Neil was jealous of the new family Graham had while his own, only his mother remaining, was months away from leaving him forever.

Her funeral was held at St Sophia's in Bayswater, an astonishing Greek Orthodox Cathedral in Central London. Sadie stood alone in vintage Chanel under the church's golden dome and spectacular frescos at the back of four hundred of the most racily dressed mourners London had possibly ever seen. The Poet Laureate did a recitation, Royal Opera singers sang cantatas, the Duchess of Kent read from Corinthians. After an hour and a half, Neil stood up to say a few words. He wore a black robe with silver piping and a gossamer-thin navy veil concealing his face throughout.

'I was in our garden once,' he said. 'Trying to catch the sun with a fishing rod. Penny watched for hours. She asked what I'd do when I caught it. I didn't know. "What is hope without intention?" she said. She taught me how to change the world.' Somehow it didn't sound boastful when he said it, just a statement of fact. 'I realised I was wasting my time because she was my sun. Her warmth overwhelming, light blinding, a life force enough to drive a galaxy. All that is gone. It's gone. Snuffed out. When I was a child I was scared of the dark. That's all there is now.'

He lifted the veil and stared out into the audience who shifted uncomfortably in their seats at such unadorned despair, before Thomas led him from the pulpit. As he walked towards his seat he saw Sadie at the back and his eyes brightened. He looked for Graham. Sadie shook her head. Neil blinked, chin quivering as the people in the front pew made room for him to take his seat.

Sadie skipped the reception at the Dorchester. At home she told Graham how broken Neil was, how he'd looked for him in the crowd.

'He needs a friend,' she said. 'He's got nothing.'

'I will never write a song like that again,' Graham said. 'And *he* has nothing?' She couldn't get through to him. His mind too bloated by the injustice.

The next day he went out to fight for what was his, organising a sit-down with Otis de Kock at the Apollo building. Graham demanded the song be taken off the album. Otis said it wouldn't happen. He insisted on full songwriting credit, one hundred per cent of the royalties. Otis said he had no proof to support his allegations of plagiarism.

'You were there!' Graham said, dumbfounded. 'Heard it there in the studio when I played it to everyone.' Otis pinched his eyes between his fingers.

'It was a session,' Otis said. 'One we paid you for.' Graham swallowed, realising why Nereus's side weren't concerned about how he'd react to them stealing his song. To get the advance for our house, he'd signed on as a hired hand. Which meant not only was he excluded from a share of royalties but that anything he played in the session, the session he'd been paid for, was legally theirs. Including his song.

'They do it so people don't come in to do a flute part and say they wrote the whole song,' Bobby told me. 'Graham should have known that.'

'I see now it was his upbringing,' Sadie said. 'Church taught him to always see the good in people. 'Course, Jesus never had to tangle with Thomas Tee.'

Though they couldn't have known Graham would come in and write an incredible song. But it seems clear that after

Danny and Fraz were pushed out of the band, they not only wanted to cut Graham out of future royalties but also to insure themselves against him claiming credit for any of Nereus's work. It was callous, cruel and, we have to assume, intentional. Thomas was definitely involved, Otis had to have been too.

'Do you think Neil knew?' I asked Sadie.

'He would have had to sign off on it.'

At one point on the tapes, Graham says, 'When people make beautiful things, you want to believe they're good people.' He was beginning to discover, more often, the opposite was true.

He stood up from Otis's desk, reeling at the news he had no legal recourse for 'Lady Theia', left the room and stumbled onto the streets of London.

'He didn't come home for two days,' Sadie said. 'When he did, it was like someone had scooped him out.'

'We were friends,' he kept saying again and again, bringing any conversation between the two of them back to the song. 'Weren't we? Weren't we friends?'

Graham refused all session work, could barely look at his guitar and managed to alienate the few labouring jobs he'd had by leaving halfway through the work day. Sadie took on work for a local seamstress and the occasional ad hoc styling job around fashion week and awards ceremonies to try to cover their bills. Leaving Graham holding the baby.

'That generation never imagined they'd have to get their hands dirty. He resented how mundane it was. I resented having to go back to work.'

'I'd see Sadie hugging Winter as she left the house,' Graham says. 'Saying sorry for not being there with her. I'd done that to her.'

It's possible Graham could have gotten over Neil's betrayal but three weeks after Penny died, *The Apotheosis of Poiseidon* was released and the whole world became Nereus Forbes.

Plastered on billboards, interviewed on every channel, headline sets, a huge world tour, Graham couldn't escape the man who'd gone from friend to nemesis in the space of six months.

In a remarkable bit of wrong-headedness, someone from Apollo Records sent Graham a first pressing of the record when it went platinum a month after its release. A boilerplate note attached saying, 'We did it! See you at the bottom of the ocean!'

He took the record up to the attic room and listened to it. When it ended he put it on again.

'I'm not on it,' he said, walking into the living room where Sadie and I were playing on the floor. 'Best thing I've ever heard and he's done it without me.'

Dr Hailee was surprised at this. 'Graham Harris is all over the album, guitar on almost every song, bass on most, some vocals, harpsichord, recorder, some drumming.'

'I suppose he meant his presence, his stamp on the album.'

'I'm just not sure I agree. He's there. Perhaps not the counterpoint to Neil as he was on *Satyrs* but his work is central.' Graham's interpretation is interesting. It might have been an indication of his depressed state of mind, but he seemed to put Neil's staggering achievement exclusively down to having shaken off the shackles of their collaboration.

'He always said I was his rock,' he says to Trevick at one point. 'But rocks can weigh you down.'

There was one part of the album though, his song, which Graham was still adamant was his sole contribution. The morning after he listened to the record, he went to meet media lawyer Harry Clyne of Clyne, Willis and Knight. Harry was not the best in the business, but was the best Graham could afford. Harry agreed that, despite the change in his contract, if Graham played the original melody and had witnesses, possibly a time-stamped recording, he had a strong case.

'Please don't do this,' Sadie said that night at dinner after he told her what he was intending to do.

'He's left me no other choice.'

'Stop! You can just stop.'

'How can I?' he said. 'How can I look Winter in the eye knowing I let him get away with it.'

'This isn't someone stealing your bike, Graham. Neil's famous. Very, very famous. You think Winter will thank you for exposing us, dragging us through the papers. That was my life. That's what my bastard father did to me. If you do this . . .' She twisted the base of her wine glass on the table, grinding the glass, almost wishing it would break. 'It will be the end of our family.'

'I'm doing it for our family!'

'You're doing it because you want to win.'

49.

Helen Grady gave me an awkward fist-bump across a table at the British Library after I told her about Graham going to Clyne, Willis and Knight. But the beam of a breakthrough was soon clouded by further questions. The letter the solicitor sent to Nereus Forbes was dated November 1974, while Graham met Harry Clyne to launch his legal action over 'Lady Theia' in the spring of 1973.

'The wheels of justice move slowly in these cases,' Helen told me. 'The side with the expensive lawyers tend to use a death-by-a-thousand-cuts strategy. Nitpick legalese, rearrange dates, obstruct it in any way they can in the hope the plaintiff will run out of money or lose the will to keep on fighting. A year and a half later, two years would be reasonably quick for a court date.'

'Is that what you think the letter was? A court date?'

'Impossible to say,' Helen said. 'Nereus was out of the country for huge swathes of 1973 and 1974. This sort of case could have run on until '75, '76 even.'

'Could it have gone on as long as 1977?' Helen drank her tea, shifted some papers. We'd met in the British Library because it was the most public place I could think of. I'd stopped the group meetings at the Crown Tavern after seeing the man in Berlin. I had no way of linking him to the Corsa or flat-cap man but I'd decided I shouldn't take any more chances than were necessary.

'If it went on that long,' Helen said, seeing I was trying to link the legal action to Nereus's death, 'I'd be amazed that nothing got out into the public domain.' I'd thought the same. Trevick's notes imply Graham was involved in some process against Nereus until at least the end of 1974 but possibly also into 1975. There's nothing in the notebooks around 1977.

'Could Graham have settled?' I asked.

'An out-of-court settlement would still have been in the record. I've looked, you and your merry men have too. We've found nothing beyond the bloody cover sheet.'

'Could it have gone south, in 1977, Nereus screwing Graham over again. The thing that finally tips him over the edge?' Helen leant back, took a deep breath.

'Like what?'

'I don't know, threats, blackmail?'

'Blackmail for what?' I didn't know. I was going to suggest something about his sexuality, that the two of them might have got together that night a month before his death, and Neil was blackmailing Graham to end the dispute. But I only thought it because I wanted it to be true. If Graham killed Neil, I still wanted it to be for love, some doomed love affair. In my head at the time that would have made it alright, if not alright then better. 'In all honesty,' Helen said when I hadn't answered. 'The case not being made public probably means it died. The people with the money normally come out on top.'

Helen thought, and the more sensible members of the group agreed, that the 1974 letter was most likely to have been Graham conceding defeat.

50.

The Apotheosis of Poiseidon is an album about a person who tries to be a part of our world and fails. It shows an outsider looking at a way of being and not only questioning it, but feeling certain their different perspective has real value. Nereus has endured because he showed people they could be gay, bi, effeminate, mermaid fetishists, that they could be whoever they wanted to be. And not only was it OK, it was better than the oppressive societal narratives we're told to aspire to.

My daughters see the world with this sort of acceptance and perhaps we have people like Nereus to thank for it. Sara wants to work in the Middle East advocating for refugees. Delphi has wanted to study music production since her dad first showed her a huge studio mixing desk — even I find all those buttons appealing. But beyond their careers, the two of them are self-assured as people. They seem to value their desires, their quirks, even their mistakes in a way I never have. They never seem tortured by existential despair, they don't see themselves as problems to be solved. I am happy to accept a fraction of the acclaim for my wonderful girls; I give more to my kind, open-minded husband. They've had a father. A good one. For their whole lives. Something Neil, Graham and I grew up without.

Neil sang to me once. I was flicking through one of the folders of Nereus images and photographed pages from his notebooks in my summerhouse. The theft of 'Lady Theia' was the most arresting motive, a thwarted legal challenge adding fuel to Graham's hatred, but there was still no evidence, nothing more than a hunch. I still didn't even know whether he was still on UK soil when Neil died. I was going over it all again, hoping I'd find something I missed.

I reached a notebook from the middle of 1975. The sketches had turned much darker, almost upsetting to look at. Tentacles, pages surrounded by borders of spiny sea urchins, dragon-like serpents blended with volcanic vents, a merman figure, Poiseidon, sitting on top of piles of cracked oyster shells – in Nereus's mythology, he becomes addicted to hallucinogenic molluscs created by contamination.

A lyric scribbled in a corner caught my eye.

'When Winter fell, she picked me up.' His talent hit me in the chest. Blending the simple with the arcane, threading it with longing. I felt like Graham, marvelling at Neil, jealous, frustrated at how easily it seemed for him. But then I noticed the word 'Winter' was capitalised. Was it possible the words weren't about the season but a person called Winter, me. I looked at the date again, I would have been three and a half. 'When Winter fell.' I tried to take myself back to a moment when I fell over, hurt myself perhaps. And then I had it, a memory swam back into my head with the quality of a long-forgotten nightmare.

It was in the kitchen of the house in St John's Wood. I was running down the hall, tripped and fell through the doorframe and began screaming. From nowhere, a tall figure arrived in front of me. He had a shaved head and *Clockwork Orange* make-up which absolutely terrified me. I really screamed. Like my life depended on it. The man knelt down in front of me and started singing. I looked into his frightening hazel eyes as he sang, hypnotised. Like he were some kind of wild animal tamer, his music calmed me down. He finished his song, cocked his head and blinked a few times. Someone else, Sadie it must have been, turned up and the man moved away.

I was in the middle of this reverie, folder poised on the desk, when I heard a rustle of leaves outside. I stared at the back wall, frightened, before shaking my head, feeling stupid. The wind, a cat. I went back to looking at the folder.

A branch snapped. I wheeled round, looked through the glass doors, but all I saw was my terrified face and the lamp behind me reflected in every pane. It was pitch-black outside but I felt sure someone was there. I stepped up to the doors, blocked the light with my hands and squinted through the glass. Nothing. Then a flurry of movement. I burst out of the room and saw a figure, shrouded by darkness, crashing through the trees and out onto the road. Someone was in my garden. They had come to my home.

I burst out of the summerhouse and ran into the kitchen where Bobby was at the table eating yoghurt.

'Someone's there!' I said. 'In our garden. Someone was in our garden.' Bobby rushed outside. I watched him walk up and down our street, phone-torch waving. I was still shaking when he came back. He wrapped me in a hug, held me for some time. Then we sat down with a bottle of wine and I finally told him everything. About the man in the flat cap, the swarthy man in Berlin, about my phone. But it was my online collaborators Bobby fixed on.

'Nereus fans are nuts,' he said. 'When anyone at work finds out who I'm married to, they lose their minds. Imagine what the ones behind their laptops day and night are like?'

'I don't think this is fans.'

'They posted Sara's uni address,' he said. ''Course they know where we live.'

'But who would? Why? I'm trying to find the truth. Surely that's what everyone who loves Nereus wants.'

'That's not what they want. They've got their versions already. Who knows what could spark someone to follow you, stalk you in your garden these days. You could probably say you don't rate "Bohemian Rhapsody" and have some crazy turn up on your doorstep. I think you need to stop.'

'What?'

'If someone's watching you in our garden because of this, don't you think it's time to stop?' I wanted to say that stopping is exactly what they'd want. But I knew I'd sound like the online conspiracists to Bobby. I suddenly saw I was behaving like Graham with his court case. Determined to fight logic, the pleas of the person I loved in the name of a righteous crusade to right some wrong.

'I don't see how what I'm doing is hurting anyone.' Bobby shuffled closer, put his hands on mine.

'People have been fighting wars for their gods forever,' he said. 'Just because we don't feel like that about Nereus, it doesn't mean there aren't people who do.' I drained the rest of my glass of wine. Bobby hadn't even delved into the fandom as I had. The bile some of them posted, the violence of their speech, their reactions to anything countering their vision of their hero made hiding in someone's bushes seem like the thin end of the wedge. 'Delphs lives here,' Bobby said. 'As do we.' He was right. Whatever I thought I'd get from finding the truth about Nereus's death, it wasn't worth provoking unstable fans who knew where we lived.

But a few days later, once the shock of the garden invasion had worn off, I thought again about Nereus being in my house in 1975, long after he'd fallen out with Graham. I couldn't see there was any harm popping down to see my mum to find out why.

51.

'We were broke,' Sadie said when I asked why Neil had been in our house. 'Bailiffs had been, landlord threatened the police.'

Graham's legal battle against Nereus shook him out of his depression. But midway through 1974, over a year after 'Lady Theia' was released, his lawyers told him there was no chance of a court date until the beginning of 1975. And, just as Helen Grady had thought, Nereus and Apollo's legal team were making it as difficult and expensive as possible. Battle lines had been drawn. Otis de Kock withheld royalty payments from *Dance of the Satyrs* and their first EP, which financially kneecapped not just Graham but also Danny and Fraz.

'Fraz was happy enough back home but I was drinking, no direction without the band,' Danny Greig writes in his memoir. 'After Graham got dropped the same way Neil did us, we were about ready to bury the hatchet. We'd phoned a few times, suggested he move back and get the band back together. But then he goes after Apollo Records. I had twins. I relied on those royalties. Graham never stopped to think how it might affect us.'

'The boys turned the whole of Whitby against me after,' Graham says. 'Horrible stories about drugs, prostitutes. None of it true. My mother was unwell by then but she would've heard.'

'I would have moved to Yorkshire,' Sadie said. 'It'd got that bad. But that door slammed shut too.'

Worst of all, with Nereus having been anointed the next messiah by the press and music business insiders, Graham was blacklisted by the industry.

'Thomas threatened anyone who considered booking me.' In a bit of circularity, Paul Denly, whose popularity had been eclipsed by newer artists like Nereus, asked Graham to produce his new album on the proviso he be uncredited and couldn't tell anyone he'd been involved. He couldn't stomach being erased from more of his work so turned him down.

'But the worst,' Sadie said, 'was the fans.' It was the heyday of band fan clubs who, back then, were tantamount to gangs. When word went round amongst the Nereids, as they called themselves, that Graham might be trying to go after Nereus in some way, the three of us became targets for some of the more extremist elements.

When Sadie took me to the park, I was two at this point, she'd notice groups of young people wearing eyeliner, parts of their heads shaved, staring at us. She was sure some followed us home once. People would knock on our door at all hours. Graham got aggressive if he was with us when it happened, once shoving a young man in an underpass, bringing him a police caution.

There was a night he was out working a security job when Sadie heard a noise downstairs. She ran into my room, picked me up, still asleep, and crept downstairs, grabbing a heavy stone vase to use as a weapon. As she got to the ground floor, she heard the sound of mumbling, humming almost. She swallowed, terrified, no mobile phones to reach Graham then. She followed the sound into the kitchen where she looked through the window and saw the garden bathed in flickering, orange light. There was a fire on our lawn, surrounded by a group of figures in hooded jumpsuits. Sadie nudged the door open and heard them singing. They were singing 'Lady Theia'. She phoned the police but the invaders were gone by the time they turned up.

'You need to stop,' she told Graham the next morning when she'd described what had happened.

'They're just kids.'

'They lit a fire in our garden, they were singing the song.'

'They're trying to scare us.'

'I am scared,' she said. 'I'm terrified. Of them, of losing the house, of something terrible happening.'

'Can't you see this is good?' Graham said, dumbfounding Sadie for a moment. 'It's all Thomas. Leaning on people not to give me jobs, mobilising fans. They're trying to make us give up the court case because they know they're going to lose.' Sadie leant against the wall, looking at Graham like he must be an alien species. 'You're deluded,' she said, an epiphany. 'I can't talk to you, you're completely deluded.'

I was shocked when she told me how Graham's legal action affected her. She told me she stopped taking me to the park, anywhere there might be young people. How she'd suffer crippling panic if she ever lost sight of me in public and that, after a few months of it, she stopped going out with me at all. It seemed so at odds with the formidable mother I remembered, that I had sitting in front of me. Though I'd spent the last two years trying to understand the parent I lost, I realised I didn't fully know the one I'd always had.

52.

After Penny's death, Nereus threw himself into work. At the end of 1973 he embarked on the epic Pacifica tour through Europe, Asia, each coast of the USA, before finishing with outdoor concerts in Marrakesh, Casablanca and Tangiers.

'Every day he had a new idea for the show,' Otis de Kock wrote in his memoir. 'All as expensive as they were impossible. But we always found a way.' The tour is seen by many as one of the greatest of all time. By the end, it included gospel choirs, thirty dancers and local brass sections and orchestras they'd bring in wherever they went. There was a twenty-foot inflatable octopus, a huge whale-model Nereus rode and, for four shows in South-East Asia, a tank with an actual manta ray on stage. All of it meant more rehearsals, more work, no downtime. 'I tried to get him to cancel dates, reduce the ambition,' Otis wrote. 'He was struggling, we could all see.'

'The chaos, the stress of keeping the batshit caravan on the tracks,' Thomas said to me in an email, 'blocked out the grief.' I wondered whether Neil was also trying to make up for not having Graham by his side. Without him the music on the tour suffered – the critical response more muted than for the album. But the over-the-top bacchanalian nature of the spectacle made it the hottest ticket in the world.

'Thank heavens for the bells, whistles and squids,' a review said in *The Times*. 'Because the band sound like they're playing underwater.'

'Graham didn't read any of that,' Sadie told me. 'Might have made him less angry. He wouldn't have let it go off the rails.'

Nereus's relentless schedule applied to his drug use too. He became dependent on cocaine and speed before the concerts to counteract the heroin from the night and morning before. Then each day the cycle would start over again.

'It was medical-grade shit,' tour manager Pete Frankom said in an *FHM* profile in 1994. 'Even still, I saw Nereus inject enough to stun a buffalo. I started cutting his coke with cornstarch, got the tip from a props guy at Pinewood. Wasn't going to let him have a heart attack on my watch.'

When the tour finished, Nereus was triumphant at the chaos, the outrage and the attention he'd garnered.

'But he was a shell,' Otis wrote. 'I began focusing on other acts. It was too sad to be around him.'

Nereus relocated to New York, hanging out at the new CBGBs and The Loft. But the city's febrile atmosphere, the result of crippling housing and financial issues, started to affect him.

'New York's when the migraines started,' Thomas told me. 'He said he could feel every violent act in the city as it occurred.'

The Nereus entourage escaped to New Orleans in the late winter of 1974.

'Not a good scene,' said Thomas. 'He was losing it, terrified all the time. Nightmares, headaches. He needed to get clean. But I loved junk, loved it. He was never going to manage it if I was around.' Thomas flew back to England for Neil's own good. According to him.

Within a few weeks, Neil had moved in with a group of Creole girls in the Mississippi Delta. He tried to kick his heroin addiction with the help of a voodoo shaman named Mama Azaka.

'Heart of darkness shit,' said Pete Frankom. 'Wild but

also, not cool at all.' Neil began seeing visions of dead bodies floating to the surface of the river, skulls in the candle-flame in their plantation house. It's rumoured he lived off nothing more than spring onions, goat's milk, steamed crawfish and psychotropic orchids which brought about long periods of projectile vomiting.

'He was less than seven stone at one point,' Pete said. The World Health Organization would have classed him as severely malnourished.

In November 1974, Neil seemed to get hold of his senses and exiled himself to Turks and Caicos to write and record his next album. He took Matthew and Thomas but that aside assembled an entirely new group of musicians from all over the world including Kittisak Chaiyapong, the Thai guitarist and pioneer of luk thung music.

'I introduced Neil to Kittisak's stuff,' Graham says. 'Would have been a dream for me to work with him.'

'We barely slept for eight or nine weeks making it,' Kittisak said to an Indonesian newspaper about his time working on *Atlantis Drained*. Matthew Salvini is quoted as saying he has no memory of making the album. But in the main, the musicians talked about the process fondly. Despite everything, Neil hadn't lost his dedication to giving his audience something they'd never heard before.

'The biggest rock star in the world,' Kittisak said. 'Trying to surpass everything he'd done. It was inspiring.'

It's hard to know what Neil made of Graham suing him for the authorship of what had become his most popular song. I couldn't find any allusion to it in hundreds of transcripts of interviews or TV clips, nor in the memoirs of those around him at the time. But his precarious mental state after his mother's death had to have been impacted by an attack from the other person he'd seen as anchoring his life.

From what I've learnt about his distaste for the business nitty gritty of his career and the extent of his addiction, it's safe to assume Neil was only dimly aware of the dark arts his team were employing against Graham's legal challenge. But it seems certain he would have known when, after nearly a year and a half of being blacklisted, fobbed off, bullied by lawyers, intimidated by Neil's fans, Graham decided he had no choice but to strike back.

53.

Back at work playing catch-up and at home with my husband's sweet if condescending concern following the man in our garden, I felt hamstrung like a maverick detective taken off the case. Having a little more space to think without my nightly hours of research in the summerhouse, I started to doubt if there had been anyone in the bushes at all. I had been alone at night, thinking about someone being murdered, having thought I'd been watched for months. However much I scanned the forums looking for an answer, I couldn't see why anyone sinister might be taking an interest in what I was doing. I became concerned I was inventing bogeymen just to prove to myself I was onto something.

Chasing phantoms from the past had got me nowhere so I resolved to work in concrete facts. If someone had a part in Nereus's death, I had to find some proof of how they could have escaped the locked top-floor room. Which brought me to the London Metropolitan Archive in Farringdon to examine what 1 Cheyne Walk might have been like in 1977.

There was no picture of the front of Nereus's house amongst the crime scene photos Bryn hung onto. But Nereus had bought it in 1974, so I wondered if I might find a promotional shot taken by the estate agent. Having spoken to the four companies still operating in the Chelsea area, I drew a blank. I went to the Kensington and Chelsea public archive who sent me to the LMA which had thousands of pictures of London streets from different eras.

But none of 1 Cheyne Walk. Delphi, who had just finished her last assessment at college, which I checked after she hoodwinked me before, begged to join me at the archive. I was in two minds about further entangling her in what had become something of an obsession, but I was days from giving up if there were no breakthroughs and thought I should at least have my best team on the job. Which was lucky because it was she who had the idea to print copies of all other Cheyne Walk buildings we could find and lining them up against a map of the road I'd had printed on two huge sheets of paper in one of the private reading rooms. All laid out, we could see the road as it was fifty years before. The gap in our pop-up street where Nereus's house should have been, a corner plot at the end of the terrace, stared at us like a lost tooth.

The sun burst from behind clouds outside, illuminating Delphi's art project, and I noticed a shadow I hadn't seen before on number 3.

'What's that?' I held the picture up. The shadow was thin but solid.

'Where's it coming from?' Delphi said, picking up the image of the opposite side of the road, trying to imagine where the shadow might be coming from – but we couldn't see anything. I picked up the picture of the top end of Flood Street, the other corner of 1 Cheyne Walk. There was a tree.

'That's still there now,' I said. 'Tall, foliage begins much higher, a long way away from the house, the other side from Nereus's bedroom.'

Delphi went to the front desk to borrow a magnifying glass and we looked at the tree more closely in the image from December 1977. Although our view was obscured by the tree's trunk, I could make out what looked like a bough, much lower than any I'd seen in real life. It extended into the front garden of 1 Cheyne Walk. It was hard to tell from the grainy old picture, but it looked thick, strong, a second trunk almost reaching up towards the sky.

'You could climb that,' Delphi said.

'I mean, I couldn't.'

'Someone big could.' We looked at each other.

Shortly after this I set about trying to track down the flight crew from Graham's flight to Nice. British Airways said they didn't keep records from so long ago but did give me the aeroplane tail code. After Insurance Stan bought four hundred British Airways flight manifests from 1977 on eBay from a collector, we found a list of all the crew and passengers. And we sent emails and Facebook messages to as many of the people we could find contact details for. I asked all of them if they'd seen Graham Harris on the flight, including a picture from the time. Unable to find the man himself, I had to know, once and for all, if Graham's alibi for that night checked out.

Because however inconvenient the thick branch overhanging the garden of 1 Cheyne Walk might have been for the homeowner, assuming that was why it was removed, for someone strong enough, it was very convenient for escaping a murder.

54.

It was a line in an interview which provoked Graham to get his hands dirty and strike back at Nereus. On a 1974 BBC appearance Nereus talks about how a visit to the Galapagos Islands had led him to see his career in Darwinian terms.

'I too was protozoa at the beginning,' Nereus says. 'Then developed into a sea-dwelling creature; with my first album *Dance of the Satyrs*, I popped a couple of legs out perhaps. Then like a primordial lizard, I shed my skin, the wasted parts of me, to emerge into this.' He shakes the rose-gold tassels of his cloak. 'But even now I'm still on a very low rung of my evolution.' The host laughs, bemused.

Graham wasn't laughing.

'I got what he was saying,' he tells Trevick. 'I was his abandoned snake skin on the floor.' He'd always given Neil the benefit of the doubt, blamed Thomas for tricking him with the contract, Penny's illness for having abandoned him in London. But it seemed Graham really was nothing to Neil. He couldn't see any reason to continue playing nice.

The next day Graham met a freelance journalist who was embedded with many of the bands at the time, offering a no-holds-barred tell-all. The journalist wanted to know about the older men Neil had slept with as a teenager, the younger girls he'd slept with more recently and of course, the orgies, but what she wanted most was the scoop about his drug use. Drugs were obviously illegal so the music industry had a widespread omertà when it came to revealing any individual's habits. This journalist wanted the *Trainspotting*-toilet grimy truth.

'Please tell me this isn't serious?' Sadie said when Graham told her where he'd been as she did laundry in the basement.

'He's trying to make it look like he's kicked on without me.' Sadie blinked, not sure how to respond. 'So when the case gets to court, and it's his word against mine about the song, no one will believe me.'

'And you think going to the papers is the answer?'

'When the world sees what sort of man he really is . . .'

'Do you really think they'll thank you for smearing their hero?' she said. 'For riling up pearl-clutching middle-Englanders like your mother against him? You think they'll take your side?'

'Sometimes you have to take a stand, for what's right.'

'What about what's right for us?'

'This is about us. We need the money.' Sadie turned back to her pile of clothes, folding. She held a clean hand towel up to her face and cried into it. 'I just want to be safe,' she said.

'Once we win, we will be,' said Graham. She cleared her throat, replaced the towel, couldn't look at him.

'Once you go public,' she said with gritted calm, 'it can't be undone.' He said nothing. She carried the pile of clothes upstairs. The two of them went to separate beds that night.

Graham left the next morning to meet the journalist. He talked about group sex he'd witnessed, men like Anton he'd seen him with when Neil was just nineteen, the conditions of Troweldun Farm, described seeing Neil shooting up with Thomas Tee. He mentioned Matthew Salvini's friendship with drug trafficker Dominik Szlonik who had extensive criminal contacts in North Africa and the Middle East. Graham revealed everything, embellished things, ornamented stories with lurid details whenever the journalist seemed underwhelmed. As he left the pub they'd met at in Camden, Graham expected to feel triumphant at the thought of bringing Neil down. He felt hollow as a dying tree.

When he got home, he saw a suitcase and three guitar cases on the front path.

He looked up at the house, saw Sadie standing in the window of their living room, holding me in her arms. They stared at each other for a moment. Graham bent down and gathered his things.

'I might have taken him back if he'd fought it,' Sadie said.

It was over between my mother and father. I wasn't even three.

Atlantis Drained

Not even the most contrary music snob could tell you Nereus's 1975 album *Atlantis Drained* is better than its predecessor. Its nonsensical themes, South-East Asian tonality and bizarre structure make it more suited to a critical-thinking seminar than a Friday night out. Nereus sounds isolated, distant, but can we really accept the most glamorous and adored person in the world as some fascinating outsider anymore? Music can be a great tonic if you're feeling down, but it should never *be* depressing. Call me a philistine, but give me songs about some recognisable emotion, love, sex, hate, stick a catchy guitar lick on top of it and get over yourself.

From *Blowing Up the Canon: An Anarchist's Guide to Pop* by Jas Peltz.

55.

Graham got a room in a boarding house at the top end of Caledonian Road. November 1974 had been mild and Graham was in his shirtsleeves as he walked to a newspaper shop on Holloway Road the morning after Sadie kicked him out. He picked up the *News of the World* and flicked to the entertainment section, looking for his exposé but he couldn't find it. Confused, he carried on searching in the main section, then further into the paper. It didn't seem to be there.

Then he saw it. Low down in the bottom corner of a page in the middle of the paper, a picture of Nereus at one of his North African concerts, the journalist's byline underneath. 'Pyramids Next for Nereus?'

The article said that after a visit to Tunisia's El Jem Amphitheatre, Nereus had fallen in love with the region and wanted to mount spectacular stage shows at some of its famous landmarks. It was a puff piece which ended saying the paper was looking forward to becoming the premier place for all future Nereus Forbes news.

'I got played,' Graham admitted. 'It was all for nothing.' The journalist had used Graham's tell-all as leverage to gain access to Nereus. I'm not in that world but it seemed the obvious play to me too. Why risk infuriating a megastar at the height of his fame with a few bits of tattle when you can use it to become his go-to press contact?

I had imagined it would be easy to find the journalist's

name in the archives by cross-referencing it with Nereus, but contrary to what movies tell you about wartime newspapers on microfilm readers in libraries, I struggled. The *News of the World* closed in 2011 following the phone-hacking scandal so I couldn't contact them directly. I went to the British Library, but several of their films of the period had become corrupted. I cursed my poorly spent taxpayer's money that night.

I put the *nereusforever* team on it. Insurance Stan bought some more ancient publications off eBay, which had become something of a trademark, but we still couldn't crack it. Until I mentioned the aborted tell-all to Paul Trevick during a catch-up.

'Sure it'd be in the clippings,' he said, as if I hadn't just told him I'd spent three weeks trying to track this person's name down.

'Clippings?' I said. He explained there was a big folder of his father's press clippings at his mother's house in Grimsby and that he'd look that afternoon.

'Marina Maxwell-Clyde,' he said when he rang that evening. 'Cursory google says she's written a book. About polo.'

'Right. Weird. Do you think we can find her?'

'In a cemetery maybe. Born in 1932.'

56.

Having lost his family and had his attempt to smear Nereus blow up in his face, Graham had nothing left but his legal action. In the winter of 1975, a court date was set for 15 April. Neil was cocooned for most of the first part of the year mixing the new album with Clive Dors and Kittisak at Abbey Road, using heroin still but purportedly more controlled with it.

Graham spent the months running up to the April court date obsessively analysing Nereus's back catalogue, making exhaustive lists of which parts he deserved credit for, compiling detailed analysis of how his ideas had shaped Neil's melodies. Without Danny and Fraz's support, he doorstepped others who'd been in the studio to speak up as witnesses on his behalf but no one would. He was at his lawyer's office several times a week, bringing new insights, points of attack, even suggesting he play his guitar for the judge. But by that point his lawyer's enthusiasm for their chances in the case, for Graham himself, had diminished to a cagey tolerance.

While Neil was insulated by fame and Graham galvanised by righteous indignation, Sadie and I were suffering.

'The fashion houses I worked for stopped talking to me after Graham went to the tabloids.'

'Even though it wasn't published?'

'Thomas made sure everyone knew.'

I have a recollection, I can't be sure if this is a projection having learnt what she was going through, but I could feel her darkening around then. She'd take to her bed, stay until late morning. When I went in to her, it felt like she'd been drained in the night. After months of this, she did what for her was the unthinkable and asked her mother for money.

'She said my father would only help us if I apologised to him for my behaviour.' Sadie's 'behaviour' being leaving home to go to art school after her well-known politician dad was exposed for having two affairs with employees her age, heaping national shame onto the whole family. 'I shouldn't have been so proud but – they'd never even asked to meet you. I couldn't do it.'

Sadie was out of options. 'I had two, maybe three weeks before we were out on the streets.' She resolved to sort Graham and Neil out herself.

'They wouldn't see each other, so I lied to them. They were both at our house within the hour. Never overestimate men, Winter,' she said.

'What did you say?'

'Just that I needed to see them.' I found this answer strange. It made sense for Graham. Although they'd separated, they still had me and shared financial problems. But why would Neil have dropped everything to visit a woman I can't imagine he'd thought much about for four years. It took me back to the thoughts I'd had trying to decode Nereus's notebooks. Sadie as Pygmalion, the perfect woman, escape, salvation. Neil would have known she and Graham had split. Although he was healthier than he had been the previous year, there was no love in his life since Penny had died, no relationships to speak of. I imagined Nereus alone in his big house in Chelsea getting the phone call from Sadie, thinking his moment had finally come.

When Graham arrived, he found Neil in the kitchen sipping tea as Sadie examined the loose stitching on the shoulder of his silver bodysuit.

'What's this?' Graham said. Neil blinked, breath catching at seeing his old friend. Graham turned to leave. Sadie leapt up and took his hand. They locked eyes, both searching the other for the simpler past they'd lost.

'This has to end,' she said.

'What he did,' he said, glancing at Neil over her shoulder. 'I can't forgive him.'

'I will not let your insufficiencies ruin Winter's life. Now sit down.' Sadie pulled a chair out from the table. Graham sat.

The two men looked at each other for the first time since the depths of night in the Highlands. Neil had more colour in his cheeks, but looked awful still, eyes so haunted it was like they'd changed colour. Graham didn't know if he wanted to hit him, give him a hug or drag him to the piano and play together. Neil seemed to be trying not to smile; whether he was embarrassed at the seriousness of the situation or genuinely pleased to see Graham it was impossible to tell.

'Neil has an offer,' Sadie said, standing in front of the back door. Graham felt a frisson in his stomach. This was unexpected. If Neil was making offers, it meant he was worried about the case.

'You expect me to roll over and take scraps because you've worked out you'll lose?' he said. 'No, you're alright.' Neil took a deep breath, glanced at Sadie.

'Your lawyers, Graham,' Neil looked past him, distraught about what he had to say next, 'have been discussing a settlement with our side for the best part of a year.'

'What?' Graham looked at Sadie, got nothing. 'That's – they wouldn't.'

'You won't win,' Neil said. 'They know that.'

'You're – you're lying.' Neil shook his head with a faraway sadness. Graham turned in his seat, astonished. As the silence ticked by, phrases from his lawyer Harry Nixon swam into his head. Lack of precedent, inspiration versus plagiarism, words like mood, vibe, his constant pleas for concrete proof.

'But you took it,' Graham said. He turned to Neil, gripping the sides of the kitchen table. 'You took it. How can – how can this be?' Neil ran his tongue along his front teeth. He seemed fidgety, uncomfortable where he sat.

'I want to give you a hundred thousand,' Neil said. Sadie sat next to Graham.

'This been sorted, has it?' he said. 'By the two of you?'

'It would pay your legal fees,' Sadie said. 'We could both buy places, no mortgage. Secure us until Winter's at school.' Graham looked from Sadie to Neil, wary like an animal in a trap. As much of a shock as it had been that his lawyers were trying to settle behind his back, Graham had known deep down he was going to lose the case. It's possible he always had. But he wanted to go to court, whatever the result, he wanted the world to see Neil for who he really was.

'Why am I here then?' he asked. 'Why haven't the lawyers settled? What's the mighty Nereus Forbes doing in my kitchen? Here to lord it over me?'

'It's a gift,' Neil said, reaching his hand across the table. 'Compensation. I couldn't put you all through a big public case you'd lose with nothing but expenses to pay. This is a better resolution for all of us.'

'Compensation for what?' Graham said, glaring at Neil's hand extended like an olive branch. 'Go on, what's it compensation for? Admit it. Admit you stole it.' Neil looked at Graham, about to say something before stopping himself.

'You weren't treated as you should have been,' he said. Graham scoffed, shook his head at what he felt was the greatest understatement he'd ever heard. He leant back, stared at Neil, waiting for him to meet his eye, and tried to decipher what game it was he was playing. Neil was always enigmatic, hard to place, but he'd never seen him be this cagey before, this considered. He was implying he was throwing Graham a bone out of the goodness of his heart, but he was concealing something. Graham had no idea what it could be.

Intellectual property lawyer Helen Grady did have thoughts on why Neil might have been willing to pay to avoid the case going through official channels.

'If they had a court date, there's a chance a settlement would go into public record. Even if there was an out-of-court settlement before the trial, it would raise speculation about what's been agreed. A financial settlement, particularly a significant one, is widely thought of as an admission of guilt. If Neil settled, it would make it look like Graham wrote the song.'

'Which he did.'

'But for Neil's reputation, his legacy, it was vital no one knew that.'

'Is that why he never admitted it?'

'One would have to assume it was.'

'So what?' Graham said, trying not to be riled by Neil's non-apology. 'You write me a cheque and I call the whole thing off.'

'You'd have to sign something,' Neil said.

'Saying what?'

'You didn't write "Lady Theia" and that you'll never tell anyone you did.' Neil meant a non-disclosure agreement. It seemed he wasn't recompensing Graham. He was buying the song, paying for his silence. Graham left the kitchen and went up to my room. He sat next to three-year-old me, the child he'd written the song for, and pressed a dark brown crayon so hard onto some paper, it crumbled into dust.

It must have felt hopeless. Knowing there was no recourse, no higher body he could go to, to fight for what he knew was rightfully his. He looked round the bare room stripped down by the bailiffs, his daughter needing safety, a roof above her head, a normal life, oblivious to how much her father was letting her down.

But imagine Michelangelo not being able to tell anyone he'd painted the Sistine Chapel? That must have been what it felt like. And on top of that, to let Neil win? The man who seemed to have everything – career, adoration, wealth he couldn't imagine. Maybe Graham laid his hand on my back, remembering the snuffling piglet in the incubator the day I was born, knowing he would never, ever write a song like that again. No one does. How would he sleep at night knowing he'd sold it to him, capitulating to Nereus Forbes again?

Twenty minutes later, Graham arrived at the doorway, holding me into his chest. Neil was still there, smoking, as Sadie pretended to wash up.

'Five hundred grand,' Graham said. Neil laughed involuntarily before seeing that Graham wasn't joking.

'I haven't got five hundred thousand,' Neil said, smiling still. He looked at me, pawing at Graham's beard. 'I could, perhaps, stretch to two.'

'No.'

'The advance on my deal, it's spent. All of it.'

'Four.'

'Any more than two would ruin me.'

'The song costs four hundred thousand pounds. We're going for a walk.' He turned, walked back down the corridor and slammed the door as he left with me. A shell-shocked Neil looked at Sadie who raised her eyebrows, shrugged.

The agreement was signed the next week. Graham sold his soul. Neil lost all he had. Sadie bought a two-bed garden flat in Marylebone and thought it was just what they all deserved.

57.

Discovering the 'grubby deal', as it's referred to in Trevick's notes, helped many things fall into place. The legal document, the purchase of Methuselah, Matthew Salvini saying Graham was responsible for Nereus's bankruptcy and the fact there's no mention of any dispute over 'Lady Theia' in decades of public discourse.

I was relieved at first. Graham had cleaned Neil out. He had secured his and his family's future. He needed to be the provider and he had provided and then some. It wouldn't have soothed the betrayal, the loss of his song, but he'd hit Neil in the only place he could. It may have been a pyrrhic victory, but it was a victory nonetheless. And crucially for me, if Graham was as pragmatic as so many people have said he was, he must have felt that they were even. That it was over. Two years before Neil died. Why go back and murder someone you've already got your revenge on?

'What if Nereus asked for it back?' Lennox from Wisconsin was on an iPad screen, Candi the activist next to me upstairs at the Crown. I hadn't been meeting with anyone in person, and if I did, always in the most public setting possible. Lennox went on. 'He's broke. Thomas Tee wants him to do nappy commercials. Salvini asks for money. Dominik Szlonik serves him his long overdue bill for all the free drugs. Then he proposes to his girlfriend who may or may not be going cool on him. Maybe that's money related too? Who wants to shack up with the guy who's a busted flush?' I wanted to jump to Greta's defence, she was far too cool to be that materialistic, but held my tongue. 'We know Nereus sees Graham a month before. Maybe he's sounding him out, seeing how his cashflow is?' Candi and I looked at each other, doubtful. 'With everyone else a horror show he gets in touch with his old pal and lays it out like – "Remember that way-too-much money I gave you? Well I need it back." Maybe he demands it, threatens more lawyers. If everything he'd done to Graham was true, it'd be enough to make me snap.'

I said nothing. I was annoyed. Although it wasn't the obvious story, speculative even, it wasn't out of the realms of possibility. The more I thought of it, the more it made sense. Sadie said Neil tried to arrange the payments in instalments but Graham refused. Even after it was all agreed, Graham had the papers for three weeks and only signed them after Sadie went round and begged him to. All Graham had ever wanted was to write a great song and have the sort of happy family he didn't. Neil had taken both of those away from him and all he had to show for it was the money.

As I left Candi and Lennox to take a long walk in the early summer heat, I imagined Neil asking for the money back in his childlike, nonchalant way. As if he'd lent Graham twenty quid to get a taxi rather than bought him off in exchange for erasing his authorship of one of the greatest songs of the twentieth century. I was boiling with rage even thinking about it.

Which is why it took me longer than it should have to notice I was being followed. I saw him on the other side of a quiet backstreet which led up to Exmouth Market. A man in a black gilet over a grey sweatshirt, thick-framed glasses. I got to St John Street and turned right, away from the walk north to Angel station. The man followed. My breathing quickened. I took out my phone wanting to call Bobby, to get someone on the line, but he was in a session in Soho where he didn't have reception. I considered Bryn or seeing if Candi was still in the area.

I decided to walk down to the busier streets of the City of London. The man followed, staying on the opposite side of the road. He could have been walking to work, to lunch. He might not have been there for me. But everything in my body told me he was. I saw an alley I knew led back to the pub and skip-walked through and out into Clerkenwell Green. The man had gone, further into town probably. I'd been imagining it. I considered going back into the pub for a gin and tonic to settle my nerves but instead started heading towards Farringdon Station.

But then the man was there on the other side of the main road. He had a hand in his pocket. It seems ridiculous to write it now, but I ran. I turned on my heels and ran the other way. But to my horror, the man started following. I must not have been going very fast because he was barely jogging and managing to keep up. As I looked back I tripped on a sign outside a shop and hit the pavement. It felt like I'd twisted my ankle. The man slowed, but didn't stop approaching.

Then the brakes of a car squealed on the road beside me. I looked up to see a black Vauxhall Corsa, passenger door open, the guy in the flat cap in the driver's seat. I looked behind me at the man who'd been following me, stopped but still staring at me, and got in flat-cap's car. Wheels spinning, the car burnt away before slowing in a snake of Central London traffic.

'Who are you?'

'Al,' he said. 'Alan.'

'Alan?'

'Sperryman.' Alan Sperryman. A. Sperryman. asperryman3.

58.

Alan said he wanted to take me to his house in Croydon and I started hyperventilating. He pulled over on a backstreet.

'People have been watching you,' he told me.

'Yes, Alan. You were the first one I saw doing it.' He seemed disappointed, before explaining himself.

'When you posted on the subreddit, about how scared your daughter was after getting that poster, I felt terrible. So, so awful.'

'Because you sent it?' He nodded.

Alan was around thirty-five, skinny, pale, sallow skin. He had psoriasis all over his arms. He told me he'd fallen in love with Nereus, his words, when he was fourteen. *Atlantis Drained* was his favourite album. No one understood it like he did. He'd been listening one night, having had a huge argument with his parents who he still lived with, and felt an almost visceral anger at the universe that beautiful souls like Nereus had been allowed to die so young. It sent him down into the pit of the internet to learn more about his death.

'Your father killed Nereus,' he told me. 'I'm sure of it.' It might sound crazy to admit this but on sensing a forensic intelligence beneath the slightly bonkers things Alan said, I found myself wanting to compare notes. But that would come later. He apologised profusely, explained he was upset when he sent my daughter the poster. He used the word 'episode' which made me think he could suffer from bipolar or another chronic mental health condition. It was at that point I suggested we go to a café. A busy one.

Once with tea, I asked him, as calmly as I could, why he'd been following me.

'I work with computers, at a repair shop in Streatham. We do phones. When you posted about strange things happening, I was sure someone was tracking you. I knew every theory about how Nereus died, plugged some of it into an AI who suggested it was most likely a private security company.' I assure you I did spend most of that first meeting wanting to walk away. But I needed answers. 'So I decided to try to see you, found out about the meetings at the Crown. I wanted to make up for what I'd sent to your family, try to be of service.' He talked like he lived in chivalric times. 'But I was too scared to introduce myself.'

'So you followed me, parked on my road. Do you understand that made me feel very scared?'

'I didn't mean to. After you saw me I stopped for a while. But one night, I saw someone else watching you.'

'The man we just ran away from.'

'No, but same sort.' I told him I'd thought someone had been watching me in Berlin, which he got very excited about.

'Why would a private security company be interested in me?' I asked. I shared what Dale had thought about the crime scene, Nereus's inside knowledge of Tabby Jocasta's brothel and its later links with senior politicians, Dominik Szlonik and his debts to the Algerian drug cartel. But of course, Alan Sperryman dismissed all of these, still certain it was Graham.

'Why are you so sure?'

'*Top of the Pops*,' he said. 'That moment. The kiss. It's a sexual awakening.'

'Neil or –'

'No, Graham. He hates it in himself but he can't help it.

You can see it all in his face. He's head over heels in love with Nereus. He couldn't have him so he killed him.' I'd watched the video hundreds of times, a sliver of me knew what he meant.

'How can you be sure, just from watching YouTube?'

'I had the same with a boy at school. He didn't feel the same and I snapped. Hurt him. Was asked to leave.' My mouth dried out. I felt certain I shouldn't have been sitting alone with Alan Sperryman. But then he told me to give him my phone and, against all better judgement, I handed it over. He took out a laptop and plugged my phone into it. We waited ten minutes. I bought Alan a brownie.

When he'd finished it he told me someone had put spyware on my phone. I asked what that meant. He explained, not without a little too much judgement for someone who'd been stalking me, it was a secret bit of software that can monitor and transmit all the activity on the phone. He was in no doubt it was what was glitching my iPhone 5.

Alan was looking at his laptop screen, green numerals that may as well have been the *Matrix* for all I understood of it, when he gave a loud 'hmm'. I asked what was wrong and he said spyware was normally put on a phone remotely, a link in a text message or email, a fake app to download. Although he couldn't be certain, the software on my phone seemed to have been uploaded 'in real life'. He asked me the last time I gave my phone to someone else.

'They checked my bag at the Reichstag,' I said. 'But didn't get my phone out. The same at airports, Gatwick and Berlin.'

'A bad actor wouldn't be able to infiltrate sites with that sort of security.' That was how Alan actually talked, for context.

Then I remembered another place, the security desk at a smart office building, many months before, almost a year. I had thought it too far back, but I traced back to when my phone started misbehaving. It was in fact, just a week or so after that visit.

'Nowhere else?' Alan asked me.

'I think, I don't know,' I said. 'Maybe, when I went to the Nereus Forbes Estate.'

59.

My brief kidnap at the hands of computer technician Alan Sperryman turned out to be one of the biggest breaks I'd had in the two years I spent searching for Nereus's killer. Finding the spyware on my phone proved someone was watching me and I hadn't handed it over to anyone else except Thomas Tee and the Estate.

I rang the Estate, not saying why, but they wouldn't put me through to Thomas or anyone more senior than the receptionist. I emailed Thomas asking to meet but got a boilerplate out-of-office in return. I even went to the building with Bobby, who was as desperate for answers as I was at the thought someone in his industry had gone after us, but we were told no one was in that day. They were winding down ahead of a move to smaller premises. The security guard who'd taken my phone was nowhere in sight. Apparently Thomas Tee hadn't been in in months. It seemed a coincidence the Estate had slowed their operations just at that point. The Clerkenwell Green foot-chase had clearly got back to them.

Bobby wanted to go to the police. Alan Sperryman didn't. He couldn't trace the spyware to Thomas and even though he could tell from the code it hadn't been downloaded remotely, a tech specialist in court could argue against that. I hadn't taken photos of the men I saw following me, or their number plates, we hadn't reported any of it to the police. It was a significant allegation without any proof. But crucially, what was the Estate's motivation? Why engage a private security operation against a middle-aged academic on a wild goose chase?

'He did it,' Bobby said. 'It's the only answer. Thomas Tee killed Nereus and thinks you're going to find out.' It had been my first thought too, of course. And again, I was amazed my first feeling was relief it wasn't Graham. Thomas had motive, he wanted control of the Estate, something he'd lose if Nereus married or realised what a malicious presence he'd become. But almost as swiftly I wasn't that pleased a murderer was doing everything he could to stop me exposing him. 'He's trying to scare you.'

'Well, mission accomplished, he has,' I said. Bobby said he wished I'd never started looking, but now I had, we couldn't give up. He wanted us to expose Thomas online or go to the papers with our suspicions.

'Then we have to prove it,' I said. The company was worth tens of millions. I'd seen his lawyers with my own eyes. I wasn't going to repeat Graham's mistakes. I needed to suppress my anger, my fear, and finish what I'd started a year and a half before. I needed to prove Thomas Tee murdered Nereus Forbes.

60.

The biggest problem was that Thomas Tee wasn't seen by anyone near 1 Cheyne Walk after he left the area around lunchtime on 28 October.

'Thomas Tee had no alibi, so to speak,' Bryn told me. 'But he was seen in his apartment building in Covent Garden by a neighbour that afternoon. We had no reason to doubt his story.' Thomas drove a conspicuous gold Bentley at the time, of which there were no sightings after he left. Sadie told me he drove it everywhere, despised public transport. Which doesn't discount it. If you're known to have a car like that, you probably wouldn't travel in it if you're on your way to commit murder.

It was possible, based upon having hired people to follow me, that he'd paid someone to do his dirty work. Dale thought the crime scene looked stage-managed which might imply the work of professionals. Thomas had access to funds through Pacifica Holdings and would have had a wealth of underworld contacts through Dominik Szlonik and further back from his wheeler-dealer father. But could I prove any of that?

It might have been because I'd focused on him for so long, with the tapes and his being my dad, but I started to wonder whether Graham knew. Why else would you leave your daughter in the country of your birth, never to return? Graham hated Thomas. If he knew what he'd done to Neil, however he felt about him by then, why wouldn't he want the world to know it?

Despite the sighting of Graham's car, he was meant to be in Monaco, so I couldn't be sure he was there the night Nereus died. But I was fairly certain he was there the month before. Neighbour Abby Grade had seen him with her own eyes and had no reason to have made it up. Did Thomas get wind of Graham coming back into Nereus's life? Did he feel threatened, forced to take matters into his own hands? I had a hunch that if I could work out what happened between Neil and Graham that night, it would help me understand how Thomas did it. Because if it didn't have anything to do with Graham, I didn't want to think about why he might have abandoned me.

After the settlement, Graham took only two months before buying Methuselah.

'He knew Neil had looked into buying it the year before,' Sadie said. The house became a sanctuary for Graham. Far enough from the London he'd grown to despise but near enough to his daughter. Crucially, its ramshackle condition gave him purpose at a time when he couldn't work, and for the first time since he was nine years old, he didn't need to. With the exception of his twice-a-month trips to London to get me and, in time, the piano lessons to the Jordanians, it was the sort of isolation he hadn't felt since before he met Danny and Fraz back in Whitby. Although it was a rest from the tumultuousness of the previous eighteen months, his solitary fixing up of the big house was a self-imposed purgatory, a choice not to live.

He must have missed music but I remember the four-thousand-pound Steinway he'd bought sitting in the big banquet hall unplayed. I suppose music represented community to Graham, playing with people the only way he really knew how to interact. But he had no one to play with. He had no one.

Nereus found himself trapped in a different way. *Atlantis Drained* divided fans and critics. Some called it a masterpiece, most found it unlistenable. It sold well in the first week but then quickly tailed off. Apollo Records were left in a difficult position in terms of his next deal. Due to his profile they would have to pay through the nose for future records, but with the album's reception, Otis couldn't be sure they'd see that money again.

'I wanted to keep him,' Otis wrote. 'Nereus was the greatest talent I'd ever worked with. I offered him three times what the accountant said I could. But then he broke my heart.'

By this point, Thomas Tee had just installed himself as Nereus's de facto business manager. His first act was to turn down Otis's offer and leave Apollo Records – a move which shocked the whole industry.

'Apollo didn't back my vision,' Nereus told the press when he made the announcement.

'I couldn't have done more for that album,' Otis wrote. 'It was a tightrope trying to make it more commercial without stepping on Nereus's toes. Ultimately, I couldn't push things to where the public needed them to be.' I found this interesting, remembering how Graham had been Otis's man on the ground, reining in Nereus's more inaccessible ideas. In the control room at Troweldun Farm he'd been shattered to realise Neil was better off without him, but the first album Graham was entirely absent from was Nereus's biggest commercial flop.

Nereus tried to sell the split from Apollo as a revolution against the industry gatekeepers, announcing he would set up his own company to run his entire operation. Big bands had had elements of control of recording and distribution before, but never touring, marketing and promotion to such a great extent. It was seen as a kamikaze business decision, a sign Nereus had lost his grip on reality.

'But with what we know now,' bookkeeper Iris said, 'it makes perfect sense. Four hundred grand to Graham, possibly putting Nereus at least two, maybe three hundred grand in the hole. They had to make that up.'

The Nereus machine was unwieldy by that point. They had musicians, drivers, engineers, tour managers, any number of assistants, receptionists, runners all on the payroll. Not to mention the staggering cost of Nereus's excessive lifestyle – he had a full-time florist on retainer, for example. The outgoings were huge, they needed money there and then. What Apollo offered wasn't enough, but an exhaustive year-long tour of the US they wouldn't have to share the profit from could, in theory, get Nereus back on his feet.

The tour was Thomas's idea. It was a debacle. They cut almost everything which had made the Pacifica tour a great success, ending up with a handful of musicians in semi-darkness stood behind Nereus in a monochrome Eastern Bloc-inspired suit. It was sold as a dynamic reinvention, 'stripped-back, uncut Nereus'. I now know it was a cost-cutting exercise. And it's possible they would have pulled it off. The US fans still couldn't get enough of Nereus. But the tour was so long and gruelling and Nereus had no pyrotechnics to fall back on, he was carrying it all, still grieving his mother, grieving the end of his friendship with Graham. It sent him back into the arms of the only reliable relationship he had left: heroin.

The first tour dates went well, there was a sense of intrigue seeing Nereus without the make-up and the outfits, the songs still wonderful. But within weeks the drug-use began to scour at him like a glacier. His eyes are huge in the pictures, lost in a face which had grown more and more skull-like. The drab outfit accentuated his paleness; in some shots he looks translucent. They began changing the outfits to cover the track-marks, tape down his mic stand because his shakes were so extreme he sent it falling to the floor most nights. His voice started failing. In one show in Cincinnati, he sat on the floor for the whole second half.

'He wanted all of life, everything, anything he could see in a room, anything he could think of,' Sadie said when I asked why Neil became an addict. 'In the middle of a concert, an orgy, whatever, he'd never be there, he'd always be thinking about what he didn't have. Drugs simplified all of that. All he'd want was junk.'

Behind the scenes, the more difficult the tour was, the more tyrannical Thomas became. He and Matthew came to blows in Baltimore which led to the only remaining member of the Satyrs getting on a boat home, leaving the band for good. Neil began avoiding Thomas, arranging actual getaway cars after concerts so he wouldn't have to face him. Which would further enrage Thomas who was drowning under the pressure of running the entire operation. For Neil, who never coped well with conflict, the acrimony behind the scenes only made things worse.

'I had to shake him out of crying fits before going on stage,' tour manager Pete Frankom wrote in his memoir.

The fans began to turn on Nereus, which was the final straw for his fractured psyche. Thomas had no choice but to cancel the tour three months early, in the late summer of 1977. Neil hid himself in Cheyne Walk alone, aside from visits from Greta Handverk when she was in the country.

I imagined Graham and Neil, stuck in their respective castles, faces at rain-soaked windows, racked with confusion at how their sparkling futures became so tarnished – how they ended up so alone. And perhaps it was as simple as that. Maybe, at the beginning of September 1977, one got in contact with the other. Perhaps enough time had passed. Graham went to Neil and they spent a night in each other's company. But a night Neil didn't mention to the trusted manager he was afraid of and that Graham wouldn't even tell his own biographer about.

61.

'Between getting the money and Graham disappearing,' Sadie said when I asked about what seemed a purgatorial stretch in the story. 'When you were three, four, five. Those were the happiest times.'

'Wasn't it hard?' I asked. 'Being a single mum, on your own.'

'I wasn't on my own, I had you,' she said. 'And I was so ready for it. I was a fantastic mother.' From my fragmentary memories I couldn't disagree. Our flat in Marylebone had a garden she planted with vegetables. We had guinea pigs, chickens for a while until they were all eaten by ravenous foxes. We went to Fortnum's, to Harrods, and bought the food she wanted. Fresh tropical fruit, tzatziki, avocados, balsamic vinegar.

'Those food halls were like Aladdin's cave, you adored it.' Despite her blacklisting, there were still people who sought out her work as a dressmaker. As Nereus's music became more challenging, those who still wanted to love him fixated on the style, the frocks, the make-up. Insiders knew Sadie was a huge part of his unique look. But she turned down offers from American bands and wealthy émigrés, choosing instead to repair clothes for people when I was asleep in the evenings before taking on a full-time job at a tailor's off Baker Street when I started at pre-school.

'I'd never been away from the public eye,' she said. 'Nor men. Either trying to get in my pants or wanting me to save them. Being able to escape all that.' She sighed, remembering it like she was tasting something delicious. 'The money from Neil was a skeleton key,' she told me. 'Finally unlocked how I wanted us to live.'

'In what way?'

'Neil, Graham, my father, my mother even, I'd seen them up close. Whatever they were searching for, trying to climb to the top or stay up there once they had, it made them miserable. All I wanted for you was a normal life. Love.' I found my breath stuttering as she said it. I'd gone into our conversations so angry with her. I'd spent my life restless, looking for answers to myself. The more I learnt about Graham, about Nereus and his early death, the more it hurt she'd kept it all from me. But my life, the loving family, good husband, the nice home, the interesting if slightly dull job, had always been her dream for me and she'd achieved it. For the first time, the walls of ice which stood between us since I found she'd kept Graham's birthday cards from me began to melt.

'Did you miss Graham after you split?'

'It improved things between us. He was better as a friend than anything else.'

'Why did he leave then?' I asked. 'Not come back. If things were steady between you.'

'I thought he stayed away to avoid the handwringing over Nereus. Grieve in private. But then he wasn't back for three months —' She straightened a wrinkle in the tablecloth before looking at me. 'I really don't know, sweetheart.'

'You honestly don't think he had anything to do with it?'

'I can't see it, can't see he would.' I paused. I hadn't mentioned Thomas and the security company to Sadie, but I had to ask.

'How about Thomas Tee? Is there any way, do you think, he could have had some hand in Neil's death?'

'Thomas? I'd be amazed.'

'Why?'
'Need backbone to take a life. Thomas Tee had all the spine of a blancmange.'

62.

I too couldn't square Thomas as a murderer. He was oily, conniving, completely self-interested. But he seemed more hyena than lion. Bobby, however, no doubt fired by his rage at the Estate threatening his career and scaring his wife, was convinced.

He had got the two of us 'war-gaming' various scenarios after I'd shared my research with him. We would play out possibilities, speculating how each player might have reacted, how it could end up in a situation where Thomas killed Neil and Graham knew enough about it never to return.

'Why give him the money though?' he asked. 'If Neil was going to win the case, which we have to assume he was if Graham was happy to give up, why not just win the case. Get legal credit for the song. Keep four hundred grand.'

I thought Neil might have been worried about appeals, doubt being cast on his authorship, or that he genuinely did want to try to do right by Graham for stealing his song. Bobby wasn't convinced. And though I came up with the reasons, I'm not sure I was either. He didn't need to pay Graham. Certainly not that much. Neil may not have liked talking about money, but getting yourself in the equivalent of millions of debt by your own volition seemed bizarre even for Nereus Forbes.

That same afternoon a parcel arrived. I opened it to find Marina Maxwell-Clyde's book. I'd ordered it when I discovered the name of the mystery journalist from Paul Trevick a month or so before. It had been out of print and thus took some time to arrive. Normally, I would have added it to one of my teetering piles of books but I had a thought that perhaps the woman Nereus turned from Graham like a Soviet double agent might have had some insight into why he would have mortgaged his future avoiding a case he would have won.

I'd googled Mrs Maxwell-Clyde and found a picture of a beautiful woman in her seventies who'd had subtle but very effective remedial work on her face. She had luscious grey hair in a Farah Fawcett style and, as I'd already assumed from her writing a book on polo, reeked of wealth. When I opened her book there was a picture of a much younger Marina on the inside jacket. Although she had the same striking bone structure, she looked vastly different because although she had her hair in the same style, it was a vibrant copper colour.

She was a redhead. Like the woman who banged on the door and windows of 1 Cheyne Walk, desperate to get in, a few hours before Nereus Forbes died. I had found the red-headed woman.

63.

Bridgeforth Manor looked more like a location from *Downton Abbey* than a care home. Situated on the south side of the Isle of Wight, my pilgrimage to meet the ninety-two-year-old Marina Maxwell-Clyde involved coming across from Portsmouth on an actual hovercraft. My taxi brought me along the cypress-tree-lined drive to the estate and I took in the bowling-green lawns, topiary and well-dressed old people playing croquet.

A staff member in what looked like a footman's uniform guided me through gilded hallways to a suite of rooms where I found Marina Maxwell-Clyde rudely dismissing a young waitress pouring tea. I could see our conversation wasn't going to be a picnic. The footman introduced me and left us.

Marina stared out the window at what I thought might be a peacock. Of course there was a peacock. I told her I loved her book, and asked if she could tell me any other stories from that time. I had told the care home I was a fan of Marina's and wanted to use some of her memories for an anthology I was writing about the 1970s. But she was more switched on than I thought possible for a woman of her age. She'd seen the email I sent, knew exactly who I was and suggested I come straight out and ask what I'd come to find out.

'I've not much time,' she told me in a voice so cut-glass, I checked my fingertips for blood. I asked why she sold Graham out after he offered her the exposé.

'Your father had no story,' she said. 'Everyone knew Nereus

slept with anything animated and no one wanted to tangle with the gay question in public. If Graham had anything more than hearsay about the drugs, any criminality, we may have been in business. As it was, using him for access became the best course of action.'

Marina described how hurt Neil had been on the phone when she told him everything Graham had told her.

'He was quite upset by the end. Said he had a better story involving him and Graham. If I was patient, meaning if I canned the exposé, I could have the scoop.' The nurse Marina had been rude to entered with a gold-rimmed bowl of pills she put down without comment before leaving.

'What was the scoop?' I asked. Marina pinched her mouth together.

'Nereus died before he told me,' she said, a sliver of despair in her rheumy green eyes. I got distracted by the peacock fanning its tail outside the window, thought of Nereus swishing his Bronze Stingray cloak and it hit me.

'Was that what you were there for?' I said. 'The day he died.' Marina regarded her fingernails.

'He left a message at my office telling me to come to his house.'

'What time was that?'

'Lord, um, lunch perhaps?' I put it into my timeline. After Thomas, Matthew and Dominik had left, after his proposal to Greta but possibly before she returned early afternoon. 'I couldn't go. I was stuck at Henley with the Duchess of Kent. I managed to slip her briefly, got to a telephone in the back office. I didn't have Nereus's home number, so I rang his office, then Tommy Tee, Apollo Records. No answer. But I knew this was it, what he'd promised me. I phoned around, other papers, my little black book, asking if they'd heard rumblings, something involving Graham Harris. No one had.'

Something twitched in my head as she spoke. The answer to a question I'd never had the scaffolding to interrogate. If Graham hadn't got the flight, if it had been his car parked on Cheyne Walk that day, what had brought him there, why had he changed his plans so drastically? I'd assumed he'd been summoned, that Neil had asked him to come. But that never really made sense. Why would he drop everything to go to a man he hadn't seen in years who had treated him so badly. But someone else, one of the people Marina had spoken to that day, getting in touch saying Neil was about to reveal some big secret about him, was a far more compelling reason for him to go.

'No one knew a thing,' Marina continued. 'Reassured I wasn't going to get gazumped, I finished with the duchess and got a cab to Chelsea.'

'But when you got to the house, they didn't let you in.'

'They?'

'Greta Handverk was with Nereus by the time you got there, fourish?'

'Greta, right. Well, neither heard me. Almost broke a window banging. Thought about climbing the tree.' I swallowed, not wanting to interrupt, but pleased I'd cracked the possibility of a route down from Neil's room. 'I was bored of the society beat. It felt like whatever Neil had for me could possibly launch things.'

'What did you think Nereus was going to say?' Marina stood, walked with a ballet dancer's gait to the bright sunlight puddling below the French windows.

'I have no idea.'

'You must have an inkling.'

'It was fifty years ago,' she said. 'You seem to know far more than I do. What do you think?' I shook my head, annoyed. 'What do you think Neil was going to reveal about your father?' I pressed my tongue against my teeth, took a deep breath.

'That he was gay,' I said finally. 'Neil was going to tell you Graham was gay and that they had been lovers. A month or so before, first week of September, I believe they had sex. Maybe before that.'

Marina sighed, sat on a sofa behind her, suddenly seeming exhausted.

'Graham was so beautiful, such talent. But life happened to him, where Neil bent it to his will. It was an ugly time,' she said. 'We were all responsible for it.' She paled suddenly, finally seeming her age, and pressed a button I hadn't noticed tied to a cord round her neck. I asked if she thought I was right, if that was it, that Neil was going public against Graham, outing him at a time when it would bring him worldwide humiliation. But I'd lost her. The footman-type arrived. My time was up.

Live at Kekova

The *Live at Kekova* album ranks up there with Prince Andrew's 'Pizza Express' interview for hubristic missteps. No one ever took the blame, but three months after Nereus Forbes's death it showed up in London record shops before being swiftly recalled. I tracked one down, so you don't have to. And . . . it's not as bad as you'd expect a concert played on a submerged amphitheatre during a Mediterranean storm would be. Nereus's singing voice is back to its best and if you can tune out the chaos of mic stands and toga-clad dancers being blown over, certain songs, 'Krack the Decks', 'Missed Abyss', sound pretty great. Then there's the new song, 'What Did We Do'. It's knock-out melody and confessional lyrics, which could be about any one of the myriad mistakes he made near the end of his life, giving a bittersweet reminder of the era-defining talent taken from us too young. As the coastguard rush on to stop the concert, you can hear Nereus shouting, 'You coward, I love you,' at the storm, himself, or perhaps his mother whose death so derailed him.

Gabbi St Jean writing in the *Guardian*, 2021

64.

If Graham received the message Neil was going to out him as gay, revealing they'd been lovers, I can believe he might have gone to Cheyne Walk and killed him. For a man defined by shame, it would have been a survival instinct. Exposure like that would have been a sort of death, a public stoning. On top of which, it was the nail in the coffin of five years of agony at the hands of Neil Forbes, the man he was possibly in love with.

The method of murder goes against it being a crime of passion, a lover's tiff gone wrong. But it did fit with former detective Bryn's reservations about the time of death forensics gave, in that he would have done it soon after his car was seen on Cheyne Walk. If Graham was there to neutralise the threat to his reputation, I could see someone pragmatic like him having made a thorough plan on the drive up.

But was it conceivable Graham was gay, or that he and Neil had been lovers, even if only that one time a month before his death? He had been with my mother, they'd had me, he'd been brought up in a religious community disgusted by homosexuality. On top of which, he never talks about sex in the tapes, seems a little perplexed by it. Though that awkwardness could give credence to some confusion about his sexuality.

Despite the ickiness for me, I needed evidence relating to Graham's sex life so endeavoured to track down the only person I could think to ask – Harriet Tausig, the sex worker

Neil took Graham to who became his confidant for a time. I'd been prepared for a long search through various archives, possibly commissioning Stan to hit up eBay again, but when I googled Harriet I found an interview and photoshoot she'd given in 2016 to *Geisha*, an upmarket, art-fashion magazine. It seemed she had never left the square mile where she'd first met Graham and had become something of an icon to those who saw 'old Soho's' heyday of sex, hedonism and debauchery as some halcyon time for London. When asked how she thought she'd achieved her treasured status, she tells the interviewer it was because she hadn't changed, whatever the world thought of her.

'If you hold your nerve long enough,' she says, 'the times catch up and you end up respectable.' There were contact details for an agent who I got in touch with, which led to us meeting for lunch at the Dean Street Townhouse.

Harriet wore a bright-orange dress suit and had dark-red flecks through her silvery hair. She looked her seventy-four years, perhaps older even, but her eyes glistened with a timeless sparkle. After having a wonderful time chatting over gimlets and multiple sterling silver baskets of thin, salty frites, I asked if she thought Graham could have been gay.

'Youngsters think they came up with gender-bending, sexuality-on-a-spectrum stuff but we did it all years before. Just weren't so obsessed with putting people in boxes.'

'Is it possible though, Graham and Neil?' Harriet went on a five-minute reverie about the size of Neil's penis which in the gentle Somerset accent she'd retained was oddly sweet. She said Neil could talk almost anyone into bed, but didn't think he'd have managed it with Graham.

'Graham liked me, you see,' she said. 'Quite a lot, I think.'

'He was attracted to you?'

'Oh yes, and me him.' I mentioned that on the tapes Graham

said they hadn't slept together the first night they met and had barely mentioned her at all after that, despite them continuing to see each other.

'We never did the deed,' she said. I was surprised. I had thought he was being coy, perhaps to cover up some overlap with Sadie.

'Could he have been confused?' I asked. 'About his sexuality?'

'Lot of gay boys came to see us, cheap conversion therapy in their eyes, I always thought. Graham never seemed like that.' I asked about the first time they met, how overwhelmed Graham was.

'That's right, he couldn't get it up.' I said nothing for a while. Harriet ate more frites. Though I could imagine religious, small-town, twenty-one-year-old Graham being intimidated by the sexually confident, beautiful Harriet, he was still my dad. I didn't want to think of the nuts and bolts of it.

'Did that happen the other times you saw each other?' I asked.

'Didn't try all that much, we enjoyed chatting. But one night,' Harriet said, 'I wanted him. Weren't many men as good-looking as Graham. I worked my charms, things still weren't as they should be in that department. He explained his mother had caught him when he was ten or eleven, pulling his plonker.' I gulped, stopped taking notes. 'She threw him in a bath in the garden, scrubbed his tackle with a brush, threatened to do it in front of the whole congregation if she caught him again. I didn't try after that. Knew it wasn't what he was coming to me for.'

We sat in silence for a moment. I thought of the boy Graham, scarred for life in an iron tub in his garden. Of course he found a beautiful, sexually progressive woman like Harriet as terrifying as she was fascinating. His not being able to have sex with her didn't prove anything.

Harriet told me Graham stopped seeing her when things began with Sadie.

'I went to the gig at Hatful House because I missed him. He told me he'd found his person. He was smitten,' she said. 'I was jealous. I was a little in love with Graham Harris.'

'Do you think Neil loved him too?'

'Neil was an addict,' Harriet said. 'Needed love like one. But love's a feeling. I'm an expert. It peaks then decays. And it's inward-facing. It can be sort of selfish. What Neil and Graham were trying to do was the opposite. They wanted to build something with their music which would touch people, connect them to the rest of humanity. Maybe the work they did together in the early days felt like love, like sex in the studio, but it was never about them. Whatever their union was, they wanted to share it, wanted the world to see them. I always hoped they would work it out.'

I walked Harriet back to the Frith Street flat she'd been in for the last twenty years. On our way, every character we came across greeted her like minor royalty. I felt my phone buzzing with multiple messages but ignored them, not wanting to be rude. We stopped outside her building and as she searched her enormous Mulberry handbag, 'a gift from a sheik with fascinating appetites', for her keys, I glanced at my phone. Dozens of messages from Alan Sperryman. I flicked through quickly, names, internet handles I recognised followed by streams of code I couldn't read. But one word kept turning up in caps with exclamation marks, as if Alan was screaming it at me.

'BOT!!!!' He wrote several times every few lines. They were screenshots from a website I'd seen before, the domain at the top – ratemyprofessor.com. I read Alan's other messages – 'cyber-attack', 'smear campaign', 'bot-farm'. The student reviews of me which were threatening my job at the university had been made up. I threw my phone into my coat pocket, turned a full circle in the street, amazed.

Harriet was staring at me. I said I was fine.

'Looks like you need a brandy,' she said, taking me up to her bijou flat, decorated with a lifetime of gifts from powerful men. We had another drink; after the gimlets I was already tipsy and I found myself telling her everything. I could see why Graham had valued her company so much. When I came to the end, I asked whether she thought Thomas killed Neil, for him to be mounting this campaign against me and my family so I wouldn't uncover it.

Harriet shook her head with a certainty which worried me.

'It's money.'

'What do you mean?'

'Always money. His masters. A rumour, years back.'

'Nereus's masters?' She nodded, tight-lipped. 'What was the rumour?'

'They wanted to sell.'

65.

I left Harriet and raced back home, where I dived onto my laptop to find evidence the Estate were in the process of trying to sell Nereus's masters recordings, essentially the royalty rights to his songs. I had no idea what my part in it was yet, but it instantly seemed more likely than what Bobby and I had thought.

A digital campaign to bring down my career, bot-farms, spyware, surveillance. It would take money, a coordinated approach to undermine whatever I was close to uncovering which would only make someone trying to cover up a fifty-year-old murder look more guilty. On top of which, I'd found no evidence Thomas was there after he left in the morning, no proof of any wrong-doing and no one who knew him at the time thought he had the capacity to kill. But the Estate protecting a huge financial windfall made far more sense.

In the last decade there's been a move by hedge funds and private equity to buy up the master recordings of the biggest acts of the past century for eye-watering figures in the tens and sometimes hundreds of millions. The artists, or their children if they're dead, get a huge lump sum while the private equity people get their money back and then some in the long term, particularly when they aggressively 'monetise' the catalogue of songs. They do this by whoring them out to every TV show, film, social media company and advertising agency, for which they get a fee and the added bonus of everyone streaming or buying the old song again, netting them even more money. Everything that Neil was always so against when it came to his work.

The *nereusforever* WhatsApp group were appalled at the prospect.

'Can't be right,' Insurance Stan said.

'He'll be turning in his grave,' wrote Iris.

'This makes me so sad,' said Dr Hailee.

'Nereus wouldn't allow this,' Stan again.

'Five hundred mill. Minimum,' Lennox thought.

'Nothing stopping the Estate from a legal standpoint,' Helen Grady added.

'BASTARDS,' was Candi's contribution.

After their initial outrage, I could almost hear the keyboards hammering as they waded onto the internet to find proof. But after many hours of sharing links with each other, searching every Reddit, subreddit, LinkedIn, music industry rag, private equity portal, social media post, everywhere we could think of, none of us came up with the slightest hint of what Harriet had heard. My co-conspirators started to lose faith, hoping the rumour wasn't true so the music they loved would remain theirs and not be debased soundtracking dogfood ads and TikTok dances.

'There would be something in the public domain,' Dr Hailee said when we spoke on the phone the next day.

The other question which came up in a few private messages from members of the group, was what our investigation, more pertinently what I myself, had to do with the Estate selling the masters? Unless it was Thomas who killed Nereus, which we couldn't prove, how would finding out the truth behind his death have any impact on their ability to do a deal for the masters.

I argued it could be about Nereus's reputation, his image

as a tragic genius taken from us too soon, but I was clutching at straws. I wanted the lawyers I'd seen in the Estate office to be selling off his incredible catalogue to the highest bidder to make sense of it all. But, as Helen Grady pointed out, 'It's an office concerned with the management of royalties for a significant public figure, I'd be more surprised if you *hadn't* seen a bunch of lawyers in a high-level meeting.'

I feared they were right. Bobby, who'd reached out to music industry friends about the sale and had also drawn a blank, agreed. Another break in the story, another burst of sunlight eclipsed because what did I have to do with the sale of Nereus Forbes's music rights?

I looked around my summerhouse the day after I'd met Harriet and wondered whether I might have gone a little bit mad. I had reams of papers, dozens of hours of recordings, of material, pictures, maps, theories, stories, created narratives, neural pathways smashed like stepped-on meringue and, though I'd learnt lots of incidental facts about my parents and Neil Forbes along the way, I was no closer than I had been two years before. It was time to give up.

I began unpinning things from the walls, putting them in neat piles on the desk. For a filing cabinet, for the attic, for the shredder, I wasn't sure.

There was a sharp crack of a tree outside, a furious rustling in the leaves. I stood paralysed by the weight of a reckoning, not wanting to turn to face whatever was coming for me after last time. A hand banged on the French door.

I wheeled round to see Bobby, waving his phone, looking distraught. It was our daughter Sara on the phone. She was terrified, almost incomprehensible. Two men in a car had been following her.

66.

We drove down to Brighton to collect Sara the moment we got off the phone with her. She was still scared when we arrived. I was almost numb with guilt as she told us she had had the sense someone had been watching her for weeks, kept seeing the same man wherever she went, but dismissed it as paranoia. Then her housemate saw the person she'd described, pale with a ginger complexion and glasses, in a car on their street. He had a camera with a long lens. She called us after she'd seen him following her home from a tapas bar she'd been at with friends from her Middle East Action Group.

I begged her forgiveness, still reeling from the idea that my looking into my parents could bring people to be surveilling my daughter in an entirely different city. Sara absolved me.

'You couldn't have known,' she said.

'None of us could,' Bobby added, following us into the overgrown garden of their student house.

'Someone was in our garden,' I said. 'They put something on my phone. I knew enough.'

'I'm fine,' Sara said, putting her hand on mine. 'We're all fine.'

But I wasn't. I'd got so lost in the past, I'd forgotten to protect my present. We went to the police. They logged our report but made it plain there was little they could do. I felt too ashamed of what I'd dragged my family into to tell anyone on my *nereusforever* group. We brought Sara home.

The following day, the girls sat Bobby and I down for a family summit at our kitchen table.

'We want to help,' Sara said.

'Absolutely not,' I said. Bobby took a deep breath. 'This was never meant to involve any of you. I should have stopped a long time ago. When you got the poster, I shouldn't have even started. Your lives, your futures –'

'This is our lives,' Delphi said. 'Your mum, your dad. That's our lives, that's who we are.'

'You don't have to do this on your own,' said Sara.

'I don't have to do it at all,' I said, looking at Bobby. 'It might be it's gone too far.' Delphi was about to argue but then Bobby stood up and marched into the garden. I thought he was taking a moment to calm himself from how angry he was with me but then the three of us saw him emerging from the summerhouse, carrying the enormous reel-to-reel tape player. I opened the door for him and he plonked it on the table.

'Mum's right,' he said. 'It's gone too far.' He pressed the play button. The four of us sat and listened to Graham's tapes in their entirety. In the following days, they waded through all my theories, my thoughts, and quizzed me on many points I hadn't thought of. It felt so nourishing having them by my side after searching on my own for so long. But at the end of all our conversations they had only one thought.

'We have to find Grandpa.'

After Delphi and I found the guitars for sale and decided Graham was alive, I'd redoubled my efforts to find him for a while. But the Milanese music shop proved a dead end as the manager who'd bought the guitars had moved back to Croatia. While Sadie, who should have been my best source, refused to engage with my questions about where the birthday cards had come from.

'Even if I'd paid attention to postmarks,' she said, 'it was thirty years ago. I can barely remember the name of the school I took you to every day.' I didn't believe her for a second. But whenever I tried to press her on it, she'd become evasive and even if I had got an answer, the chances Graham would have stayed in the same place for so long after was very slim. With nowhere to go, I was forced to stop looking. Perhaps part of me didn't ever really want to make real the figure I'd conjured out of some recordings and the memories of an unreliable mother.

My daughters, however, with an eye on some reality-TV-style emotional resolution, wouldn't take no for an answer. They reasoned whether he did it or not, he had to know something. Why else would he never return home?

I wished I'd fully engaged my two girls' help before. Watching them navigate unknown crevices of the internet like they'd been born with keyboards in their hands made me feel like a chimp picking termites out of a mound with a stick. The summerhouse got too crowded so we moved everything into the kitchen, piles of papers fighting for space against empty wine glasses and leftover bowls of drying cereal.

One afternoon, Sara suggested we go through Nereus's music again to look for clues to Graham's whereabouts in the songs. Delphi rearranged our living room into a listening studio and the two girls went through every album, every B-side, foreign export. Then they looked at Graham's music, mostly through bootlegs sent over by my *nereusforever* friends. His words never mentioned a place, weather, an atmosphere even. It was all women being angels, sacred love, clichés about 'rocking you baby'. Then there wasn't any solo material to speak of after he stopped working with Nereus. Nothing he recorded was ever pressed.

'What about "Lady Theia"?' Delphi asked when we'd combed through the final pile of bootleg Marshalls records.

'What about it?'

'His version, his words. Is there anything in there?' I hadn't shown the girls the scrap of paper Paul Trevick had given me. I hadn't shown anyone. Paul aside, I wasn't sure anyone apart from Sadie and the people in the room at Trident Studios that day had heard those words. I felt they were mine, like I'd written them even, embarrassed for anyone to read them. I reluctantly handed the sheet of lyrics to my daughters.

'His writing's like yours,' my youngest said. 'Incomprehensible.' I took the page back and they stood over my shoulder as I transcribed the song for them in block capitals.

'Could it be Spain?' Sara said as I was halfway through the third verse.

'Oh yeah,' said Delphi.

'What?' I said. 'Why?'

They pointed at the line – 'drops in the sand, arenas bland now'. In the section before, Graham takes the idea of the blood in my veins outside my body, what he'd do to protect it.

'Why Spain?' I said.

'They went to a bullfight,' said Delphi. 'Graham, Sadie, Nereus.'

'Drops of blood in the sand, an arena,' Sara said. 'It's the bit in the tapes, when they're in Europe where he seems most, I don't know, awestruck.' I looked at the rest of the words, trying to see if there was anything else.

It could have been Spain. If I'd grown up in the bitter cold of East Yorkshire, I could see myself making a life in Spain. It wasn't too far from Nice if that's where he'd flown to that day. In addition I'd seen the sketches Neil had made of the bullfighting, the arena, how he'd used the hierarchy of the toreadors in his creation of the military rankings of the Pacifican people. The visit had made an impression on them all.

'Spain is,' I said, 'well, it's a pretty big search area.' Delphi and Sara shared an eyeroll and marched upstairs to their laptops.

Within an hour, they'd identified the phrase 'with the Christians and Moors' on 'Brimstone Rattle' on *Apotheosis* and a small sketch of a huge bridge over a gorge in one of the photos from Nereus's sketchbooks from 1971. Delphi put it all, bullfighting, Moors, a bridge on a gorge onto some AI thing and it came up with the name of a town. Ronda, an hour or so into the mountains from Malaga. Hemingway had loved it, George Orwell too. In an odd bit of cosmic synchronicity, the company who made my TV used a picture of its bridge as part of the slideshow on its default screensaver. I rang Sadie immediately.

'Did the birthday cards come from Spain?' I asked. Sadie said nothing. 'From Andalusia?' Still she said nothing. 'From a town called Ronda.' Sadie let out a sigh.

67.

Two days later, the four of us boarded a flight to Malaga and drove our hire car up to an Airbnb we'd booked just outside Ronda. The town was nestled in verdant hills an hour's drive from the Mediterranean. I could see how perfect a place it would be for a man who wanted to run away from the world. Though whether from the threat of incarceration for murder or from a dead-end life and his family, I still didn't know. I hoped this would be the end.

As soon as I'd put the town out to my conspirators, it didn't take long to find Graham. Candi and Alan Sperryman, who'd met and got on famously, found an artisan olive oil press based in Ronda which supplied many of Soho's restaurants. The owner of one told them she'd asked to speak with the man who supplied the olives and was surprised to be put on to an Englishman with a Northern accent. We rang the phone number the restaurant owner gave them which was answered by a Spaniard called Pau, a manager at the olive oil press. We asked to speak to a supplier of his called Graham Harris. The man on the end of the line paused just long enough before saying he didn't know any Graham for us to know we'd found him. I explained who I was, why exactly I was looking for Graham Harris. He told me he couldn't help, but later that night, I received an email from his company. It had Mr Graham in the subject line. The main text contained only an email address and a Spanish phone number.

I couldn't speak to Graham on the phone so I wrote him an email. Graham wrote back quickly to say he didn't want to exchange messages but that if I came over, he'd meet me. He expressed no shock, or surprise at my getting in touch, merely signed off rather formally he was 'so very glad' to hear from me. We arranged to meet at Ristorante Pedro Romero, opposite what I'd discover was the oldest bullring in Spain. We were due to meet at two. I was going alone but Bobby, the girls and I had a reconnaissance coffee there in the morning. I didn't want anything to surprise me as I met the father I'd last seen when I was five.

With its Ottoman tiling and thousands of ancient bullfighting posters groaning from the walls, the restaurant was like a portal to the past. You could feel centuries of preening matadors flanked by buxom monobrowed women on the surrounding tables, Hemingway with his bunch of aristocrats and wastrels ogling them all – not too dissimilar to how I imagined Neil's rabble in their heyday. We visited the bridge on the edge of the cliffs afterwards and I recognised it from the sketches in Neil's notebooks. A fictionalised version of it features in Hemingway's book *To Whom the Bell Tolls*. Fascist sympathisers are thrown off it, a passage inspired by real events. As I imagined the young Francoists being dashed on the rocks below, knowing I was shortly to meet a man I thought could have murdered his best friend, I could feel a metaphor circling over my head with the honey buzzards.

Graham was at the café when I arrived. He was still stocky, too big for the small table, and had a long-baked tan with deep, distinguished wrinkles. He had most of his grey-white hair cut short and accompanied by a smart, cropped beard – he looked fantastic. He stood when he saw me, opened his arms before clutching his hands in front of him and blinked too much as I approached.

'Hello Winnie,' he said. The only time anyone had called

me that was in the birthday cards he'd written me. He looked like he was going to pull a chair out for me but thought better of it and returned to his seat. I sat and watched as he poured me a glass of water. I wish I could describe to you how I felt, but I was so overwhelmed seeing this person I'd made a myth in the previous two years, arriving at some kind of end point, I felt paralysed. He offered me bread, got the waiter to bring me a Sprite, it was September but still very hot. He didn't know what to do with his fingers, kept picking up and rearranging the bread basket and napkins.

After a few moments the fog cleared. I began to find his busying around the normalities of a casual lunch-date, like it was a daddy-daughter thing we did every week, just the tiniest bit endearing. Which was very annoying. I wanted to be angry with him. It was embarrassing how pleased I was to see him. He asked about my life. I told him about my career, my husband, Sara and Delphi and what they were doing. Graham's face trembled with delight as I spoke, he'd nod, trying to keep a smile from breaking out, or perhaps he was fighting back tears. It was hard to tell.

He said he'd moved to the finca he still lived in in the hills above a few months after he arrived in southern Spain at the end of 1977. He spent his days caring for and maintaining the six olive groves on his land, selling the crops to the press Candi had been in touch with. Once the harvest was over in November, he spent the colder months driving to the coast every morning to fish from a small boat he kept in nearby Estepona, selling his catch to local restaurants, eating what he couldn't sell. He kept four donkeys. When Graham got into his late sixties, he employed two brothers, Jorge and Julien, to manage the groves but, even at seventy-five, he told me he still gets out there every day to oversee things and, when the weather is clement, tries to make it out to sea.

After some time, I began to shift in my seat. I wanted to be back with my family, my real family, not this man who thought of me as Winnie, as a toddler he could have chosen to see grow into who I became. The feeling built from my feet, a prickly heat almost, I could feel the blush rising into my face until I interrupted him.

'Why though?' I asked. 'Why are you here, in Spain, on your own at all? What happened?'

He bowed his head, closed his eyes. He'd known I wasn't just coming to reconnect. A waiter came over, Graham dismissed him with a wave. He looked at me with those sparkling blue eyes, their almost alarming depth.

'Where do you want me to start?'

68.

'He sent a white and gold Bentley to the house to collect me,' Graham said. 'Saw it parked by the fountain out front when I got out of the bath.' I had told Graham everything I knew about his part in the story. About the Highlands, the song, the legal challenge, the tell-all to Marina Maxwell-Clyde, the eye-popping pay-off. What I didn't know was why he'd been seen going into 1 Cheyne Walk the month before Nereus died.

'George Niven was there, Neil's driver. He'd been sent to get me. Couldn't believe the cheek of it. Sent George back without me. But once he's gone, I thought about the pictures I'd seen of Neil in America. The state he was in. I had been worried about him. Couldn't help it. So I drove up.'

Neil answered the door, skinnier than ever, perhaps accentuated by an oversized scale-effect kimono. He seemed manic, detached as he led him upstairs to the living room. He offered to make drinks but Graham said he'd do it, concerned Neil might collapse with any effort. The kitchen he walked into was a mess, bottles, full ashtrays, drug paraphernalia strewn on every surface.

'The whiskies got Neil back into the room. It was funny, but it felt good it being just the two of us together. Felt comfortable.' I nodded, I'd had the same feeling for a moment sitting opposite Graham.

'I didn't say much. Let him talk. He said he'd given up looking for the omnichord, for now. I couldn't help laugh at that.

He did too. Then he came out with it. "I want you to come back," he said. Working together.'

'What? Really?' The acrimony between the men had seemed so febrile over 'Lady Theia', Graham bankrupting Neil, such a severing act, I couldn't imagine how they'd get in the same room, let alone try to make music together. 'Weren't you surprised?'

'I was,' he said. 'But I suppose it was what I was hoping for as I drove up to town. What I dreamed he'd ask me.' I shook my head, couldn't believe what I was hearing. 'I'd have dropped everything, how angry I was at him leaving, the law stuff, I'd have given him the song if we could have worked together again.'

'How could you though?' I said. 'He screwed you over, stole your song.'

'You don't know what it was like, Winnie. Those early days.' He took a drink of water to steady himself. 'Neil said as much that night. Thought it was the best work he'd done, the best it had ever felt.' I imagined how hearing that could have been a magical balm to the wounds Neil had inflicted.

Neil said after Penny died, Graham was the only person he wanted to see. He needed how strong Graham made him feel.

'He said he'd felt nothingness without me.' I felt something coming, a confession of love, the sense of something converging in Graham's story.

The two men drank more. Neil told him about how difficult the last two years had been. He was delighted Matthew had left, how desperate he was to try to mend things with Otis, admitted Thomas had started to scare him a little.

'What did you talk about?'

'I told him about you. I filled my days with doing up the house, that mad house I bought to get back at him, but I wasn't living then, not really. Weekends I had with you were the only bright spots.' It was heartening that I hadn't imagined how excited he seemed to spend time with me. He did love me. I was his life.

As booze overcame them, Neil and Graham talked of the future like they hadn't since the early days. Neil's obsession with Noh theatre, Indonesian shadow puppetry. Telling Graham how much he'd love playing with Kittisak, his desire to bring Kathoey singers from Cambodia for the album.

'It was a rush hearing his plans again, the places his mind went,' Graham said. Neil wanted Graham back and it felt real. 'I wanted it, really wanted it.' About one o'clock in the morning Neil danced in wearing a Sri Lankan wooden mask and a fur stole. Graham asked if it was Greta's.

'I asked if they were in love,' he said. I felt butterflies, certain this was it, a confession of love – Graham to Neil, Neil to Graham. 'He said he had been, he might be again, but like it didn't matter either way. He got this little carved stone icon out to show me, all excited. Told me it was something to do with Nefertiti, on about the Egyptians' relationship with the sun, language as visual.' Graham rubbed his thumbs into his eyes. 'And I realised, in that moment, Neil loved the little statue far more than his girlfriend of two years. But just like with Greta, his love for it would fade, perhaps come back, most likely not.' He moved my glass on the table, dragging a ring of damp across the white tablecloth. 'He made me feel so special, like I'd been chosen. When we first met but even just that night. Like being touched by God. But I finally understood, that's how everyone felt with Neil. Fans still feel like it, even those born years later. That was his genius. But I'd been on the other side of it. And when that spotlight turned somewhere else, it hollowed me out. Warped me for good.'

Neil got drunker, sloppier. Graham thought he might have escaped upstairs to his bedroom for a fix, though not in front of him. He talked about the reaction to *Atlantis Drained*. He'd raged against it at first but had come to see it was just that the world had changed. Vietnam was over, the man in the street wanted to connect after years of alienation. Neil needed to make things lighter, more accessible, more grounded.

'You're wrong,' Graham told him. 'You've got it dead wrong. You don't need to be accessible, you're Nereus Forbes.' He reminded Neil of the graphic novel he'd shown him that first night at Penny's house. How he had pitched it as a stage show, a rock opera, the biggest, most extravagant the world had ever seen. Neil said something about money, the disastrous tour he'd come back from.

'If you give them something bigger than anyone else in the world could imagine, none of that will matter.' Neil's eyes sharpened, greedy for the future Graham was painting. 'But it has to be huge, colossal. Somewhere no one has ever performed before. Somewhere impossible. Mythical. Something they'll talk about for centuries.'

Neil took Graham by the hands and danced him in a circle, feeling he was right, knowing he had to be right. He said they needed to get started right away. The music had to be all new, or at least only songs they'd done together, when it felt right. He went to get his phone book, planning to get a studio open for them in Kensington within the hour.

Neil had the phone in the crook of his arm when he turned and saw the look on Graham's face.

'I can't do it,' Graham said. 'Can't be involved.' Neil was dumbfounded, put the phone down, half-collapsed onto the sofa.

'Why?'

'I just can't.'

'I need you, Graham. I can't do it without you.'

'Nereus Forbes can never go back. It has to be you. Just you. I'm the past. It's the only way it'll work.'

Neil tried to convince him, said he was his rock, how he kept the train on its tracks, the sort of phrases he used to love to hear in the back of the Teal Eel years before. Graham picked up the little statue Neil had become obsessed with.

'I'm a bloke from Whitby who plays guitar,' he said. He held the little icon up to Neil. 'This is myth, legend, this is you. You have to be better.' Neil stared at Graham for a long time. Taking him in in a whole new light. He opened his arms, took Graham into them.

'We stood like that for a bit, a few minutes. It was goodbye.'

69.

'Sorry, what?' I said, stopping abruptly. The two of us had been walking round the stands of the old bullring to escape the afternoon sun. 'You were desperate to play with him again, why did you say no?'

'I wanted to write with Neil again. But that wasn't why he wanted me back. It was there in what he said. Talking about the "man in the street", doing something "grounded". He wanted me because he needed ordinary. I hoped what we'd had was real, that it could be again. As the night wore on, I could see I was just another means to an end. First time we met he used me to get noticed by Otis de Kock, it never stopped after that.' Graham walked to the barriers to watch young bullfighters practising their passes in the middle of the arena.

I wasn't sure his assessment of that night was right. I could see another world where Neil was grieving, unwell, having realised he was surrounded by questionable people and simply wanted the man he'd felt most comfortable with back by his side. Whatever his true intentions, it must have hurt Graham immeasurably to think himself so worthless in Neil's eyes. I joined him at the front of the stand, looked out at the teenage boys swishing their capes at a metal bull's head in silence.

'The concert, on the island,' I said. 'You made him do it. On purpose.' Graham cleared his throat. 'Pumped him full of air, fed his ego to make sure. Knowing his money problems, the drugs, his poor health. You wanted to ruin him?'

'Suppose I did.'

'Were you glad it was a disaster?'

'Not a bit. Not a bit.' We walked down to the lower level, stepped onto the sand. As the boys cheered each other, I thought of Graham and Neil holding each other in that goodbye embrace by the festoon-light of Chelsea bridge through the sitting-room window.

'You could have walked away instead,' I said.

'Should have.'

'Or not gone to see him at all, surely you knew no good would come from it?' Graham nodded, eyes on the fighters still. 'Did you love him?' He looked at me, considered his answer.

'I didn't want to. I suppose I couldn't not.'

'Did he love you back?'

Graham traced a triangle in the sand with his foot. 'Far as he could. He wanted all of life, its entirety, people too, spirit, their essence. Your mother never let him in.' He stopped and looked at me, we'd walked a little further towards the centre of the arena. 'It's why I was drawn to her. I've realised that. She was far stronger than me.'

'So you abandoned Neil first, being with her?' He smiled.

'I think I had to. He spent his life abandoned. What made him so appealing to us all.' Graham put his hand on my shoulder, the first physical contact I'd had with him in fifty years. 'But it devoured you.'

We walked back out of the stadium and into the streets. He presented an arm to me and I took it as we walked towards Alameda de Tajo, a small park that overlooked the vast gorge below.

Neil had wanted Graham back in his life. Graham had seen him teetering on the precipice of his health, his sanity, financial ruin and he'd knowingly pushed him off. If he'd wanted revenge for being cast aside for newer, shinier people, for being mocked in the press, for stealing his greatest creation, surely he got that.

I still didn't have the answer I needed. Not who killed Nereus, what difference would that make now? No, Graham seemed like so many of the best parts I'd constructed out of hearing his voice, combing through his story. He wasn't someone who would ever have chosen to be an absent father. I needed to know why he'd stayed away.

70.

We retired to a bench in the shade overlooking the gorge, carrion crows flying overhead in perpetual squawking motion. My husband and daughters would be round the pool in our apartment pretending to read their books as they worried about how I was bearing up in the heat, how long I'd been away, probably my entire mental state. I was glad someone was worrying about it, because I felt all at sea high up in the Spanish mountains.

I asked Graham outright.

'Why have you been out here hiding your whole life?' I said. *Why did you abandon me?*

He told me the story of what happened on 28 October 1977.

Just before one o'clock, Graham fired up the heaters of his Jaguar to clear the windscreen in preparation for driving to Heathrow. He was conflicted about the trip, having been due to have me at Methuselah that weekend which, he assured me, was always the highlight of his month. But he knew the Jordanians wouldn't take kindly to him saying no. He knew the food would be good, the weather nicer than it was in Sussex and was looking forward to a change from his life of doing up his house alone every day.

He went inside to get his bags and guitar to hear the phone ringing. It was Clive Dors telling him Marina Maxwell-Clyde had been calling around about something involving him.

Having seen the news about the Sunken Island concert, he was concerned Neil had worked out Graham had put him up to it and was striking back. It took longer than expected to get the Jaguar started and Graham was fairly sure he'd miss his plane. There was another flight at eight and, given their resources, knew the Jordanians would buy him another ticket.

'I decided to go talk to him. Cheyne Walk wasn't too far from Heathrow.' This seemed out of character. I wasn't sure what Graham thought he'd achieve or what he was worried about Neil revealing. Unless he hadn't been truthful with me about the physical nature of their relationship. I let him go on.

Encountering rush-hour traffic around London, Graham didn't get to Chelsea until a little before five. Nereus let him in. He was alone, rubber tubing tied around his upper arm. The two of them went up to the living room, this time Graham didn't drink. He had expected Neil to be down after Turkey but he was giddy. There was an awful smell of burnt fish and a strange energy in the air.

'I've got a new project,' Neil said. 'The best one yet.' Although Neil's eyes were wider than Graham had ever seen, blood-shot, heroin-ravaged, he seemed disconcertingly lucid. Graham started to apologise about the concert. Neil laughed it off like it hadn't happened. He was manic. Graham tried to ask about Marina, about what Clive had told him but again, Neil barely acknowledged it.

'Don't you want to know about it?' Neil said. 'My project.'

'Uh, yeah,' Graham said.

'I suppose you could call it a brand-new persona.'

'OK.'

'Daddy,' Neil said. He told Graham his new persona was Daddy. Papa. Father.

For a moment, sat on the bench in Ronda, I had no idea what that part of the story meant. I smiled, looked to Graham expecting him to go on, to explain what he meant. He looked at me, took my hand in his. Then it all came at once. Marina, a huge scoop involving Graham, revealing Neil as a father.

71.

'Holy shit, no!' I stood up and almost ran away from him as I realised what he was saying. 'You can't be . . . No!' I said, leaning on the stone balustrades over the gorge. My breath caught, heaved. It couldn't be true. It couldn't. Graham walked up and stood beside me. I turned to him, searching for some sign that he was making it up, some sick joke, but his face was stone.

'I'm sorry, Winnie,' he said.

'Don't.'

'He told me you weren't mine. That you were his kid.' It felt like someone was blowing up a balloon in my throat. 'I asked when. He said the last night at Hatful House. End of the tour. Just once.'

I didn't want to believe what Graham was telling me, that Nereus Forbes was my biological father. It upturned everything I'd ever known about myself, every fragment of identity I ever thought I understood. But I'd spent two years piecing this story together, what I realised was my story, and what he was saying fit. Graham had let Sadie down that night at Hatful House. Shown weakness which shattered her view of him as someone who'd look out for her above all else. Whereas Neil had been there for her when the men attacked her on stage. Then, when she was scared, at her most vulnerable, telling her how losing his father had left him missing a part of himself, revealing humanity under the world-conquering ego. Neil had been in love with Sadie. I'd been sure of it. He saw her as a blessed Madonna figure who might rescue him. She'd always kept her distance because she thought him like her father, chewing up and spitting out women without regard, but that night she'd seen another side of him and, as most others who'd found themselves in Nereus's room, found she couldn't resist. And the following day she left the band.

'What did you do?' I asked. 'After he told you.'

'Nothing for a while,' Graham said. 'Stared at a painting he had, a Hokusai. Townspeople bringing in the rice harvest, pointing at deer standing on the top of a hill. Got a print of it up at the house.'

'You believed him?' Graham turned away, pinched tears from his eyes. 'Did you know?'

'Not that it was him but . . . Your mother and I tried, you know, in the bedroom. We tried many, many times. Once or twice it was sort of OK. Enough to believe her when she said we must have conceived on a certain very drunken night near the end of the tour.'

Neil knew the baby was his because Harriet had told him about Graham's problem. He told Sadie about his suspicions in the hospital the day after I was born, when Graham went to get glasses for the champagne Neil brought. Sadie told Neil, just once, he would have no part in my life and Graham would be my father. Neil accepted it. She made him promise. Swear on his mother's life. He did.

'Why?' I asked, furious at the man I could no longer see as some mythical rock star but as a person, my father. 'Why did he accept that?'

'To protect me, that's what he said that night. And that he thought I'd be better at it.' I blinked, anger catching up to me, thinking how much better the Graham I hadn't seen my whole life had ended up being. 'He was scared of becoming his father. All three of us were.'

'What changed?' I said.

'He thought you needed to know the truth,' Graham said. 'It's what he told me but that was crap. He'd never done anything for anyone else before. He was hurting is all, felt abandoned. He needed a lift. He thought you could be it. Just a part of his next reinvention.' I thought of that day. The concert, the bankruptcy, the debts, drugs, Greta refusing his proposal. Although it seemed abhorrent he would upturn the life of a five-year-old to perk himself up, it was consistent with everything I'd learnt about Nereus Forbes. He hadn't thought about what it would do to Graham, to Sadie who'd done everything she could to protect me from scandal and attention.

'I was upset, thrown like you wouldn't believe,' Graham said. 'But also, I had this moment of clarity. I had to stop him going public. I thought about trying to reason with him, to make him see sense. But his eyes, I could see it. In his mind, this was it. Nereus as father. Winter his most special little acolyte. I knew what he did to people, made them fall in love with him, cast them off when he was done. I couldn't let that happen to you.'

Graham saw the tourniquet hanging from Neil's arm, remembered the candles, spoons, burnt foil, wraps of powders, syringes he'd seen when he'd been in the house a month before.

'I told Neil I wanted a fix. Thought he'd tell me no, forbid it if he was so keen to protect me. But he seemed delighted. Like it was me just agreeing with his plan to come out as your dad, ruining your life, cuckolding me in front of the world. He was on another planet. He told me the stuff was upstairs, offered to go do it but I said I would, told him to get us drinks and I'd see him up there. When he finally joined me I said I'd done mine. He took the syringe off me. I pulled the rubber tight on the top of his arm. I thought too tight but he didn't notice. I watched him stick the junk inside him and then I lay down on the bed. It hit him fast. I'd put so much in.' Neil lay down next to Graham, side by side on the bed, his eyes opening and closing slowly as the huge hit of heroin flooded his bloodstream.

When Neil's eyes stopped opening, Graham put his arm around him, pulled his body close. He held him as his breathing slowed, until it stopped, as his body turned cold.

72.

Graham stayed in the room for a couple of hours after Neil passed. He made a plan. He would try to make it look like an accident. No one had seen him go in and out. He hadn't told anyone he was going to see Neil. He undid lids of pill bottles, spilled cocaine onto the table, tried to create the scene of a drug binge. But it wasn't enough. He thought of the detective books his mother had read in secret on their holidays to Skegness. There was always a locked room. He would lock the door from the inside, then there was no way anyone would think someone else had been there. But how would he get out?

He opened the bedroom window and looked down to see the large tree-branch. He'd spent his childhood climbing trees, had bought a chainsaw recently and had been doing his own tree surgery at Methuselah. He was still strong from the building sites and thought he could do it. The street was quiet, secluded. The only danger was one of the neighbours seeing him but they were mostly older. He waited until ten o'clock when he was sure most would have gone to bed and made his descent.

'The tree was good,' he said. 'Like a hand carrying me down.' He jumped onto the balcony, then again onto the soil of the front garden, leaving the deep footprints Dale had identified in the crime scene photographs.

He drove to Dover, where he made the anonymous call to the police alerting them to Cheyne Walk, before taking a ferry to France. Graham drove long into the night until, the next morning, he found an auberge in the hills overlooking Lake Annecy in eastern France near the Swiss border.

'The waiting was agony,' he said. 'Longer it took to be in the news, more convinced I was they were coming for me. But then they announced it. That it was an accident.' Graham's plan had worked. He spent a further two weeks in France before driving on to northern Spain then, over a few months, making his way to the south.

'Did Sadie know?' I asked. Graham shook his head.

'When I didn't come back, if she'd heard about the Marina thing she could have worked it out. I didn't tell her.' I wondered. My mother was sharp as a switchblade, it seemed almost impossible she hadn't figured out what happened, but if the police are telling you the opposite you wouldn't necessarily go to murder.

'Didn't she ever reach out, when you didn't come home?'

'Your mother only wrote to me once. Had my address from the cards I sent you. She needed money.'

'When?'

'Just before the millennium. I sold the house.' I laughed. I was in my mid-twenties, doing a master's after going nowhere with film school. Mum was paying for all of it, my rent, tuition, everything. I'd never questioned how she had the money. I wanted to hate Graham for what he'd done, but he'd sold his house at the drop of a hat, as soon as Sadie asked. I thought of what he'd given up to buy Methuselah, given up the song he'd written for the daughter he thought was his.

'Didn't you want to have a relationship with us, then?'

'I always wanted a relationship with you but – knowing what I knew about you, and what I'd done.'

'But I lost two fathers that night. I would never have needed to know, and you'd got away with it.'

'My old man, what he'd seen in the war, he wore it. You

would have known, Winnie.' I flinched when he called me that. 'And look at you, your family, your home.' I'd shown him pictures, had plans to introduce him in the following days but wasn't sure I could, knowing what he'd done. 'I thought you'd be better off without me and I was right.'

'You did it all for me?' I looked at him head on. 'Neil had taken your band, your song, then he took your daughter. You wanted to destroy him for it.' Graham ran his hands over the cracked paint of the balustrade over the canyon.

'That might be right,' he said. 'But I had to think it was for you. Just to live.'

I left him soon after. I texted Bobby to tell him I wouldn't be back for some time and walked up a mountain track which led nowhere. I thought about what Harriet had said about Graham. How certain she was he liked her, that he wasn't gay even though he couldn't perform sexually. He was impotent.

He was impotent in a time of free love where sex defined everything. How intoxicating, how agonising it must have been for him living in close quarters with a wellspring of libido like Neil. Perhaps he thought he'd learn from him, absorb some of his voracious sexual desire by osmosis. If sex had to be a secondary concern for Graham, I understood why he would have thrown himself with such wild abandon into his collaboration, his meeting of minds with Neil. Making music with Neil might have been the closest Graham ever came to having sex. But he knew being around Neil was destroying him. Sadie saved him from that.

But she had desires too. Graham had said they'd tried, again and again. In Graham she'd found everything she wanted. She must have been desperate for him to be the one. But he couldn't be, not in that way anyway. A moment of weakness with the most sexually attractive man on the planet. I found it hard to blame her for what she did. But I wasn't sure I could ever forgive her for the lies.

73.

'Mum, you're his heir!' Delphi said some time after I told Bobby and the girls. I shook my head, not sure why she was focusing on something which seemed irrelevant compared to what I'd just said.

'Oh God,' Sara seemed to join her wavelength. 'The Estate think you're going to make a claim.' I still didn't understand. It had been a long day. Bobby seemed to get it.

'It has to be,' he said. 'Thomas Tee must have known the truth, and when he found out you were looking into it, employed a security company to scare you off. Nereus having a legitimate heir wouldn't just screw up the sale of the masters, they'd lose control of everything.'

'It was a rumour, we don't know it's true,' I said. 'We don't know if any of it's true.' I was grasping because I didn't want any of it, anything I'd just learnt, to be true. But of course they had to be right. If Thomas didn't kill Neil, why else would the Estate want to derail me from finding the truth? I had to sit down, gripping the leather sofa cushions beneath me like they were a pair of therapy cows. It hit me as if for the first time. I was Nereus Forbes's daughter.

The following afternoon we went up to Graham's finca. I hadn't slept the night before and hadn't thought I'd want to see him again before we left for home. But he'd invited me up as I left him, said he wanted to meet my daughters. He thought they might want to meet his donkeys.

It was as awkward as you'd imagine when we arrived. He served up fresh-squeezed orange juice and made us taste the olive oil made from his groves. It was delicious. He gave me a gallon of it to take home. We met the donkeys. Which was a surprisingly good icebreaker. We sat on his veranda together, the girls telling him about themselves. Delphi asked about certain production effects on the albums, Sara asking many more questions about the donkeys. At one point I caught Graham leaning back marvelling at the girls talking ten to the dozen, eyes moist. He couldn't believe how wonderful they were.

The mood changed when the subject turned to Thomas Tee trying to sell Nereus's music rights and the lengths they'd gone to to make sure I didn't find out my true parentage. Graham grew incensed as I told him, eventually marching down the hills in front of us. For a moment I thought he was going to go full King Lear as we watched him barking at bushes and fences but after some time he stopped, a silhouette against the orange glow of the dying sun. He strolled back to us, huge frame blocking out the sun.

'We have to stop it,' he said. I looked at Bobby, doubtful. I wanted revenge on the bastards for meddling with our family, scaring my daughter, but what could we do to a multimillion-dollar company willing to engage some high-level private security company against us? Walk up and ask them nicely? Graham saw I wasn't convinced. 'When you listen to "Found Them There", what do you hear? What is the feeling?'

'Graham –'

'It's about how hard it is to contain our love to one person?' Delphi said.

'Imagine it selling tampons,' Graham said. '"Seal of Approval".'

'How it feels to be alone,' Bobby joined in the game.

'Think of them using it to flog drain cleaner. Neil never,

ever allowed it. We could have all been richer back then, more than you'd believe. Neil knew the songs, our songs were worth more than money.' It was about legacy. Graham still felt he had to protect it, just as he'd tried to protect me. He'd killed for that. Perhaps I could find it in myself to take on some lawyers.

'We won't win,' I said.

'We've got the truth.' I cocked my head at him. It felt brazen of him to talk about the truth.

'It's tens of millions of pounds,' I said.

'Hundreds, more like,' Bobby added.

'They're not just going to take our word for it,' I said. Graham thought for a moment, before turning and hobbling inside. I looked at Bobby and my daughters, rubbed my eyes. What we were considering seemed insane.

'We can leave it,' Bobby said. 'Let the Estate get on with the sale and they'll leave us alone. We go back to normal.' I looked at the girls.

'We don't have to do anything,' Sara said. Delphi was about to disagree but her sister grabbed her arm. They wanted me to fight. But it was all so much. I wasn't sure I could.

'My mother lied to me for my entire life to make sure I wasn't just a footnote in Nereus's story,' I told them. Bobby nodded. My daughters sat on each side of me, linked their arms through mine. Graham reappeared, holding a rusted red biscuit tin in his hands.

'You could never be a footnote, Winnie,' he said, handing it to me.

I opened the box to find a plastic freezer bag. Inside it was a braid of hair.

'You took it,' I said. He nodded. I was going to ask him why but I didn't need to. It was the two of them together. I felt the hair between my fingers. Two different colours, entwined together, light strawberry-blond with a deep, dark brown.

74.

I sent the braid to a lab Helen Grady recommended the moment I returned to England. She was the only one of my *nereusforever* searchers I told about what I'd discovered in Spain. She agreed to help with any legal challenge pro bono and advised us to make no contact with the Nereus Forbes Estate until we had the results.

I was alone in my bedroom when my mobile rang, a Sheffield number I knew was the lab. A thick fog sat low on the trees in my back garden. I'd been in a state of living catatonia for the previous ten days, not wanting to believe, not wanting to engage with the implications of Nereus being my father, my mother keeping it from me, the man I thought of as my father murdering him.

I messaged Sadie the night we got back from Spain. I couldn't speak to her, see her, not yet. The text said I knew she had lied to me my whole life. I wanted her to know she'd wounded me, crippled me from ever being the authentic version of myself. I didn't tell her I'd never forgive her, but I wasn't sure if I could. I expected her to call but she didn't. Which pissed me off. When she didn't even respond for the first few hours, I tried to give her the benefit of the doubt that she didn't know what to say. But when her response arrived, I realised I'd been too kind.

'I did what I had to do,' she wrote. Through our time together talking about her past, I thought we'd rediscovered the closeness I remembered so fondly from when I was young, before I found the birthday cards. I wasn't sure we could ever recover from what I'd learnt about Neil. And with someone willing to lie so comprehensively for so many years, I wasn't sure we should.

I picked up the phone.

'Am I speaking with Ms Blakely-Harris?' a chirpy female voice said.

'Yes.'

'I was told you wanted to be phoned with the results of the sample you sent us, is that right?'

'It is.'

'We tested both hair samples. Both are human hair.' My brow furrowed, desperate for this inappropriately upbeat woman to tell me what I wanted to hear. 'And of course we tested the DNA swab from yourself. Human too, you'll be happy to hear, and there was a match between you and one of the hair samples.'

'Which one?'

'Sample B.' I blinked, trying to remember. Helen and I had unbraided the hair and put them into two separate ziplock bags, labelling them. But I had no idea which was which.

'Which was —'

'The dark hair, Ms Blakely-Harris. There was a match with the dark hair. None with the lighter one.' I fell back onto the bed, nodding to no one, feeling suddenly freezing cold. It was Nereus. Neil Forbes. My dad was Neil Forbes.

'OK,' I said.

'I'll pop the full report over in an email,' the technician said. 'Hope this has given you what you were looking for.' She hung up. I was looking for the man who'd killed a rock star but I'd found my father.

Bobby held me that night. I wept for many hours but felt

no catharsis. There were moments I felt my life had been taken from me. But the next morning the sadness, the sense of loss had burned up in the scant hours of sleep by an inconsolable fury. Helen's email summoning me to her office that morning felt like a call to arms. I took the Tube up to her ready to use the evidence and my rage to smash the Estate for what they'd done to us. But within seconds of being in Helen's office and meeting her friend Claudia, a forensic expert witness, I had the wind knocked out of me.

'The sample won't stand up,' Helen said once I'd sat down.

'What? Why?' Helen invited Claudia to field my question.

'The hair sample's fifty years old, stored in an unsealed plastic bag in a rusting metal tin. Prone to condensation, oxidation, any human material would suffer a significant amount of atmospheric degradation. All of which would be brought up in court.'

'But there's a match,' I said. 'The DNA matches.'

'The report's less clear cut,' Helen said.

'If I were on the stand with this,' Claudia said. 'Any half-decent barrister would get me to give a percentage accuracy for this and –' she placed her fingers on the report – 'I wouldn't be able to say more than about thirty.'

'But there's a zero per cent match with Graham.'

'There's little doubt Neil Forbes is your father, Winter,' Helen said. 'But a judge ruling your claim as legitimate based upon Graham's word and a very old hair sample, at a time when there's a lot of money at stake.' Three hundred million pounds we'd discovered after Helen's firm engaged an investigator to prepare our case, the second most expensive purchase of an artist's back catalogue in history. A Washington-based private equity fund, SIG Investments, the prospective buyers.

'It's not about the money, though,' I said. 'They want to turn him into a theme park. I'm – and I'm his – no one else is going to protect that.'

'If we had any chance I'd work for months on this for free,' Helen said. 'You know I would.'

'But based upon this, you won't win,' said Claudia. 'I'm so sorry.'

That night I felt like bruised fruit. I went home and listened to Nereus Forbes' records for the first time in years. Since I'd learnt the truth I felt weighed down knowing I shared genes with this creative genius who inspired millions, found myself asking how it was I'd ended up so mediocre. But as I listened to his words, his worlds, as I browsed the record sleeves festooned with incredible artwork he'd drawn, I felt grateful to be connected to him. As I peeked in at Delphi in her room making madcap beats I couldn't understand on an array of gadgets I couldn't name, at Sara in hers, working studiously on old humanitarian cases to gain the tools to make the world a better place, I saw some legacy of him in them, so perhaps there was some of him in me too.

I went back to work, trying to exist in the life I had before I knew who I was, nostalgic for the ignorance almost. Although we hadn't noticed any men in cars watching us, any more strange occurrences on our phones or computers, the sale of the masters, my inability to stop it, to get back at Thomas Tee, weighed on me in almost every moment.

I was giving a series of seminars on Orpheus, the mythological figure I'd always been most fascinated by. Every other hero found their glory through war, fighting, through death. Orpheus still lives in our world now because he made the lives of everyone he encountered better with his music. He and I both found someone we loved in the underworld. He tried to bring his wife back from the dead and I realised, having found out who my father was, I'd perhaps been trying to do the same in trying to save his legacy. But both of us had failed. Orpheus at least had his lyre. I could barely play the chords to 'Wonderwall'.

75.

It was Alan Sperryman, the man whose actions first led me down this path, who had the idea which would save Nereus's music. Bobby and I met with the *nereusforever* group, who had taken their cue from me in accepting Alan as one of our own, at the Crown Tavern a few weeks after the meeting at Helen's office. Once they'd got over the collective disbelief and fangirling at the news that I was Nereus's progeny, they set about trying to work out what we could do to stop the Estate selling off his masters.

Bobby wanted to go the press, but Lennox thought it unlikely anyone would print it, fearing claims of libel and the potentially deep pockets of the Estate. Candi suggested an online campaign, releasing the story on a Substack, sending it viral to the wider Nereus community. Dr Hailee didn't think it would get the traction required and feared US financiers would easily dismiss it as internet chatter. Alan said something under his breath that no one heard. I could tell he found the group meetups a challenge. I asked him to say it again.

'What about a book?' The man who lived his life online had suggested the most analogue idea possible. People looked at each other, unconvinced.

'Wouldn't that be the same as the papers?' Iris Derbyshire asked.

'No,' said Helen Grady, walking to the window looking down onto Clerkenwell Green. 'It actually wouldn't. No, it's –' She blinked fast as she tried to work it through. She explained that because Nereus was a public figure, because the Estate was an extension of him, anyone claiming defamation would have to prove the author of the book acted with 'actual malice' – the direct intention to harm by presenting false information. Seeing that we had evidence to support my belief Nereus was my biological father and if we stated it as a belief rather than controvertible fact, the Estate would have little recourse against us.

Within a week I'd met seven publishers with the proposal for this book. Doors fly open if you're ready to admit you're the secret love child of Nereus Forbes. Part of the deal I made with the publisher I went with, whose holding company ironically owns Otis de Kock's now mostly defunct Apollo Records, was that they'd make the press release announcing the book immediately.

Once they did, things became difficult. The Nereus Estate made a number of threats to the publisher but, thanks to the continued support of Helen Grady, attorney Lennox and Alan and Candi engaging the online community with some judiciously leaked titbits from the story, none of them came to pass. SIG Investments walked away from the deal. Rumour has it they offered a desultory amount to keep the deal alive but it wasn't enough to pay off the significant debts Thomas Tee had accrued in his years stewarding the Estate. All those blondes. All those MacBooks. Months later, Thomas would be voted off the board and faced several lawsuits for his financial mismanagement. Bobby joked I should step up and take his place. I told him I'd prefer to eat broken glass.

I began writing, trying to stick faithfully to how the story unravelled for me, but did consult Graham on any finer details which weren't in the tapes or from my research. He rented a cottage in Sussex, just for the summer months when it was too hot in Spain, he told me. My daughters thought he wanted to be close to me. We saw each other only three times in the four months it took me to finish the manuscript. I couldn't quite relax around him. Our meetings remained stilted.

He would talk about Sadie often, how grateful he was to her for doing such a wonderful job raising me. He encouraged me to try to mend things with her. It had never been his intention to drive a rift between us. I wasn't ready to face that. I made myself busy with the book, desperate to get everything which happened out of my head. Sadie had made the choice to deceive me. As I saw it, it was up to her to fix it.

A few hours after I'd sent the first draft of this book to my editor, I found a letter on my doormat. It was from a former air stewardess called Lydia Hallward who had been on the flight Graham was meant to be on to Nice. When I read what she'd sent me, I knew I'd have to make some changes to the ending.

76.

I arrived at my mother's house in Wadhurst outside Tunbridge Wells a couple of hours after opening Lydia's letter. I left straight away, didn't call ahead. No one answered the front door, so I walked around the side of the house where I found her pulling carrots from her vegetable patch. She had rabbits, chickens, just like when I was a child. She made a 'hmm' sound when she saw me. I could see from the way she held her body, hands in front of her stomach like armour, she thought I was there for the confrontation about Nereus being my dad which she'd avoided for months with her bloody-minded refusal to engage. She pointed me towards a metal table and chairs, asked if I'd like tea. I didn't.

When we had both sat, I passed Lydia Hallward's letter over. Sadie read the cover note the air hostess had written apologising for her late response to the message I'd sent out months before asking whether Graham was on the flight. Sadie looked at me, blank. Then I pulled out the other document she'd included with her letter, a telegram, and placed both on the table.

Lydia's note said she found the telegram amongst a pile of papers on the desk at the check-in gate of the flight to Nice she was working on that night. When she'd seen one of the names on it, she'd decided to keep it for her father. He was an amateur historian, in truth a bit of a hoarder, and loved any of his daughter's exciting tales of the people she'd worked for on flights – royals, politicians, actors of the London stage. At the time, she explained, being a flight attendant was seen as a very glamorous job. Lydia had found the telegram amongst a huge array of papers and files he'd put together in box-files that she had never quite been able to throw away and thought it might be of interest.

The telegram was addressed to Graham Harris, sent straight from the Post Office to the British Airways reception desk at Heathrow Airport with the word 'URGENT' repeated three times at the top. The message was brief.

'Do not get on plane. Need you. Cheyne Walk now.'

The date was 28 October 1977. The time: 4.24 pm. The wind tickled the pages on the metal tabletop. On the back of the telegram there was a small scribble in the bottom right-hand corner. It gave a Post-Office account number, and with it the name 'Mr B. Blakely'. It was this name, the former Conservative MP and Shadow Transport Minister, and not Graham's, which would have been of interest to Lydia Hallward's father.

Sadie looked up from the telegram. I could see cogs turning behind her eyes, deciding what story to tell, but then she caught my eye and let out a long breath. There would be no more lies, I thought.

'You were there?' I said, voice gentle.

'Marina Maxwell-Clyde spoke to a woman at *Tatler* my parents knew who called me to find out what the scoop could be. I knew what it was straight away.'

'How?'

'I'd been dreading it,' she said. 'Ever since you were born. Neil and I made a pact you would never know. We both agreed. He didn't want to be a father. He was terrified of it, because of his dad but also, let's be honest, I'm not sure he wanted to share the limelight. But this was Neil. I may as well have made a pact with a fox not to eat my chickens. And so it came to pass.' Sadie took a taxi to Cheyne Walk immediately. 'I only went to talk to him,' she said.

'How come no one saw you?'

'I – I thought there'd be paparazzi. I wore a blonde wig. With my work I had a cupboardful. Brushed it down to look like Greta.' It made sense of Greta returning in the afternoon but then being seen at the Colony Room so soon after. 'I know what it sounds like but I – I really did go there to talk to him.'

Neil was delighted to see her, seemed to have no inkling why she might be there.

'He insisted on giving me a tour,' she said. 'Showed me where they'd made a fire, burnt animal parts, told me they'd spent the night before speaking to Penny from beyond the grave. He was completely manic.' I noted the same word Graham had used about Neil when he showed up. Sadie told him she'd heard he was making a big statement and was concerned it was about me. Neil confirmed it was.

'He said he couldn't live a lie anymore,' she said. 'I brought up the pact we'd made but he just laughed, like I wasn't serious, like it wasn't. At all.' Neil pitched a future where we would be a happy family, promised to be heavily involved in my life. He saw me going on tour with him, singing on stage, appearing on album covers, which would chart my growth. 'He wanted you to be some "universal person" he kept saying.' Sadie showed Neil a picture of me she had in her purse, to demonstrate I was a little girl, a normal little girl entitled to a normal life, that I shouldn't have to be anything but what I wanted to be.

'"No one on earth wants to be normal," he told me.' Sadie looked around her at the drugs, the tables of half-drunk bottles, bouquets of flowers, smouldering crustaceans, at chalk symbols drawn on furniture, tarot laid out on a card table, bookshelves yawning with philosophy and esoterica. 'I realised he'd never understand, didn't have the capacity to. I looked at the picture of you. Pudgy little face, messy curls. My girl. Imagined you in the papers, growing older in his costumes, the Bronze Stingray, driving a little version of the Teal Eel around photoshoots. At twelve, thirteen, on red banquettes in private members' clubs being leered at by the great and the good. Sixteen years old, black pupils whacked out on speed, coke, smack, exhausted by everyone's fascination with being part of Nereus. It suddenly clicked. Even if I could convince Neil then, it'd never stop, I could never stop someone like him.'

'Except you did stop him,' I said. 'You killed him.' She said nothing. 'How?'

'Wasn't hard. Neil always wanted a fix. I didn't flinch as I did it, didn't shake or tremble because a mother will do anything to keep her child safe.'

'Who injected?'

'I did. He liked that. Thought it was like we were in bed together again.' I said I thought Neil was in love with her, that sleeping with him and leaving the band afterwards might have hurt him more than she realised.

'He just thought I was like Penny. I didn't take his crap, spoke my mind. That's all I was to him. He didn't know how to love women. He couldn't forgive them after what his mother did to his dad.' I asked what happened next.

'As soon as I pulled the syringe out I was hit by the gravity of what I'd done. That I'd go to prison, that you, you'd be left without a mother. So I tried to reach Graham. I had no idea the telegram would get to him, or if it did, that he wouldn't ignore it. I tried to be as vague as I could. Didn't know the account I used to pay would show up on it at all.' Sadie left Neil on the bed in his room. He seemed to be enjoying himself, no pain. She wondered whether he'd be OK. Part of her hoped she'd got it wrong, that he'd pull through and they could sort it all out a different way. He kept trying to swig from a bottle of whisky, but he started choking on it every time he did. He was beginning to lose control of certain motor functions. Sadie couldn't watch him coughing it over himself anymore so she put the bottle out of reach and left him. She waited in the living room, watching the boats glide along the Thames, no idea if Graham would arrive.

'There was a frantic banging on the door,' she said. 'I thought it was the police, perhaps an ambulance somehow, perhaps if Neil had got to a phone. I looked outside and saw that woman, the journalist, hid behind the curtains.' There was another knock on the door an hour after Marina had gone. 'I thought she was back.' But she saw Graham's Jag on the street outside and let him in. Sadie led him up to the bedroom, showed him Neil on the bed.

'Graham thought he'd had an overdose. Didn't question why I was there at first. He ran to the telephone, about to call 999. I took the receiver out of his hand and replaced it. Then he knew.' Sadie took Graham into the en-suite bathroom. She told him what she'd done and why she had done it.

'He couldn't take it in at first,' she said. 'About you not being his.'

'It was much too big to get my head round,' Graham told me later.

'He did what he'd always been most comfortable doing. He got practical.' Neil was still alive but barely, too late for an ambulance. Graham wanted to take the fall. He wanted to confess to Nereus's murder. 'I wouldn't allow it. I didn't want to let him martyr himself but more than that he had no good reason. I was worried if he owned up, the police would get it out of him why he did it, that he wasn't your father. And I couldn't have that.' So Graham had the idea to make it look like an accidental overdose. He told Sadie to leave to pick me up from school straight away, and once she got there, she was to take me out somewhere as public as possible, to make sure lots of people saw us.

'I had no idea what I was doing,' Graham told me. 'I just knew, if it had to come back to someone, it had to be me. You needed a mother.' It wasn't a difficult decision to help Sadie, to take over, to conceal a murder. 'I barely thought about that,' he said.

'Graham pretty much shoved me out the door.'

'Said that if all was OK she wouldn't hear from me again.'

'I left Cheyne Walk,' Sadie said. 'Wandered the streets aimlessly for an hour or so, head in ten different places at once, but ended up at your school.' Which explains why she was so late to pick me up that day.

'You took me for ice cream,' I said.

'Brompton's, off Marylebone High Street,' she said. 'I asked for the window table.' That made my breath catch. I remembered the sundae we had. Much bigger than anything she'd usually allow. She'd just killed the father of her child. Sadie never knew what happened afterwards. Graham confirmed the rest was as he'd told me as we looked over the gorge in Ronda. Like Graham, she spent the next two days in constant terror of the police at the door.

'It never came. Life carried on.'

'Did you ever regret it?'

'Killing him?' I nodded, barely able to look at her. 'I wish it hadn't had to be like that. But did I regret putting you first? Not at all.'

'Lying to me, never letting me know who I was, why I felt so adrift in my own life? Think that was putting me first?'

'I gave you choices.'

'Choices?!'

'To have a family, a real family, to be ordinary, not to have the supernova adulation of thousands heaped on you, but to give you the chance for some common-or-garden happiness.' Her words stung, bursts of citrus in my eyes. I wanted to hear everything she was saying as excuses, self-justification, the ramblings of a woman who'd lived with her terrible act for five decades. But, and I hated it, there was a grain of me which understood, could see why.

I thought of my family, remembered Graham at his house in Spain, how he had looked at my daughters talking about their lives as if he were witnessing one of God's miracles. I left my mother's house and drove to the cottage he was renting in Sussex. He came out and I hugged him, sank into his huge body for the first time in memory. At that moment, I wasn't sure whether I'd be able to speak to my mother again, but after the sacrifice he made for us that October night in 1977, I finally wanted to be Graham Harris' daughter.

77.

I did speak to my mother again. It was she who surprised me this time, turning up at my house ten days after I'd confronted her with the telegram. I invited her in, made tea. She told me she'd burned the telegram. I laughed. She wasn't joking.

'If you put any of it in the book I'll say you made it up,' she said. I nodded. Whatever she'd done, I didn't want my elderly mother spending her last years in prison. But that wasn't what she'd come to tell me.

'There's no easy way to say this,' she said. And I knew. Deep down, I had known before, when she agreed to finally talk about the past, however evasive she'd been until I discovered the truth myself. 'I have cancer. Throat.' Sadie had successfully fought lung cancer twelve years before but now it was back. She said it had reached her lymph nodes. It was too late for surgery and she couldn't face chemotherapy again. 'I am going to die,' she said with the only tremor in her voice I can ever remember. 'And I want you to know I'm sorry. Not for what I did.' I felt a smile creep to the side of my lips. My mother could never have just apologised. 'But that we could never be as close after you found Graham's cards, as I thought we always would be. I know that's my fault.' She told me she had a year. Maybe a little more if she did various things she'd seen on the internet.

'Careful what you read on there,' I said. 'Never know where it might lead.' I stood, walked round the table and hugged her. She turned her body into me. 'I know,' I said. 'I know.'

However sad I felt knowing she was going to die, the only family I'd had before my own children, part of me was relieved because as we held each other, I knew I'd be able to forgive her. She'd lied to me, but she'd done it to give me the sort of simple life she never had. Don't all parents try to give their children the things they didn't have, protect them from the worst parts of their own lives? And although Sadie took Nereus's life, his career was on the slide, he was penniless, miserable, alone, grasping to get back to the peak he'd been at a few years before. By dying when he was young and so beautiful, she created a legend, a canon of iconic music and transgressive style which no doubt would have eroded as he aged into insignificance. Can you honestly say Nereus Forbes would have wanted that? And can I honestly tell you I wanted to be part of the circus that was Nereus?

A few weeks later, I had Sadie and Graham to our house for a barbecue. It had been Delphi's birthday a week before and she'd requested it. For the hours running up to their arrival I had to do everything in my power not to lock myself in the cupboard under the stairs and throw away the key. I resisted.

Graham arrived first, was so grateful to have been invited, near tears. I almost wanted to shake him and tell him to get it together. He soon calmed down, busying himself by setting Bobby up with a table for the barbecued food, pouring everyone the wine he'd brought from Spain, making us a tomato salad with his olive oil which was one of the nicest things I'd ever eaten.

When the doorbell rang, I told Graham to answer it. He opened it and the two of them took in the older versions of the person they'd been in love with five decades before. Sadie burst into laughter.

'You laughing at me, Sadie Blakely?'

'I am,' she said. 'Yeah.' She walked to him and wrapped him in the biggest hug her thin arms could get around him.

'What's that for?' he asked.

'You're an idiot,' she said.

'Yeah, I know that now.' She pulled away, eyes wet with tears.

'But thank you. For what you did.'

They came into the main room where we were stood pretending not to listen with their arms around each other's waists. Sadie stopped, she leant into Graham.

'You did this,' she said, pointing to me, the girls, our wonderful life.

'We both did.' Sadie didn't look like someone in the final stretch of her life, she was glowing. And Graham was doe-eyed as he looked at all of us in front of him. It was honestly a bit much.

We had a glorious lunch, a warm late September day nearly five decades after Nereus Forbes's death. Somehow history was erased for a few hours and we were with each other, simply, a sort of family. We all drank a glass or two too much wine and lost ourselves until the evening cold sent us inside. We lit our woodburner, the girls went off to do something vital and Graham, Sadie and I sat soft and watched flames lick the glass window of the stove. Bobby was at his vast shelves of records trying to pick something out for us to listen to. I could see he was finding it daunting in front of the two former Satyrs. He stopped for a moment.

'Why didn't he just give you some credit, Graham?' Bobby said. 'For the song. It's bothered me. The lyrics are totally different, he'd only have to give you a co-credit. It cost him so much, both of you. It was your song. Why take that from you?'

Graham leant forward, heaved a sigh.

'That night,' he said. 'After you'd gone.' He nodded to

Sadie. 'To pick Winnie up. I went up to Neil's room, lay down beside him, like I told you. He was just about there still, in and out anyway.' Emotion trembled through his shoulders as he spoke. Sadie sat forward, nested hands in her lap as the room seemed to close round Graham's chair. 'I turned onto my side and asked him to sing me a song. He smiled, only ever really happy in front of an audience. He hummed at first. It was the tune of "Lady Theia" but when he sang the lyrics were different, incomprehensible in fact. He turned to me, raised his eyes. He wanted me to understand.'

'What was it,' I asked. 'What was he trying to tell you?'

'It was Greek. He was singing the song in Greek. I listened for a bit more. I didn't understand. Then I did.'

'Penny,' I said. Sadie and Graham locked eyes. He smiled.

'I'd heard her sing it, to Neil. First night I went to her house. I went to the town she was from, in the early eighties, I needed to know for sure. I asked the old-timers and they all knew it, a folk song from her village.' Sadie reached across the sofa, put a hand on the cushion next to Graham. 'I didn't know I'd taken the tune. No idea. Really thought it came from me. But Neil knew. It's why he was so angry, why he left me in London.'

'Why didn't he just tell you?'

'I don't know.'

'You told him you'd written it for your daughter,' Sadie said, arrowing a look at me. 'He knew about her. He couldn't take the song away from you but Penny was dying. It's why he gave you all that money to drop it, he couldn't let you take it from her either.' Graham took Sadie's hand, clutched it for a moment before letting it go. The song came from Penny. It wasn't hers but it came from her. Two men who loved each other more than the women in their lives falling out over a song that wasn't even theirs, that they'd heard from a woman, a mother. But perhaps it was never really about the song. It was about me. Whether Graham knew deep down I wasn't his or not, I was the thing which stood between them. The symbol of some solidity, some hope to both of them. Parented by an impotent, dedicated man trying to do better but the progeny of a potent yet entirely unsuitable father. A man, more a myth, that another mother killed to protect me from.

I went to the corner of the room, picked up one of Bobby's guitars and brought it to the sofa. I started finger-picking the chords to 'Lady Theia'. It had felt appropriate, for the moment. But I couldn't much remember it, nor could I really play guitar. I was murdering it. I could feel Bobby looking at Graham to save us all. The old man stretched his arm for the instrument.

He took it into his chest like his own child, cleared his throat, stretched his arms and began playing. His fingers moved along the fretboard, over the strings like humming-birds' wings. Miraculous sounds filled the tiny room.

I began to sing the song, his words, the words he'd written for me, those I could remember. He joined me on the chorus, not remembering his own words anymore so singing Neil's. Sadie joined in. Bobby beamed at us, Sara and Delphi appearing at the doorway to listen. Graham added a harmony line. My breath caught at how wonderful it sounded. It was a harmony the world never got to hear, a vocal line Graham would have sung again and again with Nereus Forbes, my father, if they'd only given each other the chance.

Acknowledgements

Huge thanks are due to my incredible agent Juliet Mushens for her belief and encouragement and to Rachel, Alba, Catriona, Emma and Den at Mushens Entertainment.

To Joel Richardson at Penguin Michael Joseph, for his vision and kindness, along with Lily Cooper and Phillipa Walker for invaluable work in a key editorial moment. In addition, thanks to Katya Browne, Fiona Brown, Lily Evans, Helen Eka, Jon Kennedy, and everyone else at Michael Joseph who continue to be a joy to work with.

To Amber Trentham and Adam Weymouth for their day-to-day encouragement and mutual moaning in the writing trenches.

To Alastair Coe, Greg Kelly and anyone else who's ever shaped my love of music or who has shared times with me watching gigs. And to Sam Gayton and Kim Thomé for re-igniting the joy of being in a band. Passion can't exist in the dark and you have all played a part in shaping the most important interest I have.

To my mum and brother for their continued enthusiasm and unblinking support. To Frankie the dog who keeps my lap warm as I work. To Sadie and Otis for being themselves. Nothing hits me in my soul like watching them up on stage or on the pitch doing their thing. And to the incomparable Joanna for her smile, her love, her patience and her never-ending belief in the power of creativity. Writing books is hard and you make it easier.

And finally, to my readers. Thank you. You're perfect as you are.